INVISIBLE

By Danielle Steel

Invisible • Flying Angels • The Butler • Complications • Nine Lives
Finding Ashley • The Affair • Neighbours • All That Glitters • Royal
Daddy's Girls • The Wedding Dress • The Numbers Game • Moral Compass
Spy • Child's Play • The Dark Side • Lost And Found • Blessing In Disguise
Silent Night • Turning Point • Beauchamp Hall • In His Father's Footsteps
The Good Fight • The Cast • Accidental Heroes • Fall From Grace
Past Perfect • Fairytale • The Right Time • The Duchess • Against All Odds
Dangerous Games • The Mistress • The Award • Rushing Waters • Magic
The Apartment • Property Of A Noblewoman • Blue • Precious Gifts
Undercover • Country • Prodigal Son • Pegasus • A Perfect Life
Power Play • Winners • First Sight • Until The End Of Time
The Sins Of The Mother • Friends Forever • Betrayal • Hotel Vendôme
Happy Birthday • 44 Charles Street • Legacy • Family Ties • Big Girl
Southern Lights • Matters Of The Heart • One Day At A Time
A Good Woman • Rogue • Honour Thyself • Amazing Grace • Bungalow 2
Sisters • H.R.H. • Coming Out • The House • Toxic Bachelors • Miracle
Impossible • Echoes • Second Chance • Ransom • Safe Harbour
Johnny Angel • Dating Game • Answered Prayers • Sunset In St. Tropez
The Cottage • The Kiss • Leap Of Faith • Lone Eagle • Journey
The House On Hope Street • The Wedding • Irresistible Forces
Granny Dan • Bittersweet • Mirror Image • The Klone And I
The Long Road Home • The Ghost • Special Delivery • The Ranch
Silent Honour • Malice • Five Days In Paris • Lightning • Wings • The Gift
Accident • Vanished • Mixed Blessings • Jewels • No Greater Love
Heartbeat • Message From Nam • Daddy • Star • Zoya • Kaleidoscope
Fine Things • Wanderlust • Secrets • Family Album • Full Circle • Changes
Thurston House • Crossings • Once In A Lifetime • A Perfect Stranger
Remembrance • Palomino • Love: Poems • The Ring • Loving
To Love Again • Summer's End • Season Of Passion • The Promise
Now And Forever • Passion's Promise • Going Home

Nonfiction

Expect a Miracle
Pure Joy: *The Dogs We Love*
A Gift Of Hope: *Helping the Homeless*
His Bright Light: *The Story of Nick Traina*

For Children

Pretty Minnie In Paris
Pretty Minnie In Hollywood

long before. His father had been from a family with money. They were not enormously rich, but they were comfortable, and he had left his widow and only son enough money to live well on. He was from an old, respected family whose fortune had dwindled slowly over time, but there was still enough left for his widow and son to live in a decent neighborhood in a nice apartment in the East Eighties in New York, and for Brandon to get a good education at Columbia, and go to business school after that.

Brandon had made some wise investments, and had a strong entrepreneurial streak. He invested in a plastics company that did well in the '60s. By the time he met Fabienne in Paris in 1970, he was making a considerable amount of money and living well. He was ambitious and intended to make a lot more. He had recently invested in a second company that had made a ridiculous amount of money on the hula hoop. It had been patented seven years before, and he had purchased a large share of the company that produced it. The hula hoop was cheap to make and had become an enormous fad, and had already made the company a lot of money. Investing in the company seven years later made Brandon a lot of money too, with their newest products and his other investments. He had a good head for business, and an instinct for what would sell, and what people wanted. He hadn't made a single investment mistake so far.

His mother had never recovered from his father's death during the war. She lived life in retreat, depressed, and died young herself. She had been widowed at twenty-six and died of ovarian cancer at forty-one, when Brandon was twenty-one. He had been surprised by how much of his father's money she had saved, without ever working herself. She had been a constant presence in his life, and was a the movies one day. She thought Paris was the most exciting city in the world, and was hoping to be "discovered" by a producer.

Fabienne was a survivor. She was born into hardship, from a long line of determined women. She was bold and fearless, cocky, and willing to fight for whatever she wanted. Brandon sensed that about her and admired her for it. She never complained about her early life, but he could sense that it hadn't been easy. What struck him about her immediately was her indomitable spirit, and her stunning beauty. He was fascinated by her, and came back to the café where she worked to see her every day. When he walked her home one night after work, to the place where she rented a small squalid room, she told him that her father had been American, but she had never known him. He had gone back to the States before she was born, and her mother had never been able to locate him. She had no living relatives, but seemed undaunted by her circumstances, and was certain that she would have a career as an actress one day. He couldn't help but admire her courage. She was the strongest, bravest, most beautiful girl he had ever met. She went to bed with him the second time he walked her home, and he was even more bewitched by her after that. He gave her a small gold bracelet with a heart on a thin chain when he left, and he was haunted by her when he got back to New York. He couldn't get her out of his head. All the women he'd known paled in comparison to her. He had never been in love before and thought he was now. Just thinking about her was exquisite torture, and he longed to make love to her again.

Brandon's father had died in the Pacific during the war, and his mother had died when he was in college. His grandparents had died know. He made no promises he didn't keep. He left Paris, as so many other soldiers did, with unforgettable memories of his time in Paris, leaving behind a baby he knew nothing about and never would.

Fabienne's mother realized she was pregnant two months after he had left, and tried to discover his whereabouts from the army base in Paris. His name was Jimmy Smith, she knew nothing else about him, not even his birth date. They were never able to locate him for her. He was one of hundreds or even thousands of young American soldiers who had left women and babies in Paris, and all over Europe. Marceline was hardly unusual, and her mother died soon after he had left. She tried living alone in Paris, but couldn't afford to stay there with a child on the way and no one to help her, and shortly before Fabienne was born, Marceline went to live with her grandmother in Brittany, where Fabienne grew up. Marceline died when Fabienne was only three. A truck hit her as she rode her bicycle home from work in a local bakery. Fabienne was too young to understand what had happened to her mother. She was twelve when her widowed great-grandmother died of a stroke. Having no other relatives, she was sent to an orphanage in Quimper, where she stayed until she was eighteen. And then, like a homing pigeon, she went to Paris, a city she didn't know but had dreamed of all her life. She already had dreams of becoming an actress at eighteen, but had no luck getting parts, despite her striking beauty. She got a few jobs as a model, but her figure was too full for most modeling jobs, so she supported herself as a waitress, in the café where Brandon Adams met her shortly after she turned twenty-four. She had been in Paris for six years by then, and had never given up her dreams of being in him, and asked him where he was from. He said he was American, from New York, and was in Paris on business. She could tell that he had money. He was wearing a well-cut suit, and a gold watch on his wrist. He was mesmerized by Fabienne. She was twenty-four years old, and he was eight years older. She looked nothing like any of the conservative, well-brought-up women he knew, and was stunningly beautiful. She told him that she was trying to be an actress, which he could easily believe.

Fabienne came from a simple background. She was born during the deprivation of post-war France. Her mother, Marceline, had survived the Occupation, and fallen in love with one of the American soldiers who had filled the city after the Occupation and the end of the war. She had caught his eye on the street one day, and he invited her to a meal at a nearby café. She was hungry all the time. All her money went for medicine for her invalid mother. Her father had been killed in an explosion in the early days of the Resistance, and she was making ends meet doing any work she could get, cleaning floors in restaurants, waiting on tables, and as a maid at a small hotel.

The handsome American soldier was an answer to her prayers. He fed her, brought her chocolates and stockings. He was soft-spoken and young, and kind to her. Fabienne's mother didn't know that she was pregnant when he was transferred back to the States, and he didn't leave her any information about how to reach him. For him, she was a brief wartime experience, an exotic memory he would carry with him, but knew he would never see her again. He had a girl waiting for him at home, and intended to marry her, although he never told Fabienne's mother that. She didn't need to playing with her dolls, or just daydreaming and looking out the window, wondering about the people she saw walk by.

When she saw other children, she wondered if their parents fought like that too, but she would never have dared to ask. She lived in a world full of adults, fraught with hostility, and saw other children only at school. She was smaller than the others, and they often assumed that she was younger than they were and called her a baby. She had no grandparents on either side, and both of her parents were only children, as she was, so there were no important adults in her life, except her parents.

She was made to feel like an intruder from the beginning. The only way she knew to remedy that was to stay out of sight. By the time she was seven, Antonia had perfected the art of seeming invisible, and feeling that way. She was most comfortable when no one could see her. Being noticed by anyone, particularly her parents, seemed fraught with risk.

Antonia looked nothing like her French mother, Fabienne Basquet, a fiery young woman with jet black hair, porcelain white skin, and lush lips, enhanced by bright red lipstick. She had flashing dark eyes, as large as Antonia's, and for as long as Antonia could remember, her mother had been angry most of the time. Antonia's father had fallen madly in love with her from the first moment he saw her. Only later did he realize it had been lust, not love. She was irresistible. She had full breasts and a tiny waist, long slim legs, and coiled her dark hair in a knot at the nape of her neck. It fell to her waist in a heavy dark curtain when she released it when they went to bed.

She was working as a waitress in a café in Paris when they met. Fabienne had chatted easily with Brandon Adams while she served

Chapter 1

Antonia Adams was a tiny, elfin, delicate child from the time she was born. Her father thought she looked like an angel, with a fuzz of white-blond hair as a baby, soft blond curls as she grew older, and big blue eyes. She would look directly at him, even before she could talk, as though she had something to say. She wasn't shy at first, but became that way very quickly, living in the war zone between her parents.

She knew when to talk, and when not to, and most of the time it was safer not to. She learned to disappear, to hide in the shadows, to make herself so small and stay so silent that they forgot she was in the room. And at the opportune moment, as their battles became more heated, she could slip away quietly. In their rage at each other, her parents forgot that Antonia existed, and was even in the same room with them. She had perfected the art of seeming invisible, almost like a ghost. She felt safest when no one was paying attention to her. She would sit alone in her room for hours, reading a book, or

INVISIBLE

To my beloved children,
Beatie, Trevor, Todd, Nick,
Samantha, Victoria, Vanessa,
Maxx, and Zara,

May you always be safe, protected,
and deeply loved
and valued for your
many gifts and talents.

I am so proud of you
and love you so much,

Mom/d.s.

First published 2022 by Delacorte Press
an imprint of Random House
a division of Penguin Random House LLC, New York

First published in the UK 2022 by Macmillan
an imprint of Pan Macmillan
The Smithson, 6 Briset Street, London EC1M 5NR
EU representative: Macmillan Publishers Ireland Limited, 1st Floor,
The Liffey Trust Centre, 117–126 Sheriff Street Upper,
Dublin 1, D01 YC43
Associated companies throughout the world
www.panmacmillan.com

ISBN 978-1-5290-2181-3

1 3 5 7 9 8 6 4 2

A CIP catalogue record for this book is available from the British Library.

Printed and bound by CPI Group (UK) Ltd, Croydon, CR0 4YY

Visit **www.panmacmillan.com** to read more about all our books
and to buy them. You will also find features, author interviews and
news of any author events, and you can sign up for e-newsletters
so that you're always first to hear about our new releases.

Danielle Steel

INVISIBLE

MACMILLAN

gentle woman, but being widowed so young, with a son to bring up alone, had left her shaken and scared for the rest of her days. She had been completely dependent on her husband, and eventually on the advice of her son. He tried to reassure her, but found he never could. She was a sad, frightened woman, in need of more support and protection than she was ever able to give him. He moved into an apartment near her during college, and visited her almost every day. Tormented by her anxiety, she was withdrawn and not given to overt demonstrations of affection. To the best of his knowledge, his mother never had another man in her life after her husband died, and she wasn't a warm, affectionate person, even when her husband was alive. She was a dutiful, well-brought-up, genteel woman. Passion wasn't in Brandon's nature either, so his brief experience with Fabienne in Paris hit him like a tsunami. The girls he'd known and had dated during and after college were well bred, had made their debuts and gone off to college. They had none of the rough edges and passion that Fabienne exuded like lava from a volcano. She held nothing back, in bed or anywhere else. It was heady stuff for Brandon, who wasn't demonstrative by nature, but he loved it in her, and it brought something out in him that he had never experienced before. What they had shared was unbridled passion, and he wanted more. He was certain it must be love. He had never felt anything as powerful for any woman before.

After a month of being obsessed by thoughts of her, he went back to Paris to see her again, and she seemed even more remarkable to him the second time. She was volatile, outspoken, said what she thought, did what she wanted. She was stunned when he appeared at the café, unannounced, swept her off her feet, and kissed her. She was able to get five days off from work, and they drove around the French countryside together in a car Brandon rented. By the time they got back to Paris he knew he was in love with her. He wanted her to come to New York. He couldn't bear the idea of being away from her for long, or tearing himself away from her again.

"And when you get tired of me," she said soberly, "then what happens?" She knew what had happened to her own mother. She didn't want to be at his mercy in a foreign land, and she had no intention of getting pregnant and had been careful that wouldn't happen, which he was grateful for. He was mad about her, but he wasn't ready for a child. She was enough of a surprise in his life, without adding more, for now.

"I'm not going to get tired of you, Fabienne," he said gently. He couldn't imagine it himself. How could you tire of a woman like her?

"You might," she said.

"We'll be married before then." They both looked shocked at what he said. The words had leapt out of his mouth before he could stop them, and he didn't want to.

"Are you proposing to me?"

He smiled at her question.

"Not yet, but I will. We need to figure out what to do next." She answered the question temporarily by making love to him again, which was an adequate answer for now, and reminded him of how badly he wanted her in his life. Everything that came before her seemed colorless to him now.

"What about my acting career?" she asked him after they'd made love. He didn't dare say, "What acting career?" She had admitted herself that her acting jobs had been few and far between, and had led nowhere so far, but she was still clinging to her dreams of stardom one day.

"We can find you an agent in New York." With her remarkable beauty, he thought it couldn't be hard. She needed to polish up her English first. She spoke it adequately to take orders from Americans at the restaurant, but she needed proper lessons if she wanted an acting career in the States. Her accent was charming, but her vocabulary was limited, although they did well enough with each other, and he dredged up what remained of his high school French. They managed, with bursts of laughter and kisses filling in the gaps.

By the end of Brandon's fourth visit to Paris to see Fabienne, in the space of three months, he proposed to her, with a ring he brought with him from New York that had been his mother's. It was a simple band with a pretty sapphire stone. He had an excuse to be in Paris, since he had business with a plastics company in France, but Fabienne was the main reason for his trips. He helped her with the visa process, and four months after they'd met, she flew to New York with him, and moved into his apartment on the Upper East Side, which was suitable for a bachelor and a little tight for both of them. There was no one to object to the speed of their relationship, or the impropriety of it, since he had no living parents. He married her at city hall a month later. He had researched and found an agent for her by then, who advised her to take English and acting lessons, and suggested she contact a modeling agency as well. She was a spectacular-looking girl, and her exuberance and energy came through her pores. She was excited after she met with the agent and had high hopes for her career.

Brandon worked hard, and often stayed late at his office. Fabienne kept busy, exploring New York, and taking the lessons the agent had suggested. She went to see as many movies as she could, to learn the language, and the moment Brandon came home at night, she lured him rapidly into bed. He didn't have a moment's regret over his speedy marriage to her, and he was the answer to her prayers. She was leading a comfortable life as the wife of a successful young entrepreneur who denied her nothing and was delighted to spoil her whenever he could. And she was excited at the prospect of a movie career.

He introduced her to his friends, who were dazzled by her beauty, and could see why Brandon was besotted with her. The men were envious of him, the women not so sure about her. They found her ambitious and exuberant, very outspoken, and didn't like her sexy wardrobe. She had a preference for low-cut dresses, which shocked them at first. She found his friends bourgeois, and the women too domestic, dull, and conservative. She found them all boring. He had a limited social life, and it became more so with Fabienne on the scene. Not every well-bred hostess wanted Fabienne in their midst. She exuded raw sex and they didn't want their husbands around her.

Brandon put all his energies into his work, so he had little time to spend going to dinner with friends. And he took time off on the weekends to spend with her. They went for walks in the park, movies together, and the theater occasionally. He took her out to dinner at popular restaurants, and introduced her to a life she would never have had otherwise. If it weren't for Brandon, she would still have been a waitress in a Parisian café.

She teased him at times about how restrained he was in public, and around his friends. He was a lion in bed, but chilly with her in public, and she accused him of being an American puritan. She was overtly sexual with him whenever and wherever the mood struck her, which he didn't like and told her so. It never slowed her down, and they frequently left dinner or a movie halfway through at her urging, to rush home to bed. He'd never had a relationship like theirs, or a woman he was as enchanted by. Sex was the driving force of what had brought them together, and the strongest bond they had formed, and he was enjoying it thoroughly, and thought it a good start for their marriage. In the far off distance, he could envision a house in the suburbs, and two or three children running around, but he was nowhere near ready for that yet. And she was still very young, at twenty-four, and wanted a career first, and said so openly. He didn't mind waiting a few years for their married life to take a more domestic turn. They were both young enough to wait, and agreed there was no rush. And he wanted to build his businesses first.

Things took an unexpected turn when, four months after they married, Fabienne realized that she was pregnant, and considered it disastrous news. Her English was improving, she'd been intending to contact the agent again soon, and having a baby would slow everything down and interfere with her career plans. Brandon wasn't thrilled at the news either. Abortion had just become legal in New York, and Fabienne suggested it, but Brandon didn't feel comfortable about it, and although it was years sooner than he'd planned, he wanted children with her, to establish a lasting foundation to their marriage.

It took them a month of arguments and discussions, and tears on Fabienne's part, but she finally agreed to have the baby as long as he understood that she was going to pursue her acting career, whether or not they had a child. He agreed to pay for childcare so she could, which softened the blow a little for her. With a baby, she felt like she'd be in jail.

Her plans to contact the agent were rapidly postponed. She was violently sick for most of the pregnancy, which did nothing to help her warm to the idea. She begged Brandon to let her have an abortion, as she lay too sick to get up on most days, and he refused to consider it. Nor would her doctor. It was far too late for a legal abortion. She was still throwing up several times a day when she was six months pregnant, and said she hated the baby that was making her so ill. It was the only obstacle between her and the career she had dreamed of all her life and thought was within reach now. Brandon was slowly warming to the idea of the baby, although he expressed it sparingly to Fabienne, who flew into a rage whenever he mentioned it.

She made no effort to prepare for the baby. Brandon had found a larger apartment for them when they discovered she was pregnant. It was large and sunny in a handsome building, and he had to hire a decorator because Fabienne felt too ill to take any interest in it. And it was Brandon who set up the nursery in his spare time on the weekends, while Fabienne lay in bed, too nauseous to move, and too angry to do anything to help. Her doctor said that she was one of those rare women who suffered from nausea twenty-four hours a day for the entire pregnancy. Brandon wondered at times if it was because she was so opposed to the idea of having a baby, but he never suggested it to her.

He was busier than usual for the last two months of the pregnancy. He had bought another company, which had great growth potential. It was located in New Jersey, with a factory in Pittsburgh, which he acquired with the deal. He was constantly on the road between New Jersey, New York, and Pittsburgh, and had an eye on another small company in Chicago. His ventures were multiplying exponentially, as his family was expanding.

Brandon was in New Jersey when Fabienne went into labor, and rushed home to be with her, as he had promised. The baby arrived promptly on its due date in August during a heat wave in New York. Fabienne had been lying on their bed like a beached whale for the last month, and had complained constantly about how miserable she was. He thought she had never looked more beautiful, but didn't dare to say so. She cried every time she saw herself in the mirror and was terrified the baby would ruin her figure forever. All she wanted was to have it, and get it over with. She hired a baby nurse for the first few weeks, and had babysitters lined up after that. She was planning to spend her time getting her figure back, so she could start her career in earnest by the end of the year.

She'd already been in labor for several hours by the time Brandon got to the hospital. She had gotten there by cab, while he drove to the city like a madman from New Jersey. He could hear her screaming as he rushed down the hall, and was allowed to see her for a few minutes, before he was sent to the waiting room to sit with the other fathers. When he left her with a labor nurse, Fabienne was begging for drugs for the pain, and pleaded with him not to leave her, but he had no choice. Her doctor did not allow fathers at the delivery. She had seemed so desperate that he felt guilty whenever he thought of her. A nurse told him that he could go home if he wanted, she wouldn't deliver for several hours, and said that first babies took their time. Several of the other fathers, the more experienced ones, left and returned later. Brandon didn't feel right leaving, and at midnight he was still there, waiting for news. She'd been in labor for fifteen hours by then, and the nurse at the desk encouraged him again to go home, and said they'd call him when the baby was born. He couldn't imagine what Fabienne was going through, and felt sorry for her, but there was no way for him to comfort her since he couldn't see her.

At two in the morning, he took the nurse's advice and went home to get some sleep. At their apartment, he stopped in to look at the crib in the empty nursery, and tried to imagine what it would be like to have a baby there, and whether it would be a girl or a boy. Right now, he just wanted the ordeal to end for Fabienne, so they could start their life as a family. He was sure she would adjust to the baby once it was born. It had been causing her misery now for almost the entire nine months.

He fell into a deep, exhausted sleep as soon as he lay down and was surprised when he woke up at nine the next morning, with the sun streaming into the room. There had been no call from the hospital. Worried, he called them, and a cheerful nurse told him that it wouldn't be long now, and his baby would probably arrive sometime that afternoon. He was shocked by what she said, and hoped she was mistaken. He couldn't imagine what condition his wife was in if it was taking that long. He had no way of judging if that was the norm, or if something was wrong, but the nurse had said that everything was fine before she hung up.

He had coffee and went back to the hospital, and joined the fathers in the waiting room again. There was a fresh crop of men and a few of the same faces as the day before. And one by one, they left the room, when they were told that their wives had delivered a son or a daughter. Finally, at four o'clock that afternoon, a smiling young nurse in starched cap and uniform beckoned to him, and told him that he could see his daughter at the nursery window, as she led the way.

"Is everything all right?" he asked her, looking panicked. It had been the longest two days of his life, and surely of Fabienne's.

"The baby is absolutely perfect, and your wife is doing well. She's a little groggy right now, but you can see her as soon as she leaves the recovery room."

"She was in labor for thirty-one hours," he reminded her, and she nodded.

"That's not long at all for a first baby. The baby weighs eight pounds, two ounces. That's a good size." She beamed at him and pointed as a nurse on the other side of the large picture window held a bundle wrapped in a pink blanket, and tilted her so he could see his daughter's face. She had perfectly defined features, and was exquisite, with a little duck fuzz of blond hair under a pink knit cap that kept her warm.

"She has the face of an angel," he said almost to himself. She looked nothing like Fabienne, with her exotic dark looks. The baby had a little heart-shaped mouth, and a dimple in her chin, and appeared more like him than he realized. He was tall and blond with a cleft in his chin.

"Is my wife all right?" he asked again, and the nurse reassured him with a smile. The nurse beyond the window took the baby away and put her in a bassinet at the far end of the room.

"She's tired but doing well. She'll sleep for a few hours now, and then you can see her." As he stood, still gazing at the baby that was his now, he felt overwhelmed by the miracle of birth. Suddenly, this tiny, perfect little human being was his, a daughter, the ultimate proof of his love for Fabienne. He couldn't quite believe it, and walked away with a dazed expression.

He left the hospital to get something to eat. He still found it hard to believe that thirty-one hours was a normal amount of time for a baby to be born. He couldn't wait to see the baby again and hold her himself, and to see Fabienne when she woke up. This was a landmark moment for them. They were a family now, not just a man and woman who had fallen in love. His life had new meaning. It was a very grown-up feeling, and he could hardly wait to see Fabienne and share it with her.

Chapter 2

Brandon spent three more hours in the waiting room, waiting for Fabienne to wake up. They finally came to tell him she was in her room, and he could see her. He had gotten her a private room, since she said she didn't want to be disturbed by another mother and baby. He thought it was the least he could do for her, since she was producing a miracle for him, and had suffered for nine months.

She was still dozing when he walked softly into the room. Her hair had been brushed and pulled back away from her face, her perfect creamy skin was whiter than ever, and she had dark circles under her eyes, which suggested to him that she'd been through an ordeal. Her eyes fluttered open when he kissed her, and then closed again. She was still drowsy from the drugs they had given her after the delivery, and she let out a soft moan, as he took her hand in his and kissed it.

"Oh my darling, was it awful?"

"Yes," she said, as she looked at him, still shocked by how hard it had been. Nothing had prepared her for the agonies of childbirth. "It was terrible," she said, as tears slid slowly from her eyes and rolled into her hair. "No more babies after this." He nodded and didn't know what to say. He could see the toll it had taken on her.

"I'm so sorry. She's beautiful, though. I saw her at the nursery window." Fabienne had decided before the delivery not to nurse her, and said it would have ruined her figure forever. She thought the whole idea of nursing was disgusting. She said only peasants nursed their babies in France. He didn't know if that was true or not, but many women in the States didn't nurse either. It was considered old fashioned and a little primitive, and he didn't expect her to do it. "Have you held her yet?" he asked gently and she shook her head.

"No, I don't want to. She has caused me enough pain already," she said, and he nodded, hoping she would forget it soon, and wouldn't hold it against the baby. He was sure her maternal instincts would rapidly overcome the memory of the pain of delivery.

Brandon stayed with her for an hour, and left when a nurse came in to offer her a shot for the pain. She was having cramps and eager for relief. He stopped by the nursery window to see the baby again, but the nurses were busy with new arrivals, and there was no one to hold her up again for him. They had agreed on a girl's name for her before she was born, Antonia Marceline Adams, named for both their mothers. As pretty as she was, even a few hours after her birth, he thought the name suited her.

* * *

Fabienne looked more like herself the next day. She had brushed her own hair, put on lipstick in the familiar bright red, which stood out even more in her startlingly pale face. She had lost a fair amount of blood during the birth. She had brought one of her own lacy night-gowns with her, and she had artfully concealed the dark circles under her eyes. She looked like a movie star again, and not an ordinary woman who had been through hell.

They brought the baby in while he was there, made Brandon put on a gown so he could hold her, and he sat staring down at the perfect tiny face as she slept in his arms. Fabienne watched him holding Antonia, and she quickly rang for a nurse to take her back to the nursery. She said she wanted her sent back before she woke up and started to scream. Fabienne spent the rest of the visit talking about how quickly she wanted to lose the weight she had gained and get in shape again. She spent five days in the hospital, and Brandon never saw her hold the baby. Her stomach was still slightly swollen when they left the hospital, but she was wearing a short red swing dress, which showed off her fabulous legs, and high heels. She was the only woman he could imagine who was so glamorous and sexy five days after giving birth.

The baby nurse they'd hired was waiting for them at home, and took over immediately. They had turned their guest room into a nursery, with a single bed in it, and the nurse would sleep there for the next month, at the other end of the apartment from Fabienne and Brandon's room, so they didn't have to hear her when the baby woke in the night to be fed.

The morning they came home, Fabienne lay down on their bed

and smiled at her husband, grateful that the horror of the delivery was behind her and she didn't have to care for the baby. She couldn't wait to go out with Brandon, she was free again. He stopped in to see the baby in the nursery, and Fabienne never did.

By the time the baby nurse left, Fabienne was exercising every day, and back at her acting lessons. The small amount of weight she had gained fell away easily. She had been too sick to eat much for nine months, and had gained a minimal amount of weight. She lined up a series of babysitters so she would be free every day, and Brandon could see that her maternal instincts had not kicked in yet, but he was still sure they would.

"You should take a day off to go to the park with Antonia," he suggested. It was September by then, the weather was beautiful. He thought it might help Fabienne bond with her daughter. She never gave the baby her bottle and let the babysitters do it during the day. And Brandon got up faster at night than she did for the night feed, so she let him do it, and he enjoyed the late-night moments with his daughter. She seemed like a remarkably easy baby, compared to stories he'd heard, and it was the only time he had to spend with her. He was coming home from the office late, and he was closing the deal in Chicago to add another company to his growing empire. He had a family to provide for now. He loved the idea that he was building something solid for Fabienne and their daughter.

Fabienne objected when he wanted to stop in the nursery to see Antonia when he got home, and complained that she had been alone all day. She kept the sitters as late as they would stay. She was no different than she had been before the baby was born, but it shocked him now. She was all woman, with no apparent maternal instincts. She made it clear that the joys of motherhood held no appeal for her. She had never pretended that they would. He had a wife, but Antonia didn't have a mother, not one who wanted to spend time with her anyway.

As she had said she would, when she got her figure back, Fabienne contacted her agent, and he sent her out on a few auditions. Her accent was still strong, which limited her, but her looks were undeniable. If anything, she was more beautiful after the baby than before. She looked more womanly to Brandon, and sexier than ever, although she was less interested in sex now than before. She didn't want to get pregnant again.

She got a part in a cigarette commercial, and Brandon was proud of her. Her agent hooked her up with a new modeling agency, and she got a lingerie ad. Her breasts were too big to pose for fashion editorials like those in *Vogue*. But she got enough work to keep her happy for a while, and she paid for the babysitters with what she earned. All the while, Brandon's business was growing, he traveled more and spent less and less time at home. It gave Fabienne more time to go to auditions and go-sees, but she complained when he was on the road too often and she had to take care of the baby herself at night. He was tired now when he got home, needed to sleep and couldn't do the night feedings, since he got up early to go to Pittsburgh, New Jersey, or fly to Chicago, or meetings elsewhere.

"That's supposed to be your job," he snapped at her one night when she woke him up to feed the baby, and she turned to him in a fury.

"I never told you I wanted to be a mother. I wanted to have an abortion and you wouldn't let me, even though it's legal here." It was like a slap across his face, and he left the room to give Antonia her bottle. He had never realized that Fabienne had no intention of becoming a mother, and still felt that it had been forced on her, even now that she had seen her baby. She hadn't fallen in love with her child, as he had hoped she would.

Fabienne continued to get small acting jobs that didn't require her to speak, bit parts and walk-ons mostly, some modeling jobs at trade shows, but her acting career still hadn't taken off a year after Antonia was born. Fabienne was just as disconnected from her, and had hired a young girl to take care of her full-time. Antonia was walking by then, and Brandon was slowly becoming aware that the child was a wedge between them. Fabienne blamed him for forcing the child on her. Nothing about the experience had moved her, and she had no interest in Antonia at all.

The fights began in earnest when Antonia was two. The companies Brandon had invested in were growing, and he spent less and less time at home. Antonia was an enchanting child, but Fabienne got angry every time he looked at her. She seemed to view her as competition for his affection, and accused him of loving their daughter more than he loved her. It was hard for him to believe that she was jealous of her own little girl, and it annoyed her when people stopped them on the street to say how beautiful Antonia was. Fabienne had no maternal pride. He had never understood before how fiercely narcissistic she was. And her career not taking off was a constant source of anger, frustration, and disappointment for her. She wanted to be discovered, like some of the major movie stars, and sent to Hollywood to make a movie. But she was just another pretty woman who wanted an acting career and had gotten nothing more than bit parts and minor modeling jobs. It was becoming clear to Brandon that it wasn't going to happen for her, although he never said it to her in so many words. He paid as little attention to Antonia as possible, trying not to infuriate Fabienne and cause a jealous scene. He had to harden himself to how endearing she was, and he spent as little time at home as possible, to avoid the inevitable battles with Fabienne. She blamed him for not doing more to help her acting career, but he had no useful connections, and thought she should stay home with their daughter by now, and accept her role as mother and wife.

There was a particularly ugly scene one day when Antonia was three. She was playing quietly in a corner of the living room, when Fabienne lit into Brandon for not taking her out to places where she would be seen. El Morocco and other places where famous movie people went, and she could be noticed by a director or producer. It was not a world Brandon frequented, and he didn't want to. He was traveling most of the time, and wanted peace and quiet when he came home. He was thirty-six years old, and still building a small empire, which provided them a good income. He began fighting back, and accused her of being a bad mother, and not what he expected of a wife, in exchange for what he gave her. He tolerated her aspirations and delusions about an acting career, but after four years, it had become tiresome, and he was fed up with her constant demands.

At some point when Antonia was four or five, the arguments between her parents became more vicious. They were constant by then, and since she was the subject of many of them, with Fabienne blaming Brandon for her very existence, and his blaming her for how little she did for either of them, Antonia somehow got the impression that the battles between her parents were her fault. She hadn't been shy before, but she became more reticent then, afraid to come out of her room and cause another fight when her father was home, or do something that would send Fabienne into a rage when they were home alone. She was less afraid and more outgoing when the babysitter was there.

At six, the teachers noticed how shy and uncommunicative she was at school, and called Fabienne and Brandon in to discuss it with them. She was obviously a bright child and did well in her classes, but most often, she kept to herself and played alone. She made no friends at school, and spoke as seldom as possible. She was introverted, although she observed everything around her with a keen eye. She was an observer but rarely a participant. Brandon had noticed it at home, but his years of keeping his distance from her, in order not to anger Fabienne and cause a jealous scene, had taken a toll on his relationship with the child too. He no longer felt close to her, and he was a stranger to her. She seemed to vanish into thin air at home, and hid in odd places with a book or a doll.

By the time she was seven, Brandon thought Antonia was decidedly odd and unlike other children. She had become the invisible child in their midst. He had to search for her when he came home and wasn't too tired to deal with her. Sometimes he didn't bother because whatever he did infuriated Fabienne, whose acting career had fizzled out by then. She had to beg her agents for work. She wasn't marketable, and was known now to be ill-tempered and difficult on the set. She was an unhappy, unfulfilled woman, and took it out on anyone who crossed her path. Her blatant narcissism was running rampant. Her most recent employer called her a bitch and fired her on the set.

Brandon wanted her to give up her dream of acting then, stay home, and become a wife and mother, which sounded like a death sentence to her. She was home less and less after that. And so was Brandon, as he immersed himself in work to escape his unhappy home and angry wife. Sometimes when he got home at night, Fabienne was out, and a sitter was there, and he had no idea where Fabienne was. It was a relief not to have to deal with her when he came home from a trip or late from work.

Through her acting classes, Fabienne had connected with a group of aspiring actors and actresses and often went out with them at night so they could be seen. She never admitted it to Brandon, but they went to Studio 54 almost every night, the most exciting, decadent nightclub in New York. Everyone went there, actors and models, famous movie stars, artists, and unknowns. Directors, producers, playboys, businessmen. There was a party there every night, with live animals or midgets or some wild décor. People left together to have sex, or stayed and used cocaine. Fabienne got into cocaine with her friends, and several times left with men she didn't know, and came home afterward and tiptoed into the apartment early in the morning. Brandon didn't say anything about it, but he could sense easily that she was out of control.

Antonia hardly saw her mother during her Studio 54 days. It was the wildest nightlife in New York. Fabienne met Andy Warhol and a number of famous people there, and became a regular on the scene.

Brandon was beginning to panic about her coming home late every night, and he could no longer hide from the fact that their marriage had disintegrated. Fabienne wasn't made to be a wife or mother. Their union had lasted for eight years. She was thirty-two years old, Brandon had just turned forty and wanted more than Fabienne was capable of as a wife. Antonia needed a mother, and she had neither mother nor father now. Her mother was always out, and started meeting her friends to use cocaine in the daytime. And Brandon was either traveling or came home late at night himself, too tired to deal with the complications at home. The only constant in Antonia's life was the babysitter who took care of her, and felt sorry for her. She was a kind Jamaican woman, and had children of her own. Antonia liked her, but wasn't particularly attached to her. She had seen dozens of babysitters come and go. Fabienne fired them on a whim, regardless of whether Antonia liked them or not. She'd been devastated several times when she'd lost one she'd loved, so she no longer allowed herself to get close to them. Antonia felt unwelcome in her own home, and rarely saw her parents. She knew her mother didn't like her, Fabienne said so openly.

Brandon was trying to figure out what to do about all of it, when he came home one night and found Fabienne packing her bags. He could see that she was high, and wondered how long that had been going on, and why he hadn't noticed before that it was becoming a chronic problem. He didn't see enough of her to observe if she was drunk, on drugs, or sober.

"What are you doing?" he asked her quietly from the doorway, as she threw an armful of short evening dresses into a suitcase, and dumped a load of high heels in with them. She added jeans, T-shirts, and bathing suits, and laughed when she looked at him.

"I'm going to Hollywood to be a movie star," she said, as though it were a done deal and made perfect sense to her. "I met a producer the other night, and he said he can make me a big star. He's going to get me a screen test when I get to L.A."

"So that's it? You're walking out on me and Antonia? For a screen test in L.A.? Who is this guy? How do you know he's not some phony conning you?"

"He's not," she said firmly. Her friends at Studio 54 had heard of him. And even if it didn't pan out with him, she was sure something else would when she got to L.A. She was dying, tied to Brandon in New York.

"Are you planning to come back?" he asked, and she didn't answer him, and then slowly shook her head.

"I can't be what you want. It will kill me. I need to be free again."

"What about our daughter?" he said sadly. He was beyond mourning her leaving him, or begging her to stay. Being married to her had become a living hell, and had been for years. He had hidden from it in his work. But he couldn't hide from it forever. And they hadn't had sex for almost a year. The passion between them had died even before Antonia was born, when Fabienne had felt so ill. And after the birth, she avoided him when she could. She didn't want to get pregnant again, and her attraction to him had disappeared.

"She's your daughter, not mine. You wanted her. I never did. You'd be a good father if you ever stayed home. I'm not a mother. I never wanted to be. And I still don't. She'll be fine with you." She showed no sign of regret or guilt. She was done with both of them. All she wanted now was to be free.

"So that's it? You walk out on her, and on me, and now she's mine?"

"I'll sign papers if you want me to. This is better for both of us. You'll find someone else." He wondered if she already had.

"You can't just walk out on a child, and decide it was a mistake and you changed your mind. A child is forever." He was trying to be reasonable. He didn't want Fabienne anymore either, but Antonia needed a mother, and hadn't had one so far.

"I never changed my mind. It was always a mistake for me," Fabienne said without apology.

"You don't have the right to be that selfish when you have a child." He pleaded Antonia's case for her. His words fell on deaf ears.

"If I stay, I'll die," Fabienne said dramatically. "I want to be an actress, not a wife. I always did. I told you that in the beginning."

"And you used me to come to the States," he said angrily. She was an American citizen by then. And he had provided her a very comfortable life for eight years, and indulged her every whim.

"You wanted me here," she reminded him, "and it worked well in the beginning, until she was born. That changed everything for me." Brandon was wondering what Antonia's life would be like now. But the truth was that she had never had a mother. Fabienne had completely ignored her almost all her life. And he knew he hadn't been much of a father either, in his efforts to avoid his wife in recent years. Poor Antonia seemed like a terrible mistake, to both of them. He didn't have time for her, and he didn't feel equipped to have a child on his own, and her mother didn't want her. Even he realized how unfair it was to Antonia. His business was flourishing, and he knew he couldn't be around enough for her. He'd just have to do what he could, have someone reliable to take care of her, and hope that would be enough. His own loss, if Fabienne left as she said she would, would be so much less than Antonia's. Losing a mother was enormous, and never having had one in a real sense was even worse. Fabienne wasn't capable of loving anyone but herself. He had been aware of it for years, but never thought she'd have the guts to walk away from her own child. She didn't seem to care about leaving either of them, and was leaving Antonia to her father, like some cast-off object she no longer wanted.

"I don't know if I can be around enough to take care of her properly," he said to Fabienne in a serious voice, still hoping she'd reconsider.

"She's very self-sufficient," Fabienne said coldly, "she'll be fine." He wanted it to be true, but he wasn't as sure.

"She's self-sufficient because she's had to be." He felt guilty thinking about it, but he couldn't turn the clock back, and he had to be present constantly in his business to keep a handle on it. He couldn't be around for Antonia too.

"I lost my mother when I was three and I survived," she said matter-of-factly, devoid of compassion.

"You had a great-grandmother. She only has us."

"She has you," Fabienne corrected him, and closed her suitcase. She had packed mostly evening clothes, and jeans and T-shirts.

"How can you walk out on her?" he said with tears in his eyes, suddenly overcome by the reality of what she was doing.

"I have to, to save myself." She made no move to comfort him or apologize. She wasn't sorry. She was desperate to leave. Her friends at Studio 54 were her family now. She was taking her money from her bit parts and modeling jobs, which she had kept in a separate account. She didn't want anything from him, and he didn't offer. She was sure she would make money in L.A. All she wanted now was out, from a loveless marriage and the burden of responsibility for a child she didn't want. She wanted freedom and a starring role in a movie. Her friends had said he was holding her back, and she had decided they were right.

She waited until morning to leave the apartment, and avoided seeing Antonia. Brandon gave her breakfast and then the sitter came. Fabienne was sober by the time she left. Antonia had already gone to school by then, and he was late for work. Brandon stood watching Fabienne go, unable to believe it was happening. He had a moment's flash of memory of when he had first met her and was so taken with her. He wondered now if it had ever been love, or was it just excitement and lust. He made no move toward her as she walked to the front door with her suitcase. She said one of her friends was picking her up to take her to the airport. She was flying to L.A. that morning.

"When she's older, tell Antonia I'm sorry," she said calmly. "This will be better for her in the end." He had a moment's urge to rush toward her and try to stop her, but he knew he couldn't. Nothing would stop Fabienne now. She was on her own path, thinking only of herself, as she always did, not her husband or her daughter. It was all about Fabienne, and no one else. She was following her dreams to become a star, no matter who she hurt in the process, and with little hope of seeing her dreams materialize.

The door closed softly behind her and he knew he'd never see her again. He wasn't sure if he was angry or sad, and all he could think of in the silent apartment was what he was going to do with a seven-year-old child, and no one to help him bring her up. It was overwhelming. He sat down, dropped his face in his hands, and cried, for the little girl whose mother didn't want her and for himself. He had a long hard road ahead. For himself, he was relieved more than sad. Living with Fabienne had been hell for the past several years. He couldn't remember the last time he'd thought he loved her, and he wondered now if he ever had. The lesson he had learned was that passion came at too high a price, and love was only an illusion. He knew he'd never be taken in by a woman like her again. The question was what to do with Antonia now. He had absolutely no idea. And he had no desire to take care of her on his own, but no other choice. He was stuck with her, which was how he saw it. He tried to remember how much he had loved her the first time he saw her when she was born. But that was a long time ago. And he was a different person then. He still thought he loved Fabienne, and he'd had dreams of having a real family. The dream was dead now, Fabienne was gone, and he and his daughter were strangers to each other.

Chapter 3

On the weekend, two days after Fabienne had left, Brandon explained to Antonia that her mother was gone and she wasn't coming back. He tried to explain that she had gone to Hollywood to try to be in movies, but the excuse sounded so empty even to his own ears, and so wrong, that he stopped trying to pretend it made sense and just told Antonia he was sorry. Antonia nodded, her eyes swimming in tears. She took the news stoically, and didn't look surprised. She didn't dare tell him that she had heard her mother on the phone talking to her friends about going to L.A. to become a star. She had been the victim of her mother's rages often enough that she had learned that it was best to avoid her so as not to provoke her. She kept to herself and stayed in her room whenever possible. She was sad at the idea of her mother being gone, and wondered if it was because of something she'd done. But her father didn't seem angry at her. He was very quiet and subdued, and he treated her like a small adult when he told her.

He was gone more than ever once Fabienne left. An opportunity to buy another company presented itself shortly after, and he was spending a lot of time traveling and staying late at his office. Antonia hardly saw him. He had hired Judith, a new babysitter for her, when Fabienne left. She was nicer to Antonia than the others had been, a girl from Salt Lake City, the oldest of eight children, but Antonia still kept her distance from her. She was with her all the time now, and Antonia read or played alone. Judith never mentioned her mother to her. She thought it was better not to.

Antonia wondered how soon her mother would become a star, and if she'd come back to visit then. She hoped she'd see her in a movie one day. But she didn't dare to ask her father.

Brandon didn't mention Fabienne either, and as time went on, he got angry whenever he thought about her. His sense of defeat had turned to bitterness and rage. He felt cheated by her. Antonia noticed too that her father drank more now on the weekends whenever she saw him, which wasn't often. He came home from trips exhausted and paid no attention to her. Her very existence reminded him of Fabienne. Sometimes he'd smash a glass into the fireplace, and she could hear it break from her room, or he fell asleep on the couch, and she'd see him there if she woke up early in the morning before Judith came. She'd creep quietly to the kitchen on bare feet, and pour some milk and cereal into a bowl and eat it in her room. Her room felt like the safest place to be now. Her father never went anywhere with Antonia, and let Judith take her to the park or the playground. He always had something else to do, and Judith stayed with her whenever he went away.

He didn't want the babysitter living there all the time, but she

was willing to stay anytime Brandon was away overnight or traveled. And she warmed the meals the housekeeper left for them every
day. He said he'd try to be home more often, but he wasn't. He had
businesses to run and too much to do to have time for a child. Antonia knew that about him, and wasn't surprised. She was used to his
being away. Her mother's absence didn't change that. They had
breakfast together sometimes, while he read the newspaper. And
then she'd dress for school, and Judith would arrive. Antonia was
used to taking care of herself, had learned to do her own hair, and
dress, with all her buttons done up right. Her mother being gone
didn't change much in her life, although she didn't tell her class-
mates at school. She was ashamed and thought they'd guess that
she had done something terrible for her mother to leave her. And
she wondered if her father would leave her too one day. She thought
anything was possible if she annoyed him.

Right after she turned eight, her father said they were moving to a
new apartment. He said it was bigger and she would like it a lot. She
heard him say to someone that he wanted a clean slate to erase his
memories of living with Fabienne. The new apartment was close to
Central Park, a sunny duplex with two floors, two big bedrooms,
and a maid's room for Judith behind the kitchen when she stayed
over. He took Antonia to see it before they moved in.

"Will Mommy know where to find us, if she comes back?" Antonia
said, looking worried after she saw it, and he looked instantly tense
and annoyed by the question.

"I told you, she's not coming back," he said sternly. He didn't want his daughter hoping, and being disappointed. And she had the distinct impression that he was angry at her, maybe because her mother left. She disappeared into her favorite hiding places when they got back to the old apartment. She liked her new room and it was bigger, and she had noticed convenient nooks and crannies to hide in. She liked disappearing, and when she came out of hiding, she pretended that she was invisible and no one could see her. But Judith did, and always found her. Sometimes Antonia slid under the bed and disappeared completely. She would lie there for a long time, out of sight, staring up at the box spring. She loved the idea of being invisible, and no one knowing where she was. She had gotten used to Judith and didn't mind too much when she found her. And Judith let her keep the distance she needed, without crowding her. She encouraged Antonia to play with other children in the park, but Antonia preferred to sit on a bench reading a book. And the other children paid no attention to her. She never played with them. She was very pale with her blond curls and smaller than other children her age.

She helped Judith pack her books and toys, and they moved after Christmas. Brandon was doing well with his various manufacturing businesses. In each case, he had made a careful study of a failing business in need of money, bought it, and brought it back to life again, increased production until it turned a profit, and in some cases, he would then sell the business and buy another one. His empire was growing faster than projected. He was happy with how his business was growing, and all the money he made. He had built a sizable fortune. He wasn't showy about it, but he liked knowing that Antonia would have security. He believed that was more important than spending time with her. He was building the future for her.

It was after they moved, when Antonia was eight, a year after her mother left, that women entered her father's life, and sometimes came to the apartment, usually late at night, after Judith left. Antonia could hear them laughing in his bedroom. He didn't like Judith staying if he was there, and the women would go home after Antonia was asleep, but sometimes they didn't, and she could hear him sneak them out in the morning. When he stayed out all night, which he did sometimes, Judith would stay with her. One of the things Antonia liked best about the new apartment was a closet where she could hide, under the stairs. It was her favorite hiding place and Judith left her alone there so as not to intrude on her.

Antonia only met a few of her father's girlfriends. Most of the time, they arrived after she'd gone to bed, and she could hear them, talking and laughing downstairs in the living room, or in his bedroom a little later. She met one or two who talked to her. Some of the younger ones didn't even try. They were too busy flirting with her father, the rare times she saw them. She could tell the younger ones weren't happy to see her, even when they pretended to like her. They wanted her father to themselves, which was fine with him.

She heard her father say to one of them, "You don't have to talk to her. She's good about being on her own, and she's very shy. She hides all over the apartment, and disappears for hours sometimes." But the ones she liked always talked to her, for a few minutes anyway, until her father took them to the living room for a drink, and sent Antonia away. They went to his bedroom later, or they went out together.

There was never one woman who was a constant. He seemed to have no interest in marrying again and settling down. Judith said so too. Some of them vanished very quickly, usually the loud, boisterous ones. He seemed to like the quiet, pretty ones who were younger than her mother, and he had a distinct preference for women with dark hair, like Fabienne. But Antonia thought that none of them were as pretty as her mother.

She wondered if her mother had become a star yet, and how long it would take. It had been a year since she'd left, and she and her father were managing, with Judith's help. She was young, in her late twenties, but very responsible, and she had plenty of experience babysitting. Antonia liked her because, as she got older, Judith left her to her own devices, and didn't hound her to do homework or anything else. Antonia always did her homework and school projects, no one had to pressure her, badger her, or force her. She juggled it all well, got good grades, and did well in school. Not having friends eliminated distractions, and she was diligent about her homework, and an excellent student.

When Antonia was nine, Judith left to get married and moved to California with her husband. Brandon found someone else to take her place, an older German woman. Antonia missed Judith, but after her mother left, nothing shocked her anymore. She had learned at an early age that adults were unreliable, and couldn't be counted on to stick around forever, and she didn't attach to them. She liked the new babysitter, Mrs. Schmidt, though not as much as Judith. They were on a walk together one day, coming back from the drugstore, and walked past the movie theater, when Antonia had an idea. She liked going to the movies, and it occurred to her that if she went to the movies, she might see her mother on the screen. It had been two years since she'd left, and Antonia was curious about her. She couldn't say anything to her father, although she knew he'd be upset at what she was about to do, if she could get away with it. She got a small allowance to buy candy, but not enough to pay for a movie ticket. And she'd have to figure out how to get rid of Mrs. Schmidt on a Saturday afternoon for long enough to go to a movie. Her father played golf on Saturdays and was never at home in the afternoon. He came home just in time to change for his evening plans, and then left again quickly, promising to see her the next day, after he had a date and spent the night somewhere else. He thought Antonia was getting to be too old for him to bring women home. And Mrs. Schmidt was a widow and willing to spend the night whenever he asked her to. He had never liked the intrusion of live-in help, even though he could afford it.

Antonia needed money to pay for the movie ticket, and she got it by grabbing a few bills from her father's wallet while he was asleep. He never stirred and never heard her come into his room. He was always tired and had a drink before he went to bed, so he slept soundly. She accomplished her mission in record time, and she only took a few dollars. The next Saturday, she told Mrs. Schmidt that she was going to visit a friend from school in the neighborhood, and could walk there herself, and Mrs. Schmidt believed her. She was an honest child and never got up to mischief or gave her a hard time. It didn't dawn on Mrs. Schmidt that she had never seen Antonia with a friend and she had none. Judith would have caught on immediately. Mrs. Schmidt didn't and was more innocent, which Antonia knew.

The first time Antonia put the plan in motion, it went off without a hitch. She walked to the movie house and waited for a family with children to buy their tickets, stood close to them, and as they got them and left, she slipped her money through the window and got a ticket too.

"Are you alone?" the man in the booth asked her. She shook her head and pointed to the group that had just gotten their tickets and was heading to the concession stand to buy snacks.

"I'm with them," she said clearly, trying to look older than she was. "My mom lets me buy my own ticket." He nodded and smiled at her.

"Enjoy the movie," was all he said, as she went to buy popcorn. It was a Disney film and nothing anyone would object to. She entered the dark theater and wondered if she would see her mother on the screen. It was the main reason she had come, although she liked movies too. Judith used to take her once in a while.

She didn't see her mother on the screen, but she enjoyed the movie, and she felt very grown up going to the movies alone. And it had all gone so smoothly, better than she'd hoped. When she got home she told Mrs. Schmidt how much fun she had had "at my friend's." The kind old German woman was happy for her, and sorry for her without a mother and with a father who was never home. Antonia had no family life at all, and no affection from anyone, no one to love her. Her father ignored her all the time.

Eventually, it became Antonia's Saturday afternoon routine. She always found a family she could slide in next to at the movie theater and buy her ticket. They began to recognize her in the ticket booth, but the movies were always suitable on Saturday afternoons and they never stopped her. They turned a blind eye when they suspected she was alone. She had favorite actors and actresses, and she enjoyed some films more than others. In the darkened movie house, she entered a world that transported her. She liked best the movies about families, and where people loved one another, and were happy in the end. The underlying theme for her was always hoping to see her mother on the screen, but the experience was enjoyable even though she never did.

She floated home afterward, still enthralled by what she'd seen. Being at the movies was her own private world of fantasy, and she looked forward to it all week. Sometimes she wrote stories that she thought would make good movies, and imagined which actors should star in them. Her stories were simple and always had happy endings, eventually the themes got more intricate, and she submitted them in school when she had a writing assignment and usually got an A. And when the teacher asked everyone one day what they wanted to do when they grew up, she answered that she wanted to write movies. It was the most unusual answer the teacher had had that day, and she asked Antonia if her father made movies, and she shook her head.

"He owns companies that make things, like hula hoops and other stuff. My mom is an actress."

"Don't you want to be an actress one day?" the teacher asked her, and Antonia shook her head with a defiant look.

"No, I'd rather write the stories for them," she said, and the teacher went on to the others who wanted to be doctors and nurses and policemen, two of them wanted to be firemen and one wanted to be a teacher. Antonia was the only child in her class who wanted to write screenplays. The teacher mentioned it to Brandon, when he came to a parent-teacher conference a few weeks later. The teacher thought it was a very creative career goal, and said that Antonia had talent with writing. Brandon looked startled, and his face hardened when the teacher mentioned Antonia's mother being an actress. He made no comment, and asked Antonia about it at breakfast the next day.

"Why do you want to write screenplays?" he asked with a puzzled look, and she didn't answer, afraid of his anger at her. She hadn't seen her mother in two years, and in his heart of hearts, he always hoped that Antonia would forget her, and not idealize her in some way. She fantasized sometimes that she would write a movie for her mother to star in one day, but she knew not to say it to him. He got angry whenever the subject of her mother came up, or even her name. She could see it in his eyes and the way his face tightened up. He hated it when Antonia mentioned her mother, so she didn't. There was no point getting him angry at her. He never said it, but she was a constant reminder of a union with a woman he had come to hate. He despised everything Fabienne had done, her blatant narcissism, and the fact that she had walked out on them without a backward glance. All he knew about her now was what he had found out at the time of their divorce.

She was living in L.A. with an actor then, and was working at a bar while she tried to get a part in a movie, and hadn't succeeded. At thirty-four, she was a little old to be discovered as an ingénue.

Brandon knew it was never going to happen, and maybe she had given up her dream by now, but he had no way of knowing. She had relinquished her parental rights in the divorce, and had no claim on Antonia, and had never contacted her. She was only her biological mother, not a mother in fact anymore. And much of the time, he was an absentee father. He had his own life to lead, and his businesses to run. There were the women he dated, a constantly revolving assortment of women he enjoyed for a short time, and then he moved on, having promised them nothing, and attached to none of them.

There was little time for his daughter in the scheme of his life. He was dutiful and provided for her, which he told himself was enough. Antonia lacked for nothing, and she was in good hands with Mrs. Schmidt. He intended to see to it that she had a good education, in a field that would be practical and lucrative, so she could be independent one day. He didn't expect her to stick around after college, which was only nine years away, and by then he would have provided her with what she needed. He saw her as a responsibility more than a pleasure or a person. She was a job he had taken on, and which had been cast on him by his irresponsible ex-wife when she left. He didn't expect Antonia to stay around forever and he didn't want her to. It was a big world and she had much to learn and discover. He demonstrated no affection toward her and expected none in return. He had no idea what she liked or who she was. She was like an object Fabienne had left behind, and he was fulfilling an obligation, nothing more.

There was no room for frivolity in Brandon's life, or the kind of passion he had indulged in with Fabienne. It was the last thing he wanted, and hoped it would never happen again. He was looking forward to his own freedom and independence when Antonia left. He wouldn't have to think about her then, and worry about her being watched by a babysitter, or if she was growing up well without a mother. When she grew up, he could see her for holidays, and who knew where she would live, New York or another city, or maybe somewhere in Europe. He had no desire or need to hold on to her. He had grown harder and colder after Fabienne left. He was harder with Antonia too. And the walls he built around himself were impossible for a child to climb. She knew better than to try. He had become a very cold man.

And although he never expressed it to her, Antonia could always sense that he couldn't wait for her to grow up and go away, so he could reclaim his single life in full. Knowing that made her feel like an intruder in their home, as she always had. She was an unwanted guest who had been abandoned by her mother like so much luggage, and her father had no time for her. She was a painful reminder of a bad marriage to a terrible woman. She was a beautiful child, and well behaved, but she was a burden nonetheless, and there wasn't a single day in her life when she didn't feel it. Her father never had to say it. The only way she could escape feeling like a burden to him was to be invisible. She had learned that in her first seven years with her mother, and it served her well. Knowing how unwelcome she was, she simply made herself small, tucked herself in somewhere, and disappeared. She always felt safe when she did. It was the only time she felt safe in the loveless world she lived in.

Chapter 4

By the time Antonia was twelve, she had seen every appropri-
ate current movie, some several times, and she was quite knowl-
edgeable about them. She knew all the actors and actresses, and she
still had a faint hope that she would catch a glimpse of her mother
on the screen one day. But she focused more on the stories now, the
action and the plot and how it developed throughout the film. The
stories that she wrote herself were surprisingly adult and cinematic.
She turned them in at school as her writing projects. Her father had
never seen any of them. He behaved, even to Antonia, as though she
were a duty he had inherited, like someone else's child who had
been dropped on his doorstep, and he did what he thought he should
for her. He spent very little time with her, and she felt as though he
was counting the days until she left. He reminded her constantly of
how many years she had left before she went to college, as though
she was supposed to be counting the days too.

At twelve, she was allowed to go to the movies alone. He trusted her to choose wisely, since she was a sensible child who never gave him any trouble. Having been rejected by her mother, she never wanted to give him any reason to reject her too, or send her away to school. She liked living at home, and the freedom she had there, since only the babysitter paid attention to her. And now her father gave her the price of admission to the movies. She no longer had to steal money from his wallet, although he never figured out that she had, since she took so little.

She looked younger than her age, because she was small, but the people at the movie theater knew her well now, and expected her Saturday visits. They gave her free popcorn or a box of candy once in a while.

Other than the movies, she went to school, where she got good grades. She went ice-skating occasionally. Her father let her go to ballet class for a year, but it took too much time away from her studies, so she gave it up. Her life remained solitary. She had no close friends at school. She was always separate and alone, ashamed of not having a mother and a constantly absent, indifferent father. She couldn't explain it to anyone and didn't want to.

She looked somewhat like her father, who was a handsome man. She had more delicate features and was beautiful, though she had none of the smoldering, exotic appearance of her mother. That was a relief to her father. He never wanted to see that face again, even on his child. But Antonia was nothing like her. She had her own elfin appearance and beauty. She took French in school, in honor of her mother, and her father questioned her about it. She lied and told him the Spanish class was full. He didn't want her idolizing her mother in any way. She still dreamt about her mother at times, and remembered her raven-haired, striking looks and dark eyes. But often they were frightening dreams of her mother screaming at her. Antonia had no gentle memories of Fabienne. There had been no happy times. The best her mother had ever done for her was ignore her. When Antonia had caught her attention, it was never for a good reason, and ended in a jealous rage.

When Antonia was twelve, her father dispensed with Mrs. Schmidt's services. He told her she was too old for a babysitter now, and Mrs. Schmidt was getting older and becoming frail. Their house-keeper still came to clean the house daily, while Antonia was in school. She left things for Antonia to eat, and she knew how to cook enough simple things to feed herself if necessary. When her father went away, a neighbor looked in on her to make sure she was all right, and wasn't sick or getting into trouble. She was used to being alone now, and most of the time, she went to bed before her father came home. Or he didn't come home at all. She felt obligated to take care of herself and not be a burden to him. She always felt like an uninvited guest in someone else's home. Fabienne had imprinted that on her early and the impression hadn't changed. With Brandon busy with his own life and successful businesses, he had little time for a child. It might have been different if Fabienne had stayed, and Antonia thought they might have had a home life then, but it hadn't worked out that way. She missed the idea of it, but it was something she had never known. She existed in a solitary world and always had. Babysitters had provided the only affection, and they were gone now.

She wrote her stories at night after she finished her homework. In many ways, she was an exemplary child. Brandon's friends told him he was lucky, and wondered how he had achieved it, but Antonia knew she had no leeway to misbehave. Who knew what he would do if she did? He might send her away forever, since she knew he didn't want her around.

When he was home, she read late into the night sometimes with a flashlight, so he didn't know she was awake. The stories she wrote all had happy endings. They were the books and movies she liked best. She liked the ones where everyone ended up safe, and loved, and happy, and left you smiling at the end. It was what she wanted her life to be, not the solitary one she led.

At thirteen, she felt as invisible as she tried to be. Even at school. The boys had no interest in her, since she was small and had no womanly attributes yet. Some of the girls in her class were fully developed by then. She looked more like nine or ten than thirteen, so they paid no attention to her. And the "cool" girls at school had formed cliques by then, and never included her. They acted as though she didn't exist, and she tried to pretend she didn't. Even some of her teachers paid no attention to her as she sat quietly at the back of the class. The taller students in front of her blocked her view. She didn't care. She listened to the classes carefully and took precise notes to study later for tests, at which she excelled.

She saw less and less of her father then. His businesses were booming. The eighties were good to him.

A year later, when she turned fourteen and started high school, she heard him come home late at night several times, and she heard a woman's voice. He hadn't done that in a long time, and it sounded like the same woman every time. By breakfast the next morning, the woman was gone, and Antonia wondered who she was. She finally saw her one Saturday. She was at the breakfast table, and her father introduced her as Lara, and offered no explanation as to who she was. Antonia didn't ask. The three of them sat together in silence at the breakfast table. Antonia was about to leave and go back to her room when Lara spoke up. She was an attractive blonde and was slightly older than the girls he used to bring home. She looked like she was in her mid or late thirties. She wore her hair in a stylishly cut bob and had green eyes. She was wearing blue jeans and a crisp white shirt, and was appropriately casual for a Saturday. She had big gold bangle bracelets on her wrists. Brandon didn't seem enamored with her, but he appeared comfortable with her, as though he knew her well. She had a warm smile when she spoke.

"What are you doing today, Antonia?" she asked as Antonia was about to leave the kitchen. She was surprised that Lara had spoken to her. Her father never asked about her plans.

"I go to the movies on Saturdays," she said politely, hesitating in the doorway.

"That sounds like fun. Maybe I could go with you sometime." Antonia looked even more shocked at that, and almost asked her why. "I love going to the movies." Antonia smiled shyly at her, and didn't know what to say.

"So do I," was all she could think of and left as quickly as she could before her father got mad at her.

"We should go with her sometime," Lara said gently to Brandon, who looked at her over his paper with surprise, didn't say a word, and went back to reading again, as Antonia quietly slipped away down the hall, and disappeared to her room. She heard her father's voice in the distance before she closed her door.

"You don't need to do that, you know."

"Do what? Offer to go to a movie?" Lara was surprised. It seemed like a harmless suggestion to her.

"Make friends with her. She's used to being on her own. She's very independent, and very shy. She probably goes to the movies with her friends."

"Do you know that? Have you asked?" She was startled by his reaction to her speaking to his daughter, and how little he knew about her himself, or seemed to care. It was a side of him she hadn't seen yet, and was startled by.

"No. She's been going to the movies on her own for years. I have no idea who she meets there."

"You should. Why don't we take her to dinner sometime?"

He scowled at that.

"At her age, I'm sure she'd rather be with her friends." Introducing Lara to Antonia had been a big step for him, and so was letting her spend the night. They'd been dating for a year, and he'd been extremely cautious with her. Fabienne had made him gun-shy about long-term relationships, and had driven him back into his shell. He never wanted another relationship like theirs, and he still felt extremely burned by it. She had left him after several unhappy years, and abandoned him with a child to raise on his own.

He was forty-seven years old now, and had no desire to marry again. All he wanted to do was get Antonia through the next four years, see her off to college, and concentrate on his businesses as they continued to grow. His dreams of a house in the suburbs and more children had vanished with Fabienne. He knew now that they were a fantasy that wouldn't suit him anymore. His life had taken a different turn. He no longer trusted women, but Lara was an exception to the rule. She was an independent woman with her own business in real estate. She never pressured him and wasn't intent on marriage, so he had gotten more involved with her than he had with any woman since Fabienne. He had taken a long time to introduce her to his daughter. Lara hadn't pressured him about that either. She was an easygoing woman who was content as she was. She had lost a brother when she was very young, and it had convinced her that she never wanted children of her own. She had watched it almost kill her parents, and age them overnight when he died. She was content to date Brandon, with no particular promise about the future, and he had told her early on that he had one child from his first marriage and didn't want more. He said he didn't have the energy for a child or a wife, and she accepted that. But Antonia seemed like such a quiet, lonely child that it touched her heart. She knew that her mother had left them seven years before, when Antonia was very young to lose her mother. Brandon always insisted that she was fine, but Lara couldn't help wondering if he was right.

"Would you mind my going to the movies with her sometime if she wants to?" she asked him directly and he hesitated, and then nodded.

"I suppose it would be all right. But you'll find that she keeps her distance. She disappears all the time. Most of the time you either don't notice her she's so quiet or you can't find her. She vanishes like a ghost. She's a little odd, and very much a loner." Lara suspected that Antonia had had no other choice, with a workaholic father and her mother gone.

They left at lunchtime to go to a new restaurant Brandon wanted

to try, and had promised Lara he would take her to. And the following Saturday, Lara was at breakfast again. They had no plans that
day and it was raining. Brandon said he had a little work to do, and
Lara invited Antonia to the movies. She didn't know what to say, so
she said yes, not wanting to be rude. She wondered why Lara was
making an effort with her, since her father never did. She seemed
nice.

They walked the few blocks to the movie theater together, and
Lara treated Antonia to the tickets, which surprised her too. Antonia
had asked her on the walk over if she had children, and Lara said
she didn't.

"Your father is very lucky to have you," she commented, and Antonia wasn't sure that he'd agree with her, but it was a nice thing to
say.

"I'll be going to college in four years," she said, as though to reassure her that she wouldn't be around forever. Her father reminded
her of it constantly.

"That's still a long time off. You don't need to think about that
yet," Lara said kindly, and then paid for their tickets, and treated
Antonia to popcorn and candy, which seemed very generous to her.
She usually had enough money for one or the other, not both.

They enjoyed the movie, which was a current box office hit. It was
just the kind of movie Antonia loved, with family in the story and a
happy ending. They were both smiling when they left the theater
and Lara could see how much she had enjoyed it.

"Did you have a family like that, growing up?" Antonia asked,
feeling brave, and curious about her.

"No, I didn't. I had a brother who died of a brain tumor when he was twelve and I was nine. My parents got divorced after that, and my father moved to another city, so I grew up with my mom and didn't see my dad very often."

"My mom left when I was seven," Antonia said on the walk back to the apartment. "My father doesn't like to talk about her. He hates her. She's an actress and she lives in L.A. Or at least she did. I don't really know where she is now. I never see her."

"Your father told me a little about it," Lara said discreetly. He had told her about Fabienne and their disastrous marriage when they started dating, when he told her he never wanted to marry again. "A lot of people have complicated childhoods. More than one realizes," Lara said gently.

"My dad grew up without a father, he was killed in the war."

"We all have baggage of one kind or another." Lara smiled at Antonia. She liked her and thought she was a sweet child, and more mature than she appeared. "What do you like to do, aside from go to movies?"

"Write," Antonia said immediately. "I like ice skating and horses, and I used to do ballet. I want to write screenplays one day. I want to go to USC. They have a great film school. My father wants me to study economics or something more practical. I hate math."

Lara laughed. "So do I. I studied architecture, dropped out when it got too mathematical for me, and went into real estate instead. You never know what you'll wind up working at in the end. You just have to keep an open mind and see what you like doing when you know more about it."

"I think law school would be okay with my dad too, but I don't want to be a lawyer. I know I want to write. I get good grades in it in school."

"I'd love to read one of your stories sometime," Lara said carefully. She didn't want to rush her or crowd her, but she suspected that Antonia was starving for attention and affection. Brandon had been nice to her so far, but he was not a warm person. His marriage to Fabienne had left him unwilling to let anyone in, including his own child. He had admitted it to Lara several times, and didn't plan to change.

They had gotten back to the apartment by then, and Brandon was waiting to take Lara out. He noticed how expansive Antonia seemed as they chatted when they walked into the apartment, but Antonia fell silent as soon as she saw him. He and Lara left a few minutes later. Antonia thanked Lara again for the movie and the treats.

"We'll do it again whenever you want," she said before they left. Antonia was still smiling and looked wistful to see her leave, which touched Lara's heart.

Lara talked to Brandon about it in the cab on the way to her place. She had invited some friends over for drinks, and he helped her get ready for them. He did more at her apartment than he did at his. She had a beautiful apartment downtown, with a river view, and it was handsomely decorated with things she had collected on her travels. He felt warm and comfortable there.

"She's a lovely girl, Brandon. I had a really nice time with her."

"She never gives me any trouble," he commented, "and she does very well in school." He sounded proud of her, although he never admitted it to Antonia. He was old school that way.

"She needs more than that, I think. Being a good student and staying out of trouble is not enough. She has dreams for the future, and I think she needs someone to talk to."

"That's a mother's job at her age. It's not my strong suit," he admitted. Lara liked his honesty, and when he relaxed and let her in, she liked how smart he was.

"You have to wear both hats in your case. You have no other choice." He didn't answer. The choice he had made years before was not to engage with Antonia, because she was Fabienne's daughter, but she was his too. He forgot that at times.

"She seemed very chatty with you," he commented finally. "She never is with me."

"Maybe you could spend a little more time with her," she suggested gently. "I don't mind if you'd ever like to bring her along with us." But that wasn't something he wanted to do. He compartmentalized his life, and it was already a big step that he had brought Lara home, let her spend the night there, and introduced her to Antonia. He didn't want to get in any deeper than that. And if the relationship didn't last, there was no point letting Antonia get attached to her. That wouldn't be fair to her either. Lara could guess that those were his thoughts.

They had a nice time with her guests that night. They were mostly her friends that he had come to like and a few of his. All of his friends were still married, he was the only divorced man in their group. Most of her friends were married too, with a few who were holdouts like her, who had never married. It was a congenial group.

He spent that night at Lara's, after the guests left, and he knew Antonia would be fine by herself. She sat alone at dinner that night, thinking about Lara. She had enjoyed going to the movies with her, and was interested in what she'd said. Her home life seemed pretty sad as a kid, with her brother dying and her parents getting divorced and her father moving away. But she seemed like a happy person. She wondered if her father was serious about her. It didn't seem likely. She hoped she'd see her again.

She wrote a story that night about someone like Lara. The story was sad because of her brother dying, but in her story, the father came back at the end, which made it happier. And the parents got back together. She liked the story a lot, and put it in a folder to take to school. She might show it to Lara one day, when she saw her again.

Lara went to the movies with her several times after that. They talked about the movies afterward and Lara was impressed by how sophisticated Antonia was about the nuances of every film. She said something about it to Brandon, and he looked irritated the moment she did.

"I don't want her going into the movies as a career. Her mother was a wannabe actress, with no talent I might add. That was bad enough. Her ambition and obsession about it ruined our lives."

"Writing screenplays is not the same thing. And what if she has talent? You can't force her in a direction she doesn't want."

"If you open that door, it can lead to something else, like acting. I won't let her do that." He was adamant, unreasonably so, in Lara's eyes.

"She's not her mother, Brandon. She's an entirely different person. And she's part you. You can't punish her for what her mother was."

"Yes, I can," he said stubbornly. "I don't want anything related to acting or movies anywhere near my home." He had never recovered from his marriage to Fabienne, and refused to discuss it further. But he did allow Lara to spend time with Antonia occasionally, and he was always surprised to see how well they got along. They had a relationship that he had never had with her. Whenever Lara was at the house, Antonia seemed much less inclined to disappear, and stuck around to chat with her.

"She thinks she's invisible," Lara explained to him one day.

"Invisible? That's ridiculous. What makes her think that?"

"I don't know. I get the feeling that she thinks it's what you want, never to be bothered by her. She's afraid you'll get mad at her and send her away."

He looked shocked. "Why would I do that? I've hardly ever gotten angry at her."

"I think it's a leftover from another time, when it was safer not to be seen." Antonia had told her about her parents' fights, but Lara didn't share that with him.

"I used to feel that way about Fabienne. I just stayed at the office as late as I could. It's a habit I've never managed to break since." He worked long hours, as Lara knew too. She had to wrestle with him to get him to leave the office and spend an evening with her.

"She didn't have that option so she hid, and convinced herself she was invisible. And that way she felt safe."

"And now?" he asked. He was getting to know his daughter

through Lara, and she was a competent interpreter. More so, because she liked them both.

"You said it yourself, old habits are hard to break. She feels invisible at school too. She feels different from the other kids. She looks younger and she's not in a clique of mean girls, and she's been embarrassed for years not to have a mother. You know how kids are. They can be hard on each other."

"I felt that way about not having a dad at a boys' school," he said, looking misty-eyed at the memory. He hadn't thought it would affect Antonia as much, but clearly it had. "Antonia and I really don't know each other," he said sadly. "Maybe we'll do better when she grows up."

"You don't have much time left," Lara reminded him gently. "She's almost there. High school will fly by, and then she'll be gone, in college, and she won't come back much. I never did." She had fled her depressing home as soon as she could.

"My mother died when I was in college so I never got the chance to come back. There was no one to come back to," Brandon said. She realized then, more than ever before, that he had lived in a state of emotional deprivation for years, and then Fabienne had come along and blown him wide open, and burned him badly while he was vulnerable, and he had been shut down ever since. It was terrible luck for Antonia. Lara was trying to slowly pry him open, for his sake and her own, but it was a hard battle she hadn't won yet, and she wasn't sure she'd ever succeed. Fabienne had done a lot of damage before she left. But as long as they were dating, Lara continued to chip away at him. Sometimes it worked and sometimes it didn't. But he made several awkward attempts at conversation with Antonia, and was surprised at how much he learned about her, particularly when they talked about films. She always drew the parallels with real life and was amazingly astute, just as Lara had said. She didn't seem to disappear quite as often, especially when Lara was around. Their growing friendship touched him, more than he wanted to admit.

In the summer before her sophomore year in high school, Antonia, who would be turning fifteen in August, went away to camp in Maine for two months. Her father had sent her there every summer, ever since her mother had left. He didn't know what else to do with her. It was a sailing camp and she was a good sailor, but she admitted to Lara before she left that she didn't want to go, didn't enjoy it, and felt like an outcast there, but her father insisted on sending her every year.

"I'm terrible at team sports," she confessed. "I'm too small and I'm lousy at sports anyway, so no one wants me on their team. Softball, baseball, touch football, field hockey, I suck at all of it. I always make the swimming team, but that's about it. They draw straws about who's on what team, and the losers get me. And honestly, I don't really care if they win or lose."

"So you become invisible again while you're at camp?" Lara asked her, and Antonia grinned.

"Yeah. I guess. I don't want to go again next year, but he'll probably make me."

Lara passed the information on to Brandon, but it didn't do much good.

"What else am I going to do with her in the summer? I only take two weeks off myself, and when I do, I need a break. I can't entertain a kid for two months, while I'm working. I've had her on my own since she was seven. I've been sending her to camp ever since, and it's one of the best. Kids even come from Europe to go there."

"Maybe so, but she hates it. None of them want her on their sports teams. The only thing she likes to do there is swim and sail."

"I know. She's told me that every year." For eight years.

"You could take a little more time off and rent a house somewhere. You've said yourself that she's good at entertaining herself."

"Renting summer houses is what married people do. I'm a single man with an almost fifteen-year-old daughter. She's better off at camp for two months, with other kids and lots of planned activities." But Lara didn't agree. She was doing something more exciting herself, and going to Greece for three weeks, with friends, as she did every year, to Spetses, a romantic, rustic, tiny island she'd fallen in love with years before. And she was going away with him for two weeks to Shelter Island, to stay in a house he had borrowed from friends who were going to Europe. He was upset about her going to Greece, but didn't want to complain. He had a busy work summer ahead, and she didn't want to sit in the sweltering city waiting for him.

They had a wonderful time in the house on Shelter Island, and she left for Greece immediately afterward. She came home tanned, and relaxed, with stories about the good time she'd had, and he stunned her the night she came home. She was happy to see him, and they fell into bed, made love, and lay in each other's arms afterward. He was technically a good lover although not a warm person.

"I've missed you terribly," he admitted, which was unlike him, and she could tell that he had missed her and was thrilled to have her back. Antonia was due back from camp in two weeks, and had sent him the regulation postcard once a week that was required. Brandon was warmer with Lara than he'd ever been, and she teased him that she should go away more often, if this was the welcome she got when she returned. He couldn't keep his hands off her, and held her close.

"I've done a lot of thinking while you were gone," he said softly, nuzzling her neck. She wondered if he was going to ask her to move in with him, but she knew that was too bold a move for him, and he didn't want to set that example for his daughter, as he had told her several times in the nearly two years they'd been dating. She couldn't guess what he had in mind. He looked her in the eye then and said in a soft voice, "Will you marry me, Lara?" There was silence for a minute as she tried to absorb it. She had never expected to marry him, and the arrangement they had suited her. She wasn't asking for more. She was about to turn forty, and didn't mind being single at all. She had made her peace with it long since, and in many ways, it worked for her. She liked her independence, and she didn't want children.

"What did you just say? Are you serious?" she asked him, looking him in the eye as they lay there in each other's arms, but she could see he was.

"I never thought I'd get married again, and I wish I'd met you first, instead of that monster. It's taken me years to get over her, and I finally have. I want to be married to you, if you'll have me." He kissed her then and it was a long time before they came up for air.

"I might if you promise to take a month's holiday every summer. In that case, I'd consider it, and maybe a week at Christmas to go skiing."

"We'll be free in three years," he said as an inducement. "Antonia will be in college then."

"I don't need to be free of Antonia," she said. "I love her. You're a package deal, as far as I'm concerned. I've never actually been that keen on getting married. It always seemed too risky to me, but I'd consider it with you," she said, and kissed him gently on the lips.

"Is that a yes?" She nodded, and he kissed her, and made love to her again a moment later. They were both smiling afterward. "Does this mean we're engaged?" he asked her, still breathless.

"I think it does," she confirmed.

"I don't have an engagement ring for you yet," he said. Fabienne had left with his mother's sapphire ring, which he would have liked to give to Antonia one day. He suspected that Fabienne had probably pawned it. She had refused to return it.

"I don't need one. I'll take your word for it."

He made what he thought was a daring suggestion then. "Let's just do it, right away, would that be okay with you?"

"It sounds perfect," she said dreamily, lying next to him.

"You're okay with that, no big white dress or fancy wedding?"

"I'm too old for that, and my parents don't speak to each other, which would be too complicated. My father is remarried to a woman my mother hates. I can't deal with them. When do you want to do it?"

"Yesterday," he said happily. It was all working out better than he'd hoped.

"What about Antonia? Shouldn't she be here with us? I don't want to upset her, or make her feel left out." She already felt alienated enough and left out of her father's life.

"I think she'll be thrilled, and I'd rather it be just the two of us. I've been married, and you never wanted to be. Why don't we just do it, and then pick her up at camp?"

Lara looked worried about it, although a simple civil wedding appealed to her. But she didn't want to start their life off on the wrong foot.

"I think we need Antonia's permission," she said seriously.

"Oh God," he said, and rolled his eyes. "What if she says no?"

"Then we'll wait until she says yes."

"I don't want to wait," he said, pouting like a little boy.

"Neither do I, but I don't want to hurt her feelings. Let's call her and ask."

"Now?" He sat up in bed, looking shocked. "We're not allowed to call her at camp except in an emergency."

"Good. Tell them it's an emergency," she said happily, and he went to get the number out of his wallet with shaking hands.

"This is crazy. We're asking a fifteen-year-old for permission to get married."

"She's the only family you've got, and the only one who matters."

He looked worried then. "Do I have to ask your father for permission?"

"Definitely not. He's a curmudgeon, and he'd probably tell you

you're making a terrible mistake, and would say no. Just Antonia." He had already put the camp number into his phone and it was ringing. Brandon gave his name and Antonia's, and said it was an emergency and asked to have her called to the phone. The person who answered responded immediately that they would get her right away and to hold the line. They didn't ask what the emergency was.

They waited a full five minutes and Antonia sounded breathless and worried when she answered. She'd run all the way from her cabin.

"What's wrong, Dad?" At least he was calling himself, so she knew he was alive. If he was dead, she had no idea what would happen to her. She thought of it sometimes.

"Nothing. I didn't know how else to reach you. I'm sorry if I scared you." For an instant she had worried too that he had heard that her mother was dead, but she didn't tell him that. He put her on speakerphone then. "Lara and I have a question to ask you." She waited to hear what it was, and couldn't imagine. "We want your permission to get married. We wanted to get your okay first."

Antonia let out a piercing scream which turned into a whoop of joy. "Yes! Yes! Yes! When?"

"Now, soon, tomorrow, we thought we'd just go to city hall and do it before you come home, and pick you up at camp. You're okay with it?"

"I give you my permission, and I love you both." Brandon couldn't remember the last time she had told him she loved him, or that he had said it to her. Maybe he never had.

"We love you too," Lara volunteered for both of them.

"So do I," Brandon added, and meant it. He felt closer to his daughter than he had in years. Lara had gently shifted the dynamic between them and changed their lives.

"You don't want a big wedding?" she asked them, and Lara answered.

"I'd feel stupid in a big white dress. I'd rather do it this way."

"So would I," Brandon added, although he'd gotten married at city hall before. But this felt entirely different. He and Lara were both grown-ups and knew what they were doing, and who they were marrying. They'd had two years to get to know each other. Brandon knew this wasn't a mistake, and Lara did too. And so did Antonia.

"See you in two weeks, Mr. and Mrs. Adams." Antonia giggled. "I can't wait to see you both."

"We love you," Lara said again before they hung up.

The next few days after that were a whirlwind. In the end, she did wear a white dress, a simple cotton eyelet one, and carried a big bouquet of white daisies. They spent five days at an inn in Vermont as their honeymoon, and picked Antonia up at camp in Maine as promised. She threw her arms around both of them when she saw them, and had her duffel bag and trunk packed and ready to go. Brandon put them in the SUV he had rented, and they headed for New York. His dreams of having a family had come true, just with a different woman. A much better one this time. It was a new beginning for them all.

Chapter 5

The rest of Antonia's high school years were a different experience thanks to Lara. Brandon worked a little less than he had before and spent more time at home, and Lara had a busy career with her real estate business too. They all had their jobs to do, and Antonia had high school to get through and kept her grades up so she would get into a good college.

She still kept to herself some of the time, the attention that Lara gave her was unfamiliar to her. Lara tried not to intrude on Antonia, once she moved in. Antonia had spent so many years with no one paying attention to her, and no one to talk to, that Lara's kindness was overwhelming at times, but Antonia was grateful for it. They became movie buddies every Saturday afternoon, and Brandon tried to communicate better with Antonia, but it didn't come easily to him. No matter how hard he tried, and how different she was from her mother, Brandon couldn't separate her in his mind from Fabienne. She was a constant reminder of his terrible experience in a disastrous marriage.

"It's not her fault, Brandon," Lara said when he admitted it to her. "She's not her mother."

"I know she's not," he said, "but I can't separate her from the memories." Antonia sensed it too, and it made her sense that she should be invisible, in order not to upset him. He and Lara were so happy together that she still felt like an intruder at times. She knew that her father was waiting for her to leave, so he could be alone with his wife.

The time came soon enough. She was spared camp the next year, and Lara convinced Brandon to rent a house in Water Mill on Long Island for a month, and they rented it the following summer too. Lara improved the quality of Antonia's life immeasurably. She had never wanted children of her own, but she loved Antonia as she would have her own child. She was a wonderful stepmother, and Antonia was only sorry that she had come into her life so late.

With strong grades, she applied to several Ivy League colleges. She applied to USC, for their film school. She still wanted to write screenplays after she graduated. But she had several backup schools, since her father didn't want her on the West Coast. No matter how much she begged and Lara cajoled, he was adamant. So, she applied to NYU's Tisch School of the Arts, for their classes on film. It was her first choice.

She was accepted in March, for the fall semester, and Brandon stubbornly said he wouldn't let her go. He wanted her to go to Columbia, as he had, to Barnard, the women's school, or any other school. But not film school at NYU. They had a division for actors too, and he was sure she would be seduced into the acting division, and wind up an actress like her mother, and he flatly refused to let that happen.

"I have no interest in being an actress," she insisted to him, and he wouldn't listen, to her or Lara. She was about to accept a school she didn't want to attend, two days before NYU's deadline, when he and Lara had a showdown. It sounded suspiciously like one of his battles with Fabienne, but Lara was fighting for Antonia's right to attend the college she wanted. Antonia felt guilty to be the cause of dissent between them, and was filling out the acceptance form to her backup school, when Brandon walked into her room, stone-faced.

"I give up. You can go to NYU," he said in a voice so low she almost couldn't hear him. She turned in her desk chair to look at him as he stood in the doorway. He didn't want to fight with Lara over this, and somehow she had gotten through to him, and was almost willing to risk their marriage for it. She had never fought so hard for anything in her life.

"Do you mean it?" Antonia stood up and stared at him, and rushed to hug him as he nodded. Lara had finally won the war when she pointed out to him how he had punished Antonia all her life for reminding him of her mother, and how unfair it was. He knew it was true, and finally conceded.

"Yes, I mean it," he said in a gruff voice, as she hugged him. "But don't ever tell me you're becoming an actress. I'll never speak to you again if you do."

"I won't, Dad. I promise." There was no chance of it, and he knew it too. She wanted to write, not be an actress. And she was nothing like her mother.

Lara helped her pack to move into the dorm on Washington Square. Brandon came too, to set up the room. He hung pictures, while Lara made her bed. Brandon set up the stereo and the computer and carried her bicycle up the stairs, while Antonia hung up her clothes in the tiny closet. She had a roommate from Virginia, Betty McCabe, who was going to be in the Tisch School of the Arts too, and wanted to be a playwright. She had already written two plays, which had been produced in summer stock that summer. Her parents and younger sister had come to settle her in and looked like nice people.

Lara reminded Antonia to call if she needed anything. They were a short ride uptown. Brandon stood looking stiff and awkward when it came time to leave. He hadn't expected to care, but he was filled with emotion, to be leaving the daughter whom he hardly knew and had kept his distance from all her life. She was taking to the skies now. It was too late to undo the past, but there was hope for a better future, with Lara to assist them.

Antonia felt awkward with him too, and thanked him again for letting her go to school there, and Lara for convincing him. He had hoped for this day for so long, after the responsibility Fabienne had left him to shoulder alone, but now that it had come, he had tears in his eyes and a lump in his throat, and wished he could undo the last eighteen years, or at least the last eleven. Lara could see what he was feeling and felt sorry for him. He had shut Antonia out for years, keeping himself from her, and she had lived without warmth or protection for most of her life, but their bond to each other had been slowly getting stronger since his marriage to Lara. She was the best thing that had happened to both of them. She had humanized Brandon, after the holocaust he had been through with Fabienne. Antonia had paid a high price for it too. Both her parents had cheated her of a loving childhood.

Her reward for it now was that her dreams were beginning to come true. This was the first step toward the career she wanted as a screenwriter.

She loved all her classes and professors, whom she found fascinating. She bought all her books and the materials she needed, and went to the library to start working on her first paper.

She left the library just before closing time, and saw a tall, handsome boy with dark hair coming down the steps at the same time. He looked vaguely familiar, but she couldn't place him. She had seen so many new faces in the past few days. She didn't know if they were in the same class, or she had just seen him on the street, or in a hallway.

"Hi, I'm Jake Burton," he said as they reached the street together. She looked cautious before she answered. "We're in the same dorm. I saw you when you moved in with all your stuff." He smiled easily at her. "I'm in the Department of Drama. What about you?" It was the famous acting school that was part of the Tisch School of the Arts.

"I'm doing screenplays, or I want to." She smiled at him then, still hesitant.

"What's your name?" He had to pry it out of her. In new and overwhelming circumstances, her old shyness had taken over.

"Antonia."

"I'm from San Francisco," he said confidently. It occurred to her that he would be a gorgeous actor one day. But she wasn't interested in romance. She just wanted to get her bearings, get settled at school, and do a good job there. She got on her bicycle and rode away a minute later.

She saw him again at the grocery store nearest the campus two days later. He was wearing a dark blue V-neck sweater and black jeans, and black Converse high top sneakers. She'd been in the library since her last class, working on a screenplay. He wound up behind her in the checkout line, and chatted with her again. She couldn't tell if he was hitting on her, or just being friendly, but he made conversation easy, and they talked for several minutes as they waited in line.

"How's it going?" he asked her with a broad smile. He reminded her of a big friendly puppy wagging his tail, and she smiled at the image.

"It's intense. They're already giving us assignments." She was beginning to wonder if she was good enough for the school. It was harder than she'd expected.

"They're giving us a shitload of work too. I have two acting classes and an audition tomorrow. I thought I was ready for this. I took acting classes all through high school. Now I'm not so sure."

"Me too," she said, relieved to be able to say it out loud. He was the only person she knew so far, other than her roommate, who was pleasant, but Betty was out all the time, and had friends in the dorm, so Antonia hadn't seen much of her since she'd arrived. It was a big urban campus, which made it harder to meet people, with everyone rushing around and many students living off campus.

"What's your screenplay about?" he asked casually as they approached the cash register.

"It's a short piece, just one scene between two men in a concentration camp, and one is about to die."

"Wow, that's heavy," he said, impressed.

"I've never done anything like it. I like happy endings," she said with a grin. The class was being taught by a famous Hollywood screenwriter, who was a guest lecturer for a semester.

"I'll invite you to one of our plays, if I get a part," he said, as she finally reached the cash register, paid for her groceries, and said goodbye. He caught up with her on the sidewalk a few minutes later and offered to carry the bag back to the dorm for her. The groceries were heavy, and she finally handed them to him, grateful for the assistance. They talked all the way back to the dorm about their classes.

His room was on the floor above hers, and he stopped at her door and handed her the grocery bag. "Do you want to have dinner sometime?"

"If I get caught up," she said vaguely, and he nodded.

"Yeah, me too. If I get a part. They pile on the homework here. I kind of expected it, but it's even heavier than I thought. I guess if we survive it, we'll be ready for the real world." She nodded and unlocked her door. Her roommate was out as usual. She thanked him again, and he waved as he headed for the stairs to his floor. There was no question, he was a good-looking boy, but she had no time for romance now. She headed straight for her desk, and got to work on her screenplay.

She didn't see Jake again until the following week, when she was leaving the library again. He was walking by when he saw her.

"Hey! I got a part!" he said, beaming. *"One Flew Over the Cuckoo's Nest.* We're putting it on in the studio where I take class. The performance is a week from Saturday. Can you come?"

"I'll try. I've got two big assignments," she said. The upperclassmen always said that you could tell the freshmen by the look of terror in their eyes.

"I think they're trying to kill us," Jake said, pulling a PowerBar out of his pocket. "Sorry, that's breakfast and lunch. I haven't had time to eat all day." She laughed. She hadn't either. "If you come to the play, we can have dinner after, if you want." She hesitated, not wanting to encourage him for a romance she didn't have time for. She was running from one class to the next, and then rushing to the library to do homework. She had called Lara once to say she was okay, but had had time for nothing else. Dating was out of the question. She didn't see how anyone could manage it. "I'll check in with you closer to the time," he promised, and took off on a skateboard he'd been carrying. She wished she had Rollerblades sometimes to get places faster. She was using her bike a lot, but even that didn't seem fast enough.

A week later, Jake knocked on her door. He looked tired and had a stack of scripts under his arm. "Are you catching up?" he asked with a warm smile.

"Not really. I feel like the last skater in the Ice Follies. I don't think I'm going to catch up for the next four years." She was panicked about it.

"I'll give you a ticket to the play," he said, as he handed her one. "Come if you can. If you can't, I understand. No pressure."

"Thanks, Jake," she said, happy to see him again. At least he was a familiar face in a sea of unknown ones.

In the end, she left the library at six-thirty on Saturday, and decided to go to his play. She had the ticket in her backpack, and slipped into a seat in one of the studios where they held classes and small performances in the Tisch building. The play started on time, and Jake was powerful in the role he'd been given. She was stunned by how talented he was, how professional, and how convincing he was onstage. It was a masterful performance by all of the players.

"You were fantastic!" she told him when he met her in the hall afterward. She had waited for him.

"I screwed up about four times, and blew my lines."

"I didn't notice," she said honestly.

"Do you have time for a pizza? I'm starving. I threw up before the performance."

"Sure. I've got to go back and work after that, though."

They walked a few blocks to a pizza parlor bursting with students, but they found a small table for two, and each ordered a pizza. She ordered a small Margherita and Jake an extra-large with everything on it, including anchovies. When it arrived, she looked at it in horror.

"That looks disgusting."

"Yeah, doesn't it. I can hardly wait to eat it," he said, and she laughed. "So tell me your story," he said with a huge slice of pizza heading toward his mouth.

"No story," she said simply. "Four years of high school and here I am."

"No documentaries, never ran for public office, no national awards, or two years in prison? How did you get in here?" She laughed at the image and shook her head with a mouth full of pizza. "Brothers? Sisters? A boyfriend? Parents you love or hate? Your mother's a drug dealer and your father's in rehab?"

"No brothers, sisters, or boyfriend." She'd never had one but didn't tell him that. It made her sound like a freak. She'd had a few dates in high school, but no serious romances. "No broken heart, no rehab. My mother was . . . is . . . an actress. My father's a businessman. My parents divorced when I was seven, and my mom moved to L.A. I grew up with my father in New York, and I have a fantastic stepmother, who talked my father into letting me come here. He wanted me to be an accountant or a lawyer."

"No evil stepmother? Christ, you're disgustingly normal. No drama there." There was more drama than she was admitting to, but she didn't know him well enough to tell him. He was destroying her comfortable position of being invisible. He wanted to see and know everything. "Okay, my turn. A sister, two half-brothers, and two stepbrothers, who are twins. My parents are divorced, but still love each other, even though they're married to other people. Sometimes we all go on vacation together, which is insane. My mom's a psychiatrist, my dad runs a newspaper, my stepfather is a novelist, and my stepmother was an artist but is now addicted to plastic surgery. They're all crazy, and most of the time I love them. No one in jail or rehab yet, but I'm sure we'll get there. My stepbrothers are only five and still have a long way to go. My whole family thinks it's funny that I want to be an actor. I grew up in a three-ring circus, but they're all pretty nice people. My stepmom is a little weird, but my father is happy with her. It's a wonder he even recognizes her. She gets a new face every year." Antonia laughed. He seemed surprisingly normal, considering the cast of characters, and by the time he had finished describing them to her, he had eaten his entire pizza. She was still working on hers.

"They sound like a lot of fun. My life was pretty quiet, until my father remarried three years ago. It's better now."

"Do you go to see your mom in L.A. a lot?" he asked, curious, and she paused for an instant, and then answered.

"I haven't seen her since I was seven."

He didn't look shocked, just matter of fact. "That's a long time. Do you talk to her?" She shook her head. "Sounds like a bad divorce."

"Pretty much. She's French. They met in Paris, and got married pretty quickly. Not such a great idea. She left to go to Hollywood to make movies."

"Has she been in anything I've seen?" He was a movie buff too, like Antonia.

"Not that I know of."

He nodded, and changed the subject. "And no boyfriend? That's hard to believe."

"Not really. I was working on my grades so I could come here, and I was never one of the cool girls."

"Have you looked in the mirror lately?" She smiled at the question. "Pretty impressive. You don't need cool with looks like that. I went out with the same girl for three years in high school. She's at USC now, at film school."

"I wanted to go there. My father wouldn't let me."

"It's better here. New York is a blast. I love it."

"I've lived here all my life. I thought L.A. would be cooler, and I thought maybe I'd run into my mom somewhere." She had never admitted that to anyone else, but he was easy to talk to.

"It's a big place. My ex and I are still friends, and she has a new boyfriend. We kind of ran out of gas senior year, and once we knew I was coming here, we decided to hang it up and stay friends before we screwed it up long distance. That's a tough one to pull off. We didn't want to do that." It sounded sensible to her too.

They walked back to the dorm after dinner, looking at the people on the street, the noise, the shops, the street vendors, and the crowds jostling one another on the street. They'd had a nice time together.

"I haven't been uptown yet," he said.

"That's where I live. It's a lot quieter than this. This is more fun." He left her at the dorm, and said he was going to meet a friend at another dorm, and he thanked her again for coming to the play.

"You were fabulous," she said again, and went upstairs to do homework. It was Saturday night, and everyone was out, including her roommate, but she had work to do, and wanted to get a good grade. She had enjoyed her evening with Jake. He seemed like he'd make a good friend, and she didn't think he was pushing for more either. It was just nice having a new friend in an environment as unfamiliar as this. She was sure she'd see him again soon. And with that, she pulled her reading assignment toward her, grabbed her highlighter, and got to work.

* * *

As Jake had predicted, she got invited out on a date by a boy in one of her classes, and she turned him down. She said she had too much studying to do, but she wasn't interested in him anyway. Her excuse had been true.

Lara came downtown to have lunch with her after she'd been there for four weeks. The time had flown, and she had gotten A's on two of her papers, and was excited about it. She hadn't heard from her father, but didn't expect to. Lara wanted to be sure she was coming home for Thanksgiving, and Antonia promised she would. She was having too much fun and was too busy at school to go home before then, which Lara understood. After years in isolation with her father, Antonia was loving the college experience. She had joined a study group and liked the people in it. The students were a diverse group from all over the country and all over the world, and it was a whole different experience from being an outcast in high school with no friends. It didn't matter anymore. She loved NYU. It was the right school for her.

Jake was loving it too. He was going back to San Francisco for Thanksgiving, and told her she had to come with him sometime. Their friendship was well established, and there was an unspoken agreement between them that it wasn't a romance. They liked being friends, and a romance might be short-lived.

She felt like she was traveling to another country when she went home for Thanksgiving, and was surprised to discover that her father had turned her bedroom into an office for when he worked at home on weekends. Lara had been uneasy about it, and afraid that

Antonia would be upset. She said she wasn't, but Lara sensed immediately that she felt displaced. Her bed and her furniture were still there, but he had moved everything around so it worked better for him. It made her feel like she didn't belong there anymore and it was someone else's room. Lara thought they should move it all back for the Thanksgiving weekend, but Brandon didn't want to. It made Antonia feel invisible again. The waters had closed over her quickly as soon as she left. Not so much with Lara, but with him. This was what he had waited for, for years.

Lara set a beautiful table for Thanksgiving, and they had a delicious meal, as they always did, and her father was talking about going skiing in Aspen over Christmas or right after. It wasn't clear if Antonia was invited or not. They were meeting friends of Lara's there, and Antonia wasn't sure that was how she wanted to spend her Christmas vacation.

"Nothing is decided yet," Lara said firmly, with a meaningful glance at Brandon, who didn't get it, or pretended not to. He was finally a man without a child underfoot, and acted like it. He was enjoying the empty nest, but officially Antonia still lived there. It was her home too.

They asked about her classes, and she told them how much she liked NYU. Her father was impressed by some of the guest lecturers, who were important filmmakers. They had told her at school that they were expected to find summer jobs in the film industry, and the employment office would help them. She was excited about it, and her father said maybe they'd go to Greece that summer instead of renting a house again, particularly if she wouldn't be there. They seemed to have alternate plans that didn't include her for every occasion. She felt as though she were being pushed out of the nest, instead of spreading her wings.

Lara scolded Brandon for it when they went to bed that night, and it almost started an argument between them. "She doesn't come home anyway. She hasn't been here since we set her up in the dorm two months ago. What does she expect?" he said. But Lara knew he'd been planning to set up the home office anyway.

"She's been busy," Lara said fairly, "but she still expects to have a place here. This is her home."

"We haven't moved. It's all here. Her bed is still in her room. She's sleeping there, isn't she?"

"Yes, under the window, with your file cabinets all around her. How would you feel?"

"Like an adult. She's moving on, and we have a right to enjoy our freedom too. Aspen would be fun for Christmas, and I've always wanted to go to Greece with you. And Water Mill is boring. She's going to be working this summer anyway."

"She could join us on weekends if we rent a house again. I don't want her to feel that we're shoving her out the door. That wouldn't be right. She's only eighteen." Their relationship had just started to get warmer, and he was being insensitive again. It upset Lara, and Antonia was crying in her room that night, looking around her, at the office furniture her father had crammed into the room, and no one had warned her. It had been a shock when she opened her bedroom door and saw the state it was in. Lara understood it perfectly. And as usual, Brandon didn't.

She and Lara went to the movies on the Friday after Thanksgiving, and saw a terrific new film, *Steel Magnolias,* with a star-studded female cast. It was deeply moving, they were still talking about it when they got home. The three of them went to Elio's for dinner on Saturday and had a good time. It was less stressful than Thanksgiving had been, and Antonia was used to the mess in her room by then. But she had no place of refuge anymore. Her bedroom had been turned into an office supply depot. She couldn't even get into her closet and was living out of her suitcase.

She left Sunday morning after Lara made breakfast for them. She saw Jake when he got back from San Francisco that afternoon. He had been eager to get home, after a 7.6 earthquake in October. Their house had only been slightly damaged, but he wanted to see the city. And an entire segment of freeway had collapsed, and many people had been killed. He'd been watching the World Series when it happened, and saw the screen go wobbly and then black. His family had reached him quickly to tell him they were okay. But it was reassuring to see the city again.

"How was your Thanksgiving?" he asked her, tired from the trip. He had gone out with all his old friends the night before. Everyone was home from college for the holiday. Antonia seemed a little subdued to him.

"It was okay. My father turned my bedroom into a home office. I could hardly move in the room and there are file cabinets in front of my closet. I guess he was pretty anxious for me to leave." She had always felt it, but now the evidence was clear. "They're already making plans for next summer that don't include me, but it doesn't really matter. I'll be working anyway." And then she glanced at him shyly, embarrassed about something. "Can I ask you a crazy question? And don't be afraid to say no. I just had an idea over the weekend. You said I should come out to visit sometime. How would this Christmas be?" He looked startled but not unhappy about it. In fact, he was delighted.

"Are they making plans for Christmas too?" He didn't like the sound of it for her, and felt sorry for her.

"My father is. He wants to go to Aspen to meet friends of theirs and go skiing. My stepmother says it's not definite yet, but my father really wants to go. I could probably tag along, but it sounds uncomfortable. It's all couples their age. I'll feel like hair on the soup, as the French say."

"Great expression." He grinned. "My family is completely nuts, but they would love to have you. The more the merrier is their theory about everything. You'll never be able to keep straight who's who and who's married to who. But I would love it if you come home with me. Consider it a firm invitation. There will always be room for you at my house. My family's not going anywhere. They're too dysfunctional and disorganized to move our whole army on Christmas. So definitely plan on Christmas in San Francisco." She smiled and looked relieved. She didn't want to screw up Lara and her father's plans, or force her way into anything. And it sounded like fun for them. Jake's invitation was hard to resist.

She called Lara and told her the next day, and she sounded unhappy about it. She was afraid that would happen, when Brandon talked about wanting to go to Aspen for Christmas.

"We *don't* have to go," she emphasized to Antonia. "Your father was just talking. You know how he is."

"He sounded like he really wants to go. And it'll be fun for you too. We can have dinner and celebrate some night before you leave, or when you get back."

"Antonia, I don't want you to feel that you don't have a home anymore, and that we're not here for you, on holidays or any other time." But that was the truth. They weren't. Her father had a home office now instead of a bedroom for her, and the freedom he had dreamed of for years. She was no longer an intruder, and barely a guest in their home. It had come as a shock when she saw the evidence of it, but it wasn't entirely a surprise.

Lara reported it to Brandon that night, and he wasn't embarrassed or remorseful. He was pleased, even when Lara expressed her concern. He brushed it off.

"Don't be silly. She'll have a good time in San Francisco with her friend, and we'll see her when we get back. It's not like she believes in Santa Claus anymore. She's a college girl, Lara, she needs her freedom too."

"She needs holidays with us, and a home to come back to. I don't want her to feel like she doesn't belong anywhere. And you were already talking about Greece next summer. How do you think that makes her feel?"

"Like a free woman, and all grown up. She's not a baby anymore."

"We all need to feel like babies at times, and she needs a home. She's not gone yet. I don't want her to feel we're pushing her out the door."

"There's a bed in her room, isn't there? She can sleep here whenever she wants. And the new home office works for me. I get to spend more time at home with you. That's a valid reason for changing her room around."

Lara didn't argue with him, but she hated how insensitive he was at times, and she knew he was always ambivalent about his daughter. Half of her was his, and the other half was Fabienne's, which he couldn't stand. But you couldn't split the two. She was one person, and while he was rejecting the part that reminded him of Fabienne, even though Antonia was nothing like her, he was rejecting the side that was him too. And to him, going to Aspen with friends was a way of avoiding the issue entirely, and having a good time. She didn't believe in Santa Claus, as he said, but Lara knew that Antonia needed a father. He felt he had given enough for eighteen years, and now it was his turn to enjoy himself. Lara loved him, but she hated the excuses he made for himself sometimes, especially at his daughter's expense.

But the die was cast now. Antonia was going to San Francisco for Christmas with Jake. They were going to Aspen. Lara just hoped that Antonia would have a good Christmas. It was the least she deserved. She'd had so little from her father until then. And no family life whatsoever.

Chapter 6

The day after the Thanksgiving weekend, Antonia booked a reservation on the same flight as Jake, going to San Francisco before Christmas. He was flying business, and her father agreed to do the same for her. It was going to be fun flying together, and she was excited to meet the family he insisted was crazy, the parents and stepparents and all five of his siblings. His sister had graduated from Harvard Medical School, and had just started her residency at Stanford Hospital. He said that it was a miracle she wasn't on duty on Christmas Eve or Day, and was coming home for a night with her boyfriend, a resident too. He explained that he and his sister, Eloise, were the oldest of the kids, and the others were all younger. His half-brothers, Jamie and Seth, whom they referred to simply as brothers, were twelve and fourteen, and were just reaching the right age to get into trouble. They were his mother's children with Jake's stepfather, the novelist, Ian. Jake's "real" father, Bob, was the publisher of the largest San Francisco newspaper, had written a novel himself (he said his mother liked writers), and had married a woman, Genevieve, who had been a talented graphic designer and retired to devote herself full-time to the identical twins she had decided to have at forty, before she married Bob, using both an egg and sperm donor and a surrogate to carry them. She had married Jake's father when they were a year old. They were six now, and monsters, according to Jake, Dennis the Menace times two. And for recreation, now that she had two full-time nannies thanks to Bob, his stepmother had become addicted to plastic surgery, and had Botox, fillers, duck lips, and a new chin. She'd had breast implants put in, and liposuction twice. According to Jake, she looked like a Barbie doll, but beyond anyone's comprehension, his father seemed happy with her. Even though the twins, Zane and Zack, were little terrors, his father claimed that having small children again made him feel young.

He filled Antonia in, writing all their names on a napkin on the flight to San Francisco, and a diagram to show who was related to whom. "Eloise's boyfriend is John, from Hong Kong. Don't try to remember all the names. I can barely remember them myself. My parents got divorced when I was three, so I don't remember a time when they were together. I've lived with that insanity all my life, at our house anyway. I was thirteen when my father married Genevieve. I thought she was great looking before, but she's a work in progress. My mother says it's a disease. She should have married a plastic surgeon, but my dad thinks she's great. They're thinking of having another baby by surrogacy, using my dad's sperm this time, so that would be more half-brothers or sisters if they do."

They took a cab from the airport, which Antonia paid for, since she was staying at his house for the next ten days. They were going back to New York on New Year's Day, after spending New Year's Eve with his high school friends, whom she was eager to meet.

He mentioned that his mother had canceled her patients for the afternoon so she could be at the house when they got home. It was a half-hour ride from the airport, and the car stopped in front of a large, sprawling Victorian house that occupied two whole lots, and Jake explained it was a historical landmark his parents had restored. They needed every inch of it now when the family got together, although his father and Genevieve and the twins didn't actually stay there, but they spent all holidays with them, and always had, so the children didn't have to be separated. Ian had always been fine with it. He and Bob were good friends. He said his mother, Lea, had had Eloise when she was in medical school herself, and Bob had been a junior sports reporter in L.A. They had moved to San Francisco so Lea could do her residency in psychiatry at UCSF, and they had decided to stay. His father had gotten a job at the local paper, and had worked his way up to publisher.

The house had a dignified beauty to it, like a grande dame. They made their way up the front stairs on Clay Street in Pacific Heights. It was clearly one of the nicer residential neighborhoods, and as they opened the front door, they could smell cookies baking. His mother came out of the kitchen to greet them at the front door in an apron, with a small smear of chocolate on her face, and bright red hair. She put her arms around Jake and hugged him, obviously thrilled to see him. Then he introduced her to Antonia, who felt instantly shy in a strange house, about to be surrounded by people she didn't know. But his mother hugged her just as exuberantly, and told them to come to the kitchen for a cookie before they went upstairs.

The kitchen was huge with a big round table in a bay window. It was filled with sunlight and good smells.

"Don't let this domestic scene fool you, my mother only bakes cookies and brownies, and can only cook eggs. We have caterers for holidays, and we all learned to cook for ourselves." But the cookies smelled delicious, and they helped themselves to one, while she put the pans in the sink and smiled at her son with pleasure.

"I put the boys in together," she told him. "Antonia can have Seth's room. There are clean sheets on the bed, and she'll have her own bathroom that way." There were six bedrooms, one for Lea and Ian, one for each of the four children, and the sixth bedroom, on the top floor, was where Ian wrote. It had a spectacular view of the bay, and they'd had it soundproofed for him. Antonia had never read any of his crime novels, but she had heard of him.

Lea said he was upstairs working, but he had promised to finish by dinnertime, and take a break for the next week. She smiled warmly at Antonia, and told them to help themselves to whatever they wanted in the fridge, but they had eaten enough on the plane on the six-hour flight.

"Where are the boys?" Jake asked with trepidation. They were like an explosion of arms, legs, and sports paraphernalia the moment they walked into the house.

"Seth is at soccer practice, and Jamie's at a friend's house. They'll be home at five, so we'll have peace until then. Eloise and John won't be here till Christmas Eve. She's on duty till then." It all seemed very civilized to Antonia, and cozy and warm. A few minutes later, Jake took her to her room, which was neater than usual, but filled with trophies, and autographed photos of sports figures, most of them from local teams. Her room was two doors down from Jake's with a bathroom in between. He showed her around upstairs, and the view of the bay from his parents' room. Everywhere she looked were warm, cozy rooms and inviting spaces. The house appeared well filled and well used.

She put her clothes in the closet on the hangers they'd left for her. When she visited him, Jake's room was only slightly more grown up and less cluttered than Seth's. His older sister still had a room at home too, that was very girly with flowered chintzes and matching wallpaper in dusty pink. Antonia noticed that there was no office equipment in it, although she had left home years before to attend college and medical school. Everyone had their own spaces, the same rooms they had grown up in. It was a house set up for children and the people who lived there, no matter how seldom they came home. The difference with her home struck her immediately.

They took a walk down Sacramento Street, and saw the shops decorated for Christmas. It was a real neighborhood with large comfortable homes. There were children playing in a park across the street. It looked like a wonderful place to grow up, unlike the fast-paced urban life of New York, with cars honking and traffic rushing by. There was no traffic here. All the offices and the financial district were downtown. There were no skyscrapers, and you could see the sky. It felt like a sleepy little city.

They went back to the house and moments later the front door flew open. There was a clatter of equipment being thrown down, shoes with cleats flew in all directions, and both boys had arrived home at the same time. Seth was tall with his mother's red hair, and Jamie still looked like a little boy and headed straight for the cookies he could smell in the kitchen, with a quick hello to Antonia.

"Hi, Jake," he said as he flew by, and Seth seemed happy to see him, and smiled shyly at Antonia. They both looked like nice boys, and she could see the resemblance to Jake. Antonia followed them into the kitchen, and sat at the round table with them, and Lea came in to remind them to get their things out of the front hall before someone fell over them.

They went to their rooms after several cookies, and as soon as Seth got to Jamie's room where he'd be sleeping, he turned the stereo on and the music was blaring. Jake had his stereo on too, and their mother reminded them to turn it down to something more civilized. Then she went to her own room to check messages and return calls. She was taking time off from her practice until after the new year, so she could enjoy her family and spend time with them. Just seeing them, Antonia envied Jake the family atmosphere he had grown up in. She wondered if he realized how lucky he was.

Ian came to see him as soon as he came downstairs when he finished writing, gave him a bear hug, and welcomed Antonia warmly. That night they all had dinner in the big country kitchen. They ordered Chinese food, and conversation was constant around the table, interspersed with laughter as they told Antonia funny stories. She loved both of Jake's brothers, and Ian was a warm teddy bear of a man. His hair was disheveled and he had a beard. He corrected the two younger boys gently but firmly, and after dinner they all went to their rooms to settle down, call friends, watch TV, or do whatever they wanted. Jake came to check on her, tucked into Seth's room.

"Are you doing okay?"

"I couldn't be happier, and they're not crazy at all, they're terrific!" It was a house full of love. It filled every space and reverberated from the rafters.

"They're on their best behavior for you. Wait till the boys get into a fight and start throwing things at each other, and my dad's two little monsters arrive on Christmas Eve and Day. My mother says they're both hyperactive, and Genevieve thinks they're fine."

Antonia loved Eloise, when she and John arrived the morning of Christmas Eve. They all had lunch together and went for a walk on Ocean Beach. The fog was hovering just beyond the coastline, and you could hear foghorns in the distance. It was such a picturesque little city. Antonia loved it, and she and Eloise had a long talk about their favorite movies. Lea had let the young people go out alone. She let Jake drive their Suburban and there was room for all six of them, Lea's four children, and Antonia and John. They came back in good spirits with bright pink cheeks from the wind at the beach. It felt like a city and the country and beach combined.

At the end of the afternoon, they all went to their rooms to dress for dinner. Caterers were setting up for the meal, and they were going to use the formal dining room for Christmas Eve. It was a traditional menu of turkey and stuffing and all the fixings. It smelled delicious while they were cooking. Antonia took a short black velvet dress out of the closet and high heels. She took a bath and did her hair, and when she knocked on Jake's door, she was wearing the velvet dress, with her hair French-braided and long down her back, and little pearl earrings, and he was wearing a good-looking dark gray suit, and a shirt and tie.

"Wow! You look gorgeous," she said as she admired him, and he did the same.

"So do you. You clean up pretty good." He still couldn't understand why she didn't have a boyfriend, except that she didn't seem to want one. She was a stunning girl, but their relationship had gone in a completely different direction by then, and they both liked being friends.

They were standing talking just outside his room, when they heard the front door slam, followed by screaming and laughing, and it sounded as though an army had arrived.

"My dad's here," he said with a grin. "The two little monsters," he said as they headed for the stairs. Bob and Genevieve were at the foot of the stairs talking to Lea, as the twins ran around them, nearly knocking over furniture and objects until Lea called them to order and told them to slow down. Antonia laughed when she saw them. They were exactly as Jake had described in matching blue corduroy suits with little red bow ties, and standing next to them was a woman who looked like a Barbie doll. She was wearing a white satin suit with silver trim, and high-heeled silver shoes. Her features were perfect and seemed artificial somehow, and when she smiled at Antonia, nothing on her face moved except her mouth, which had huge, puffed-up lips in a permanent pout. She had a perfect figure, and surprisingly large breasts for a woman as slim as she was. Antonia remembered Jake's description of her. But when Antonia spoke to her, she could understand some of Genevieve's appeal. She was incredibly nice, and warm and friendly to Antonia, as they chatted and the twins ran wild.

Jake's father was completely enamored by her, and he and Lea chatted easily, and she gave him a warm hug when he arrived. They seemed to be the best of friends, and there was no animosity between the ex-spouses or the new ones. They were one big happy family as they moved into the dining room a short time later. Lea had set out place cards with the adults at one end of the table, and the children at the other. Bob and Lea's older children, Eloise's boyfriend, and Antonia sat between the two couples and the younger children.

There was constant conversation at the table, and laughter, the food was delicious, and they had flaming Christmas pudding, doused with brandy. It was a perfect meal, and as far as Antonia was concerned, they were a perfect family, enjoying the evening together, across generations, with old and new marriages represented and their children. They gathered in the living room to play charades afterward, which was fun too.

Lara called her from Aspen to wish her a Merry Christmas and make sure she was all right. Antonia left the table to talk to her from the kitchen.

"I'm having a wonderful time," Antonia said, glancing at Jake as he walked past. He was happy she had enjoyed the evening. She got along with everyone, everybody loved her, and she had been the ideal guest, joining in every aspect of the evening. She even played a game with the twins before they fell asleep on the couch during charades.

Jake and Seth helped carry them to the car while Antonia finished talking to Lara. She and Jake walked upstairs together after she thanked Lea and Ian for allowing her to be there and giving her such a happy Christmas in their midst. Jake kissed her on the cheek when he left her in Seth's room. Having her there had made it a better Christmas for him too.

Jake woke Antonia the next morning on his way downstairs in his pajamas to open gifts with his family in front of the tree. She joined them a little while later, and was surprised to find two gifts for her too. One of them was a sweater Lea had bought for her, and the other was a book Jake had gotten her with famous screenplays in it that he thought might be useful to her. She loved them both. They had breakfast in the kitchen before the caterers arrived to prepare lunch. They were having local crab, which they always had on Christmas Day. The lunch would be more informal than dinner the night before, but it was just as spirited and jovial, and they had gifts for Bob and Genevieve and the twins too when they arrived at noon. They wore jeans and sweaters on Christmas Day. Everyone was in a good mood. Antonia told Jake it was the best Christmas she'd ever had.

She called her father and Lara in Aspen before they sat down to lunch, and Lara was relieved to hear her still in good spirits and having fun with Jake's family. They were enjoying Aspen too.

By the time Jake and Antonia left San Francisco to fly back to New York, she had met most of his old friends, had some serious talks with Lea and Ian, gotten to know Seth and Jamie, and even thought the twins weren't as bad as he said. She liked Jake's dad. It was hard to get to know Genevieve. Her remodeled face was distracting, and her conversation superficial most of the time, but she wasn't a bad person, and Antonia agreed that Jake's father seemed very happy with her. They had mentioned wanting to have another baby through the same complicated process she'd used before, and Jake's only comment was that he hoped it wasn't twins next time. His whole family was sad to see them leave, and neither of them wanted to go back to New York.

They slept most of the way back, and took a cab to the dorm.

"I can't thank you enough for taking me. It was the best Christmas of my life, and I love your family. They're the nicest people I've ever met," she said, as he left her at the door of her dorm room, and headed up the stairs to his own. It had been a good Christmas for him too, with old friends and new ones, and his crazy combined family, who seemed better to him when seen through her eyes. He couldn't imagine his own family going to Aspen without him, and leaving him high and dry. He was glad she had come with him. Sharing the holiday with her had added something to their friendship. They had a memory to share now.

They had classes the next day and they both knew they'd have a lot of studying to do, as they started a new term and new classes. He had another play to audition for at Tisch. They were almost halfway through their freshman year, and it was off to a great start.

* * *

96

In January, Antonia went to the employment office to start looking for a summer job. It took them a few weeks, but they called her and asked her to come in. They had something that had just come on the list that they thought might interest her. A major film studio in L.A. wanted an NYU intern to be a gofer on the set of a movie that would be filming there in the summer, and to work in the main office when they didn't need her on the set. The job was for ten weeks, and worked perfectly with her schedule. She had to find her own accommodations, and the job offered no pay, which many students couldn't afford. But her father gave her a healthy allowance, which she could use while she was in L.A. She was to report for work on June 15. It was exactly what she wanted, her dream job. They had two other candidates for it listed in the employment office, but they thought the lack of pay would be a problem for both of them, particularly with no living accommodation offered.

They called her the next day, and told her that she had the job if she wanted it. She thanked them profusely, and felt as though she had won the lottery.

"Hollywood, here I come," she said when she hung up. She wanted to celebrate, and called Jake immediately. He was going back to San Francisco for the summer, and looking for a job there. She called him, but his answering machine picked up, which she knew meant he was in class. She left him a jubilant message about the job.

She was going to try to locate her mother once she got to L.A. She had no idea if she could find her, but she had to try. All she wanted was to meet with her once, just to see what she was like. She hadn't seen her in almost twelve years, they were strangers to each other

Danielle Steel

now. But her mother was a missing piece of the puzzle that her life
had become. There were questions she still wanted answers to. She
wasn't going to tell her father if she saw her. It was something she
had to do for herself. For twelve years, she had wanted to know why
her mother had left and never contacted her again. Her father had
never explained it to her and the mere mention of her mother still
sent him into a rage.

Chapter 7

Antonia spent a weekend with her father and Lara before she left for L.A. in June. She had to move all her things back from the dorm for the summer. The dorm rooms were made available to students in summer programs, and she would be assigned a new room in the fall. She piled everything from her dorm room into her bedroom, along with her father's office equipment, and it looked like a warehouse by the time she got it all in. She could barely get to her bed, and she had to pack her suitcases for L.A., to add to the mess. But it gave her a chance to see them before she left. She wouldn't see again until the end of August. She would be turning nineteen while she was in L.A. It didn't bother her to spend her birthday away from home. Since it was in August, she was usually at camp in Maine anyway, or had been for many years, from seven to fifteen.

Her father and Lara were going to Greece, and had decided not to rent the house in Water Mill again. They were excited about their trip, and Antonia was thrilled about her internship in L.A. Her father had added to her allowance so she could get a decent place to stay in a safe neighborhood. She was going to rent a car, since public transportation was poor in L.A.

She felt like she was camping out in their apartment for the weekend. With her bedroom turned into an office, and now a storeroom, there was really no place for her to stay. They could have used a three-bedroom apartment to give him an office, but he loved the apartment they had. Lara was sad that they wouldn't see her all summer, but she knew it was going to be a great adventure for Antonia. Her father told her to take a good look at it, because if she stuck to her plan to write screenplays after college, she might be living there one day. The prospect of her moving three thousand miles away didn't seem to bother him, which Antonia noticed too. He never seemed able to bridge the gap between them. There was an emotional void in him that she was increasingly aware of as she got older, and a lack of fatherly feelings toward her. She had always blamed some inadequacy in herself for it, but she was beginning to wonder if there was something missing in him. Or habit. Maybe he had avoided any strong emotional tie with her for so long, whatever the reason, he just couldn't find the connection anymore.

She said goodbye to them before she went to bed on Sunday night, and left the apartment early Monday morning. She took a cab to the airport with her two suitcases filled with summer clothes, most of them suitable for work. She had a reservation at a small hotel near the studio they had recommended to her, and she had given herself a week to find a small furnished apartment, or a room somewhere. She felt very grown up flying across the country for a job, and searching for an apartment on her own. She'd never done anything like it before. She knew no one in L.A., except her mother if she could find her. It would be like finding the proverbial needle in a haystack. She was going to call actors' agencies, and search through directories by name. Anything was possible. The only thing she knew was that her mother would be forty-four years old now. She was going to search under her maiden name of Basquet and her married name. She suspected that she didn't use her father's anymore, since she'd left him twelve years before, and it couldn't be a fond memory for her either.

The flight to L.A. was uneventful, and she arrived at the hotel at noon local time. The hotel was small and battered looking. The room was barely bigger than the bed, but it was cheap, in a safe neighborhood, and there was a pool.

She had lunch at a coffee shop nearby once she dropped off her suitcases, scoured the real estate section of the newspaper while she ate, and circled four or five apartment listings. She called for the apartments from her hotel room, and two of them had already been rented. After lunch, she picked up her rental car. She had to take out extra insurance because of her age, but they were willing to rent to her. Her father had given her a credit card for major expenses. She rented a small, unimpressive Ford, but it would get her where she needed to go. They gave her a map of the city and neighboring counties, and she set out to see the two apartments. Both were in seedy-looking buildings, and the apartments were awful. She went back to the hotel, and took a swim in the pool. There were no hotel guests visible. She assumed they were all at work, or out for the day.

She called two realtors and they had nothing for her either. She wasn't worried. She knew she would find something sooner or later. And on Friday, she did.

It was a small residential building in West Hollywood that rented out furnished studio apartments by the month for reasonable rents. It was small and modern and clean, tucked in between Spanish-style buildings. It was within her budget, and she rented a room on the second floor, with a view of the neighbor's garden and a large palm tree just beyond it. It wasn't fancy or even pretty, but it had everything she needed, and it was more than adequate for two and a half months.

"Welcome home," she said to herself, as she dropped her suitcases in the apartment and went to look at the kitchen. It had a small fridge, a double hot plate, and a toaster oven, which was all she needed. There was a diner nearby and a Mexican restaurant up the street, where she suspected she'd be eating most of her meals. The apartment came with linens, and there was a Laundromat down the street where she could do her laundry.

She hung her clothes in the closet. A noisy old air conditioner kept the one room cool, and she was sorry the building didn't have a pool, but that would have been a luxury she couldn't afford.

She knew Jake was back in San Francisco by then, and she wondered if he had found a job yet. He wasn't looking for anything related to acting. He just wanted something that would pay him enough to make pocket money for school in the fall. He was willing to do almost anything.

She spent the weekend exploring L.A. by car, and checked out the studio location so she'd know where to go on Monday, and wouldn't be late. The studio had a huge parking lot for employees where she could leave her car.

She finally reached Jake on Sunday and told him all about it. He said he'd found a job as a busboy at the Fairmont Hotel on Nob Hill. It sounded like a cushy job to her, and he was going to spend three weeks in August at his parents' house in Lake Tahoe before he went back to school.

"Maybe I'll come to see you in L.A. before I go up to Tahoe," he said before they hung up. She loved the idea, and wondered if he'd get around to it, between his job and family and their summer plans. She promised to tell him all about her internship as soon as she started.

She reported to work promptly at nine the next morning, after parking in the employee lot. She went to the main studio office, and asked for the person whose name she'd been given. She was a serious-looking woman wearing a shocking pink silk blouse and white slacks, with her hair in a neat French twist. Antonia had worn a black cotton dress and flat shoes in case she had a lot of running around to do. She looked businesslike and efficient, and very young, with her hair in a ponytail and very little makeup. She didn't want to stand out. Her first assignment was to deliver a manila envelope to the third assistant director on the set of the movie they were making. The woman she had reported to drew a quick map. The studio lots looked like a maze to her, as she started out to find the set where she had to go. It took her fifteen minutes to find it, and the day was already blazing hot. When she reached the right place, a security guard stopped her. She told him her mission and who the envelope was from and he let her through, and told her to be very quiet when she entered the set. The cameras were due to start rolling any minute.

As it turned out, they already were, and she had to wait half an hour before they allowed her on set to find the third assistant director. He was slouched in a chair when she found him, studying the shooting schedule for the day. He opened the envelope and saw that it was the script changes for the day that had to be delivered to all the actors and the principal director. She had seen the list of actors working on the film, and wondered if she'd see any of the stars. She guessed that they were probably in their dressing rooms.

He sent her to another assistant to give the script changes to, and the girl thanked her pleasantly and asked her if she was new. The third assistant director had hardly looked at her.

"I'm a summer intern," Antonia said softly. "Today is my first day." She was scared, but excited to be there. And she didn't want to make any mistakes on the first day.

"That's how I started too." The girl smiled at her. "Good luck!" Antonia thanked her, and made her way back to the office. She got lost twice and had to double back, but she got back to the main office an hour after she'd left.

"Mission accomplished," she reported to the woman in the pink blouse. She sent her on a similar mission to another set, where a different movie was being made.

She was sent out four times in the sweltering heat by lunchtime. She felt wilted by the time she got back to the office after her fourth delivery, but at least it was cool there.

They gave her a heavy metal box to deliver after that, with a padlock on it. It was money for one of the directors on set. The woman in charge of her told her she could go to the employees' commissary for lunch after she made the delivery, and to be back in an hour. It didn't give her much time to eat since it took so long to get around. The studio was as big as a small city, or so it seemed, as she hiked across hot pavement and found the studio where she was supposed to go. They took the box from her, and she headed for the commissary. She had seen signs along the way.

It was a giant tent, with a whole cooking area, long tables with plated food on them, and refrigerated cases with salads and dairy products, and another one filled with drinks. There were at least a dozen people setting up the food. She took a salad and a bottle of water and went to sit at one of the tables. And a few minutes later, a good-looking blond boy came and sat down across from her, with a hamburger and a Coke on his tray. She wondered if he was an actor. He was handsome enough to be one. There were attractive people everywhere, and it was impossible to guess what their jobs were.

"Mind if I sit down?" he asked her after he did, and smiled at her, and she shook her head and ate her salad. She noticed that he was wearing a striped T-shirt and jeans, and sandals. He looked like he was going to the beach. He seemed very confident. He dropped a script on the table, and ate his hamburger. She guessed him to be about her age. She could sense him watching her, and she finally got up the courage to ask him the burning question.

"Are you an actor?"

"Yes, but not here. I'm a drama student at Northwestern. I'm a summer intern. What about you?"

"I'm a summer intern too. From NYU." They smiled at each other and the coincidence that they wound up at the same table on their first day.

"It's a fantastic place, isn't it? I hope I get to make a movie here one day," he said hopefully.

"Me too. I want to be a screenwriter," she said shyly. He was surprised she wasn't an actress. She was pretty enough to be.

They chatted for a few minutes while they ate lunch, and finished quickly. "I have to get back to work," she said, and he did too. "I have to go to the main office."

"Me too," he said easily, "I'll walk with you." She tried to match his strides as they walked back, and she could feel the back of her dress getting damp in the hot sun. "I'm Jeff Blake by the way." She introduced herself, and they arrived at the main office five minutes later. She was beginning to know her way around. He reported to a different person and was sent out on an errand immediately, while she waited for her next assignment. At least she knew one person now. The boy from Northwestern was undeniably handsome, and had been pleasant to talk to. They were both awestruck by their surroundings.

Her next mission was easier. She was to report to the movie set she'd been hired for, and ask what they needed her to do. The woman in charge of her had wanted to see if she was reliable first, and she had been so far, and came back quickly each time and didn't dawdle. She seemed bright and efficient. The interns were often smarter than the employees, and they tried harder.

She went to the set then where she had made the first delivery, and she was told that the directors were in a script meeting with the writers, making changes, and the cast members were in their trailers having lunch. It left her nothing to do until they all got back, and she sat in a chair and waited patiently for an hour, and then the directors returned and continued conferring, and half an hour later, the cast appeared.

"We're out of water," one of the directors said, "send one of the gofers out to get more. It's hotter than hell today." He gestured to Antonia and told her where the giant refrigerators with the bottles of water were kept. He pointed to a cooler to carry them in, and she left immediately to get the water. She was nearly staggering when she got back with the cooler filled with bottles.

"That's a heavy load for you," the main director commented sympathetically. He was the only person on the set who had spoken to her and noticed her. He smiled gratefully when she set the cooler down beside him. He handed the bottles out to the other directors and whatever crew and cast members were standing near him, until the cooler was empty. "I hate to ask, but we need more. I'll send one of the boys with you." He pointed to a light technician who wasn't doing anything and told him to help Antonia bring more water. They made two trips together.

"Gofer for the summer?" the light man asked her. He could spot it a mile away. She nodded. "Wear shorts tomorrow, and don't wear black if you're going to be standing around in the sun all day." There were big umbrellas in stands on the set, but they were for the crew and the actors and directors.

"I thought I'd be working in the office," she explained, and he smiled at her again.

"They'll have you running all over the place. That's what the gofers do here." She was a glorified errand girl, she realized, but she was excited about the job anyway, being this close to famous actors and directors, making a major movie. It was a unique opportunity for her to see how it all worked. "The gofers are usually actors and actresses waiting to be discovered. Are you an actress?" She shook her head.

"I want to be a screenwriter one day," she explained, as she had to Jeff Blake at lunch.

"I'll get you one of the scripts if you want."

"Is that allowed?"

"No, but it's not a big deal. I'll grab one for you if I see one hanging around spare." She didn't want to break the rules and get fired on her first day. He set the cooler down for the second time then, and went back to work with the light crew, and she thanked him for carrying the cooler for her.

The main director sent her to the office an hour later. She felt as though she was melting by then.

"Tell them we need blue script changes for tomorrow," he said, handing her an annotated script with the writers' changes, many of them at the request of the actors who didn't like a line or a word.

She was a little dizzy from the heat when she got to the office and gave them the script and his message. They sent her to do some filing then, and at the end of the day, they had her insert the new blue pages into fresh copies of the script, so they'd be ready for them on set in the morning. And at six o'clock, they let her go home. She walked to her car, drove to her apartment, and lay in the air-conditioned room, thinking that it was going to be a very long summer, running back and forth from the set to the office a dozen times a day. Her first day as an intern had been exhausting, but she was determined to do whatever they needed, and do well at the job.

She took a shower and lay on her bed, too tired to even go out and eat, and there was nothing in her fridge. All she wanted was a gallon of water to drink and a night's sleep. And half an hour later, she was dead to the world.

Antonia and Jeff Blake crossed paths again several times the next day. He was friendly to her every time, and their missions were similarly undistinguished, running things back and forth from various sets on the studio lot to the main office or various crew members. They asked Jeff to do physically heavier things because of his size, although the locked cash boxes they entrusted to Antonia were heavy too. There was nothing glorious about the job, and it taught them nothing more about the movie business, they were simply in proximity to it, like being a busboy or a valet car parker at a restaurant with a great chef. But once in a while they did get a glimpse of some major star in a dressing gown at hair and makeup, or on the set. And just being there and absorbing the atmosphere was exciting. But Antonia wondered several times if she would have been smarter to do what Jake had done, get a menial paying job. She hated being dependent on her father for every penny. But she was here now, and decided to make the best of it.

She used any time off she had to call acting agencies she found in the Yellow Pages and ask if they represented a Fabienne Adams or Basquet, and they never did. In her forties now, she wouldn't be modeling. Antonia went to the library and looked in the phone directories of every county she could think of, and found nothing.

The DMV might have had some trace of her, if she was in the area, but Antonia had no access to those records, nor to police files. She checked the county public death records and didn't find her either. She realized too that things might not have panned out for her mother in L.A., and she could have gone back to France. And Antonia didn't have any idea of how to search there. She thought that she might hire a detective agency one day, when she could afford to, and try to track her down. But for now, her mother's trail was cold. She could also accept that if her mother had wanted to contact her, she would have by now, and there had never been even the slightest sign from her, not even a postcard or a birthday card or a note. And Antonia hadn't gone anywhere. They had moved after she left, but were easy to find, their phone was listed, and she still lived in New York. For whatever reason, Fabienne wanted no contact with her daughter or ex-husband.

Antonia and Jeff from Northwestern saw each other often in the course of the day. He was always chatty and pleasant, and she was feeling particularly down and defeated by the search for her mother one day when she ran into him at lunch. She had called the last acting agency by then. She had known it wasn't realistic or even likely that she would find her mother, but she had hoped she'd get lucky and find her anyway.

"You look like you've just lost your best friend," he said as he set his tray down on her table, without asking, and sat down next to her. Sometimes she found him a little too friendly, but they were both in the same boat and commiserated at times about the job and the weather, which was relentless. The smog was so heavy on some days that they could hardly breathe while they ran around. She hadn't taken to wearing shorts, but she wore the lightest clothes she had with her, and even that didn't help. She wore sundresses, and was always tidy and immaculately put together despite the heat.

"No, my mother," she said under her breath in response to his comment about looking like she'd lost her best friend.

"For real?" He was startled and she shook her head.

"No, just kidding. What have you been doing today?" She hadn't seen him all morning.

"Helping some of the sound guys move equipment. Why is everything in this place so damn heavy?" She laughed at the comment, and had thought it too, although they gave her a lot of envelopes to deliver, which they saved for her, and used Jeff for the harder, more physical jobs. "I can't wait to go back to Chicago. It gets hot there but nothing like this. And just being here, getting sneak peeks at a bunch of actors, isn't teaching us anything. I had a shot at a job in Disneyland, wearing a Goofy costume, or Pluto," which were their taller characters. "I thought I'd die of the heat dressed as Goofy for two months. I'm just as hot here, and Disney would have paid me. I was going to try and get class credit for this. The only thing this prepares us for is to work for a courier service. And at least they ride bikes and make tips." He looked totally fed up and she sympathized, but she still thought it was a good opportunity. Maybe at some point they would have them do something more intelligent than they had for the first few weeks. She tried to be cheerful, cooperative, and willing and do the best she could, and everyone had been nice to her so far. That was something at least.

"Do you want to have dinner tonight?" he asked her, sounding discouraged. She was too, and the heat was horrendous, but she tried to be a good sport about it.

"Sure," she said, thinking it might raise their spirits. She had spent very little money so far, except for the rental car and her furnished studio apartment. She hadn't gone anywhere, or done anything, and by the evening, most of the time she was too tired and hot to even eat. "Let's go somewhere air-conditioned," she said, and he laughed.

"Yeah, like standing in the meat freezer at the local butcher. I could go for that. Where do you want to go?"

"I don't care, just so it's cool."

"I don't have a car, so I can't pick you up."

"I do, I can pick you up so you don't have to take the bus. Where do you live?" She said it to be helpful, and he looked pleased.

"I live on the wrong side of Hollywood Boulevard, in a fleabag motel, the cheapest I could get. What about you?"

"I have a tiny, ugly furnished studio apartment in West Hollywood, but the ancient air conditioner works."

"We can get takeout, and eat there if you want," he said easily, and she shook her head. She would have with Jake in a heartbeat, for the pure practicality of it. But she didn't know Jeff well enough to invite him to her apartment.

"No, that's okay. I don't have enough plates." It wasn't true, but served the purpose as an excuse. "There's a Mexican restaurant down the street from me, which is pretty good, if you like Mexican." They both did, and she didn't know any other restaurants in L.A., and neither did he. She said she'd pick him up at seven, and he agreed, and the office sent him on a long mission after that, to unload furniture off a truck. She spent the afternoon in the air-conditioned main office, collating scripts with different colored change sheets for the various sets. But at least she was cool while she worked, and felt fresher than usual at six when she left. Her supervisor liked her and felt sorry for her, so she'd created the project for her.

She drove home after work, showered, and changed quickly. She wore a turquoise sundress and gold sandals Lara had bought for her at Bergdorf in New York, and she looked clean and pretty when she drove to Jeff's address. There were hookers walking up and down the street in front of his hotel and for a good distance on either side of it. It was exactly the kind of place her father hadn't wanted her to live, but Jeff was in less danger than she would have been. He looked tired and rumpled when he walked out of the hotel and got in her car.

"You like my neighborhood?" he asked her, as a hooker walked by and offered them a threesome, and referred to Antonia as Little Bo Peep, because she seemed so young and innocent. She drove away and made a face. "The hooker who has the room next to me is pretty nice. She gives me leftover Chinese food once in a while, since we don't have fridges and can't keep it. The place is full of cockroaches and rats. And the other night, she offered me a free blow job. She's new and said she needs the practice." He said it as a matter of course, and Antonia was shocked. No man had referred to that with her before, as though it was an ordinary subject, and she didn't comment. She looked upset for a few minutes, but by the time they got to the restaurant, she had recovered. Maybe he thought he was being funny, although she was not amused by the comment.

The food was even better than she'd realized, and they both ate a full meal, despite the heat of the day, and the hours he had spent unloading a truck full of furniture into a warehouse. The restaurant wasn't air-conditioned, but there was a slight breeze that night, as they sat at a garden table and talked about their respective colleges and early lives. Jeff had two brothers and a sister older than he was, his parents were divorced, and he'd grown up in Ohio, and liked Northwestern a lot. His father worked for an insurance company and his mother was a high school chemistry teacher. He said he wanted to go to New York after he graduated, be an actor and make a lot of money. He was quick to pick up the check, which she thought was generous of him. She had thought him cocky when they first met, and a little smug about his good looks. His hair was longer than it should be, but it was sexy on him, and there was no denying he was a handsome kid, and he knew it. But he seemed nicer as they sat at dinner that night, and a little more modest than he had before. The grueling conditions of their boring job had taken a little of the starch out of him. He showed her the blisters on his hands from what he'd done that day.

"You know, maybe in a way, we're lucky," she said, after she thanked him for dinner and they left the restaurant. "They only hire two college interns every summer from all over the country, and we're it. It's kind of an honor."

"To drag boxes around, and unload truckloads of furniture?" He looked disgusted. "More like slave labor. We're working for free. I could have stayed in Chicago and gotten a job that paid me decently. We're not learning anything here."

"Humility maybe," she said softly. "Whatever we do after we graduate, we'll have to start from the bottom." They were driving past her apartment as she said it, and she pointed the building out to him. "That's where I live."

"That's good news," he said hurriedly. "I'm desperate to go to the bathroom. I needed to go all through dinner, but I hate scuzzy public bathrooms. Would it be too rude to ask you to let me use yours for a minute? I'll never make it home."

Faced with what he said, she didn't feel like she had much choice. She couldn't let him pee on the front seat of her car. She thought for an instant if she felt safe letting him use her apartment for a pit stop, and she decided that she did. He was a decent kid and they had known each other for several weeks now. He had never done or said anything out of line, other than the blow job comment when she picked him up at his hotel.

"Okay," she agreed, slowed the car, and parked on the street, as she always did. She hopped out of the car, and he followed her. He acted like it was urgent, so she hurried to get her keys, and ran up the stairs to her apartment, unlocked the door, and pointed to the bathroom. He rushed in and slammed the door. He was out a few minutes later with a big grin on his face.

"Thanks, Antonia. That was a real emergency." He sat down on the couch then without being invited, and patted the spot next to him. "Why don't we hang out here for a while. I'm in no rush to get home. I don't have AC, you do."

"I need to get to bed, or I'll be dead in the morning," she said apologetically, and he reached out with a long well-toned arm and pulled her down next to him.

"I'm not stopping you from going to bed." He grinned at her, and she didn't like the look on his face suddenly. "That actually sounds like a good idea to me." She stood up again and looked down at him sternly.

"Come on, Jeff. Let's go." She left no doubt in his mind that she wasn't interested, or playing with him, which made no difference to him. He grabbed her hard then, pushed her onto the small couch, dropped his full body weight on top of her, and pinned her down. He was crushing her, and he was a big man. He was six feet three or four with broad shoulders and strong arms. She couldn't move an inch as he held her down and pulled up the skirt of her sundress, got to her underwear effortlessly, and started to pull it down.

In an instant, she knew that she was in trouble, and he wasn't going to free her. There was a heavy chipped glass ashtray on the narrow coffee table, which she didn't use since she didn't smoke. She grabbed it, and hit him on the side of the head with it. He let out a scream and loosened his grip enough for her to escape, run to the door, open it, and head for the stairs. "I'm calling the police!" she shouted as she ran down the stairs, and he followed her a minute later. She turned and could see blood trickling from his forehead. She realized that she could have killed him, but it had never occurred to her. She was just trying to avoid getting raped.

"I'm calling them first, and charging you with assault," he shouted at her. They were both on the street by then. He had left her door open, the keys on the table, to chase her down the stairs. He lunged at her and she ran away. She was faster than he was and lighter on her feet and he was hurt. She could see that he wasn't bleeding much, but he was definitely injured. "I paid for dinner, you bitch!" he shouted after her, and he stumbled into the street as a passing cab slowed to see if he wanted a ride. The taxi stopped, and he grabbed the door handle. "Fuck you, Antonia Adams," he shouted back at her, as the cab pulled away and she ran back into her building and up the stairs on shaking legs. She ran into her apartment, locked the door behind her, and sat down on the couch. There was blood on the ashtray and the coffee table, but it had been the only thing that saved her. She was shaking all over, and too shocked to even cry. She was sure he would have raped her. She didn't know what would happen next, or if he would report her to the police, but she'd had no other choice to protect herself. She realized how fortunate she had been that he hadn't, and she realized now how stupid she had been to fall for his bathroom ploy, and take him to her apartment. She didn't know him as well as she thought. And he thought that the price of a Mexican dinner justified having sex with her, whether she wanted to or not.

She lay awake for most of the night afterward, and wondered what would happen if the police showed up at work, if Jeff pressed charges. But she went to work on time the next day anyway. She was quiet and subdued, accepted her assignments to take things to the set. There was no sign of the police. At lunchtime, her supervisor advised her that Jeff, her student intern counterpart, had had a family emergency, and had to leave and go back to Ohio. He had said he wasn't coming back. She wondered if he was as afraid of her calling the police as she was of his accusing her of assault. It had been self-defense in her case, but who would believe her? Women's claims of rape were dismissed all the time. It would be her word against his, and he was visibly injured, she wasn't. He hadn't even torn her dress or left a mark on her. But it had been a powerful lesson to her to be more careful in the future, and not so trusting.

She didn't comment to the supervisor, discretion seemed like the better part of valor, as her father often said, and she went back to doing her job, grateful that Jeff was gone and he hadn't raped her.

Chapter 8

By the time her internship ended, the summer hadn't been a total success. The job was menial, though it got a little better after Jeff left, and as they trusted her more, they gave her a few more meaningful tasks. But the job had been billed as a gofer, which was all she was. She didn't learn anything, except not to trust men she didn't know well and never to take them to her apartment. As a career move, the internship had been a waste of time, and she didn't earn a penny.

Jake had earned very decent money as a busboy, but it had done nothing to enhance his acting career. He'd had a good time with his family at Lake Tahoe, and he had never made it down to L.A. to see her.

She had found no trace of her mother, which had been one of her main goals. So it was a disappointing summer, and a relief to go back to New York. Jake was flying in the night before school started, and she arrived a few days before. Their rooms weren't available yet, and they were both ecstatic to discover that they would be in the same dorm again, a different building from their old one, but the sophomore dorm was nicer. Some colleges still separated men and women in different dorms. NYU no longer did, and they had some truly wonderful buildings in the area.

Since she arrived before their rooms were ready, Antonia had to stay at her father's apartment again. Her room was an even bigger mess than before. Her father had brought more files from his office, which were piled up in boxes on the floor. Their empty suitcases from their trip to Greece were scattered all over the place, and a full set of kitchen crockery they'd bought in Italy had just arrived and was still in crates, crowding the room even more.

She and Lara had spoken a few times, but Antonia hadn't talked to her father since she left New York. She looked tired, pale, and had visibly lost weight. Lara suspected it hadn't gone well, and asked her about it when they were alone.

"It was kind of a bust. I was just a delivery/messenger girl. It was hotter than hell, and I didn't learn a thing about movies or writing screenplays." She told her about Jeff then, and Lara was horrified, but proud of how she had defended herself. It would have been a disaster if he'd prevailed.

"Good for you!" she praised her. "What a smart move!"

"He said he was going to call the police and charge me with assault, and he could have. I really hurt him. But he never did."

"What a little bastard," Lara said angrily, and put an arm around Antonia's shoulders.

"I shouldn't have let him in."

"No, you shouldn't have. You'll know better next time, and thank

God he didn't rape you." It would have been a tragic summer for her if he had. Similar experiences had happened to Lara's friends when they were in college, and more than once to her. Some guys just thought they had the right to do anything, and got away with it. "I'll try and get your room back in better shape," she said when they moved on to other subjects. Antonia didn't tell her father about the near rape, or she suspected he'd never let her take another summer job away again.

Her room at her father's apartment seemed almost beyond salvation by then, and the message in it was clear to her. It had become a dumping ground as well as her father's home office. There was no room for her anymore, or her belongings. She couldn't even get to what was there. It was an ordeal extricating what she had left there in June and needed in school. She took it back to school herself this time. Jake had said he'd set up her TV and stereo. By sophomore year, parents didn't usually go, and Brandon said he was relieved. Lara was willing, but Antonia said she could do it herself. Her father rented a van for her to use, she drove it all down to the Village, and met Jake on the street. He looked tan and relaxed after his three weeks in Tahoe. Antonia looked as though she had been through the wars. The heat in L.A. had been record-breaking all summer, and she was pale and thin and worn out.

He helped her unload the van, and carried everything upstairs for her. She had told him she'd do the hanging and decorating, make his bed for him, and put his clothes in the drawers if he would do all the heavy lifting and technical stuff for her, and there was a lot of it. It sounded like a good trade to both of them. They were finished by early afternoon, went for a pizza, and took a walk in Washington

121

Square Park. It was a beautiful late summer day. She had told him all about her job over lunch, and he was sorry for her. And she told him about Jeff's attempted rape. Jake was incensed.

"What a shithead. You should have called the police."

"They probably wouldn't have believed me. And he got hurt and I didn't. I would have gotten in trouble, and I couldn't prove what he did."

"Thank God," Jake said gratefully. If there had been proof, it would have been rape. "You did absolutely the right thing to clobber him. You were damn lucky!" He hated the thought of what could have happened to her, and was enormously relieved it hadn't. He gave her a big hug as they left the restaurant. "I'll be your body-guard from now on." She didn't usually need one, and nothing like it had ever happened to her before. Jeff had taken her by surprise, and taken full advantage of her trust and innocence. It had been a huge lesson for her. She'd heard stories like it on campus the year before, during freshman year. Assaults of that kind were common in colleges, workplaces, even on dates with boys girls knew. Lara had told her that she had to be very careful from now on. Clearly, there were bad people everywhere, and good ones too. No matter what the circumstances, drunk or sober, Jake would never have done any-thing like it. But some men did. It made her wish she were invisible again. She'd had an easy time in high school, where boys paid no attention to her. She hadn't even had a date for her senior prom, and hadn't gone. She felt like a total loser, but it was easier. Now men paid more attention to her. She looked older and her beauty was more evident. She was still small and delicate, but she looked like a woman now and not a child, which attracted bad guys like Jeff, as well as good ones. Being "invisible" had been simpler. She'd never felt beautiful before, and she didn't now. Her mother had always told her she wasn't, even as a child, and her father never complimented her, but she was a woman, and for some men that was enough to treat her as easy prey.

Jake admitted to her that he'd dated a girl while he was working at the Fairmont. She was a beautiful Mexican girl, one of the maids, and a student at Berkeley. She was smart and wanted to go to law school. They'd had fun, but it ended when he left, and they both knew nothing would come of it. He was going back to New York, and there was a senior she liked at Berkeley. It was just a summer fling, and neither of them had tried to make it more, which seemed sensible to Antonia.

Sophomore year was harder than their freshman year had been. Antonia signed up for more classes, hard ones. She was taking a lot of writing classes, and had endless assignments. Jake was working harder too, and they were both struggling for good grades and had less time to play than the year before. More was expected of them sophomore year.

She never went home for the weekend, as it was too complicated staying at the apartment now, with all the junk in her room. Lara said that every time she made order of it, her father brought home more. She could still sleep there, if she was willing to climb over all the boxes, and she couldn't bring anything home. She felt like she'd been evicted, and in a way, she had.

She turned down the few offers of dates she had. Jeff had put her off from dating, for a while anyway, and she said she had too many assignments and didn't have time.

"You can't live like a nun," Jake scolded her.

"I'm only nineteen. What do you want me to be? A slut?" She was afraid to go on a date now, even a simple dinner. What if something horrible happened again?

"You could try for something in between."

"Yeah, later," she said. She always had a good time with him and for now it was enough. Good grades were more important to her.

She decided not to go to San Francisco with Jake for Christmas this year. She'd hardly seen her father since school started in September. He and Lara were staying home this year, and she had a lot of writing assignments to do. She was going to stay in the dorm, and spend Christmas Eve and Day with her father and Lara, and the rest at school, working in the library.

Jake tried to convince her to go home with him.

"I'd love to, it was the best Christmas of my life, but I can hardly keep up with my writing assignments, and I feel like I should spend it with my dad and stepmom since they'll be here."

"Christmas won't be the same without you," Jake said sadly. "My mom said so too. Genevieve and my dad have a surrogate who's pregnant with his sperm and a donor egg. It sounds disgusting, and they're bringing her to dinner. Genevieve just had surgery, she had her eyes done again. She wants to look 'fresh' for the baby. Ian finished his latest book, and my mom thinks Eloise and John might get engaged. You'll be missing all the fun!"

"I *love* your family." She grinned. "Maybe I can come again next year."

"You'd better!" he warned, and she was sad when he left, but she felt virtuous staying in New York to work on her assignments.

Christmas with her own family was as dreary as she remembered it. Her father wasn't crazy about the holidays, and didn't like too much fuss, or the apartment overdecorated. He said it was all commercial anyway. Lara was closing an important deal for the sale of a townhouse in the East Sixties, and was on the phone constantly.

Their family was small, and her father wasn't the embodiment of the Christmas spirit. By nine o'clock on Christmas Eve, they were in their room, and Antonia was in hers, draped over a pile of boxes, wondering what she was doing there. She was sorry she hadn't gone to San Francisco with Jake. She could just imagine the loving chaos there. He called to tell her that his mother had been right. John and Eloise had gotten engaged, but were going to wait two years to get married, until they both finished their residencies. And he added, "Dad and Genevieve's surrogate is a *babe*! She's twenty-two and she's done it before. She says she loves the money, and think, if I go out with her, she won't get pregnant! She already is!"

"You're disgusting." She was laughing at him, and knew he didn't really mean it.

"Trust me, she's hot!"

"For the kind of money they must be paying her, I'm sure there's some sort of no-sex clause."

"I think it's just no booze and drugs, and only organic food. I'll have to ask my dad if there's a no-sex clause," Jake said, laughing.

He told her about everyone else then, and she was grateful to have someone to talk to in the quiet apartment. Brandon kept it a very restrained, subdued Christmas. Lara did her best to liven it up, but Antonia's father made it clear that he didn't like holidays, and put a damper on them. He said they had been depressing as a boy after his father died, and he saw to it that they stayed that way now.

Antonia spent Christmas Day with them, and was relieved to go back to school that night. The dorm was silent and empty. She didn't have a roommate this year, so she had the room to herself, and could work. She headed to the library the next day. She got a lot done before everyone came back from their holidays. And she was thrilled to see Jake when he returned. He brought her a Christmas snow dome, with Santa Claus standing on one of the spires of the Golden Gate Bridge. He had given her gift to her before he left, a beautiful leatherbound first edition of *Winnie-the-Pooh*. And she had given him a handsome black leather backpack, which he was already using. Her father had given her a check and said that he didn't know what she'd want, so a check was easier, and Lara had given her a gorgeous black and white cashmere Dior sweater. Antonia was going to save it for a special occasion. One thing she always realized and was grateful for: Her home life was emotionally deprived, but her father was financially generous with her. It was his substitute for love, which he was incapable of, for her.

Before everyone came back, she spent New Year's Eve alone in her room, and was asleep by ten o'clock. Her father and Lara had flown to the Caribbean for a week, to a new hotel. She hadn't planned to spend it with them anyway. And her father would never have invited her. She was still the unpleasant reminder for him of a past life, and he treated her accordingly.

In January, she went to the employment agency to put her name down for a summer job again. She wanted a better one than she'd had the year before. She wanted to learn something this time, and make a little money. They also suggested that she contact the studio where she had worked last summer, and specify what she wanted. With some successful history with them, they might have something better for her, and they knew her. So she wrote to the head of HR and her supervisor from the year before. She didn't expect to hear anything for a while, and she was too busy to think about it, turning her assignments in.

She went ice-skating with Jake once, and the rest of the time she worked on her writing assignments.

On the first of February she got a phone call from the university employment office. They said they might have something interesting for her, and asked her to come in.

She went in the next day. She sat down, looking a little leery.

"The studio you worked for last summer is going to be producing Hamish Quist's latest movie. They're shooting next summer. They would want you for three months. June, July, and August, which works with our school dates, if that works with any other plans you have. He apparently likes to have an army of people to support him. He brings personal assistants, and the studio supplies some others. They have an opening for an assistant to an assistant to an assistant. You'd be way down the line, and it's not a glamour job. But you might learn something this time, you'd be closer to the action, and it's not a big salary, but it's a paid position. Apparently, you made an excellent impression on them last year, they say you really stuck with it in less than ideal conditions. So they'll consider you first if you want it." The employment counselor was smiling at Antonia when she finished, and Antonia rose right out of the chair and almost hugged her.

"Yes! Yes! *Yes!* I'll take it. Tell them I want it."

The counselor told her the salary then, which was minimal but decent. "And there's housing for Mr. Quist's assistants. You'd get a room in whatever accommodation they have, not the best one obviously, but at least you won't have to pay for it. Everything else you pay yourself, airfare, meals, car rental, expenses, etc." It was a *much* better deal than she'd had the year before, and she loved Hamish Quist's movies. He was a *major* British producer/director.

"I've seen *all* his movies," she blurted out. "Tell them I want the job."

"They're waiting for you. They won't give it to anyone else until we give them your answer. And, Antonia, I'm really happy for you. I think this is your reward for sticking it out last year, even if you didn't like it. Sometimes that happens, you do the right thing and the reward comes later." Antonia was beaming as she floated out of her office. She called Jake from the nearest payphone and told him immediately. He was impressed too, and thought she deserved it. She worked harder than anyone he knew.

"Hamish Quist is big stuff," he said, and Antonia knew it. "Can you get me a starring role maybe?" he teased her, and she laughed.

"Yes, if he lets me write the screenplay!" They both knew that neither of those things was going to happen. She'd be lucky if she even got to talk to the famous director. More likely she'd be picking up his dry cleaning.

"You're a glutton for punishment going back to that studio," Jake commented.

"It was just a crap low-level job, with no pay and terrible weather. It wasn't all their fault."

"And you nearly got raped as a bonus," he said.

"That won't happen this year. I get housing, with his other assistants. It'll just be a room, but that's all I need." It had occurred to her too that she could try again to track down her mother. But she didn't know where to look this time. She had exhausted all her avenues before, and had come up with nothing.

The job was worth going to L.A. for. It sounded perfect as a next step. The next day the employment office called to tell her she had secured the job. The studio had confirmed. She was going back to L.A. to work for Hamish Quist, even as a lowly tenth assistant. It didn't get better than that.

Chapter 9

Antonia completed sophomore year successfully, and was on the flight to L.A. right on schedule on the first of June. The plan was different than it had been the year before. She was to go by cab to the house where Hamish Quist's assistants were staying. It was in the hills, in a canyon, across the street from the house they had rented for Hamish Quist himself, so they were near at hand, but not underfoot. He was bringing two assistants with him from England who had worked for him for years. They had hired a topflight American production assistant, a highly experienced woman they were paying a fortune, and at the bottom of the food chain, Antonia would be there to serve all of them, with anything they wanted her to do. She had to be available at all times, her official workday ended at ten P.M., but could be extended as long as they needed her. She was to start at eight A.M., as directed by the three main assistants. There was no official day off, and she would be notified if and when they could give her free time. Considering the house and the duties, they were paying her a minimum but decent wage. It sounded like a lot to her. She was to wear respectable, "non-suggestive, non-revealing" clothing at all times, which wasn't a problem for her either. She had brought her best summer dresses and nicest shoes, along with clean, untorn jeans. Lara had helped her put her wardrobe together and approved. Hamish Quist was a big deal.

When she reached the address, a houseman in uniform directed her to an apartment over the garage. He said it was the old chauffeur's apartment, which Antonia didn't mind. The houseman informed her that he came with the house, which was owned by a European director who had bought it four years before and never used it since, so they rented it out.

The chauffeur's apartment was decorated in bright, multicolored floral chintzes and looked freshly done. She had a small bedroom, a living room, an immaculate bathroom, and a kitchenette. There was maid service to the rooms, so she had no housework to do. It was a first-class luxury experience and nothing like what she'd had a year before. There were some basic things in the refrigerator, a few bottles of wine, and the houseman left her after he set her two suitcases up on luggage racks.

"I believe the other ladies are expecting you in the main house in half an hour," he said politely, which gave her time to shower and change if she needed to. She washed her face, brushed her hair, changed her shoes, and walked up to the main part of the house in a navy cotton skirt suit that looked businesslike, and navy pumps with low heels. She looked like a secretary in a bank, or an attorney. She could always dial it down later, but she wanted to start out more formally until she met the others. She pinned her long blond hair up in a bun, with a few soft wisps around her face that she could never control. They made her look younger and a little sexier, although she wasn't trying to achieve that effect.

There were two women sitting in the living room drinking wine, when the now-familiar houseman let her in. She could hear British accents, and they both turned their heads when she walked in. One was wearing black slacks and a white silk blouse, the other jeans and a crisp men's shirt. Antonia's outfit wasn't totally off the mark. None of them had the sexy, casual style typical of L.A. They looked professional and clean. Both had long hair smoothly pulled back, little makeup, and no jewelry. The younger of the two smiled and stood up when Antonia walked in, and walked over to shake her hand.

"Hello, I'm Margaret. I'm the lesser half of the British team. This is Brigid, the senior member of staff, she's been with Hamish forever, and we all work for her." She grinned and the slightly older British woman laughed.

"I think it's the other way around most of the time," Brigid said after shaking Antonia's hand, and they invited her to sit down in the elegant living room. "We all work for Hamish, he's the boss and we do everything we can to make his life easier."

"And I'll do whatever I can to help you," Antonia volunteered. "It's an honor to work for you, and for Mr. Quist." Antonia was very quiet and humble, as she always was, with no inclination to show off. She was very grateful for the job and it showed.

While they were talking, another woman came down the stairs from the upper hall. She was six feet tall, had dark chestnut hair and dark brown eyes. She seemed to take in everything at once. She had a wide smile, and was all American. She smiled at Antonia, and sat down with the rest of them.

"I'm Angie, local talent," she said to Antonia, "to help everyone find what they need in L.A. I'll be doing the troubleshooting on the set, while Brigid and Margaret work more closely with Mr. Quist. They're his familiar team. We ought to be able to cover any and all problems, and solve them, between the four of us." She included Antonia on the team and she was flattered. Antonia looked more grown up these days, she was turning twenty in August, but she was decidedly the youngest member of the group. She felt for a minute as though she were being interviewed by Charlie's Angels, one of her favorite television shows growing up, but it hadn't been on in years. The women who formed Hamish Quist's team of assistants were smart, beautiful, well dressed, and looked as though they could handle anything. It really was an honor to be hired to assist them.

"When is Mr. Quist arriving?" Antonia asked politely, not sure if he already had.

"Tonight, around ten, on his own plane. We start meetings tomorrow, with the writer, the actors, to get the bugs out of the script, and any technical problems we need to address. We'll probably be in meetings for two or three days, and he'll meet with the insurers. We'll handle all that," Brigid said confidently as the head of the group, "but some of it will filter down to you. We'll keep you informed when we need you. He likes to move fast, but he's a kind man to work for. He's the best." She smiled at the others and Margaret nodded. Angie hadn't met him yet, but the women who worked for him raved about him, which counted for a lot. Brigid said he wasn't a diva, he was reasonable, brilliant, unassuming, modest, and drove himself very hard.

Brigid and Margaret got up after a while to start getting his papers ready for him, and Angie left them to make some calls, to set up appointments that he wanted and had already requested. They told Antonia that she had nothing more to do that day, but to be ready for a tsunami the next day.

There were three cars for their use, and they said they didn't think Antonia would need one, but she thought it might be smart to have one if they needed her to do a quick errand, so she went back to the place where she'd rented the Ford the year before, and got one again.

She got back around dinnertime, and there was a spread set out in the dining room of the main house. This was very luxurious living, which she hadn't expected. She thought it would be more rudimentary. But what she had seen so far was far from that.

She heard a car drive to the house across the street that night, around ten-thirty. She peeked through her blinds and saw a tall thin man leap from an SUV and hurry into the house carrying a briefcase. All she could see was salt and pepper hair, a safari jacket, and jeans. The luggage went in through the garage, and she was sure it was her new boss.

She was ready the next morning at eight, fully dressed in white slacks and a man's striped shirt, and fancy sneakers in case she had to do a lot of errands. She walked up to the main part of the house, and all three women were dressed and ready. Hamish Quist walked in three minutes later, although he wasn't expected. He was wearing almost the same thing as Antonia, and shook hands with all of them with a warm smile. He had a handsome, chiseled face and deep blue eyes.

"Shall we?" he suggested, and led the way to the dining room, which they used as a conference room. He gave each of them a list of what he wanted. He let them decide what to delegate to Antonia, but she took careful notes anyway, so she'd have all the information she needed.

He left twenty minutes later, and said he'd be at the studio at nine-thirty, and wanted to start their first meeting with the writers by ten. As they had warned her, he was moving at full speed. Antonia knew he was in his early forties, had been married twice, and had no children. He had married famous actresses, and according to the press had been generous in both divorces. He'd received two Academy Awards as a producer, one as a director, a Golden Globe, and countless British awards.

He had smiled several times at Antonia, as though to encourage her, but he spoke to the others and gave them distinct, precise orders that made it crystal clear what he wanted from them. He was very organized, and had a hand in every aspect of the production. He was directing and producing it himself with some major stars.

They all disbanded a few minutes later after he left, and Antonia waited for further orders. When they took off for the studio shortly after, they told her to follow them in her car and park in the studio lot, all of which she did. And she met them on the set immediately. It was a far cry from her low-level job the previous year. She was privy to information here, was considered part of a team, and had sat in on a meeting with Hamish. She couldn't wait to see him work as a director. There was so much she wanted to learn.

For the next two weeks, Antonia went nonstop. They gave her plenty of errands, some of them menial, like getting control-top pantyhose for one of the stars. She had to deliver scripts to the main office, take notes to the hut where the writers were working, bring pages back to Hamish Quist for his approval or changes. She had to find a vet for one of the stars' dog, and her favorite lipstick shade at Chanel. She wouldn't go on without it. Some of it was mindless, and other aspects were vitally important, like anything to do with the script.

A week later, they came to a dead halt when Hamish wanted to add a walk-on part, without lines, to a scene of a young girl emerging from a swamp alive, after everyone thought she'd been murdered, and a man had been falsely convicted and gone to prison for it. He wanted someone ethereal, clearly a woman and not a child. She had been held captive by someone else, and managed to escape. She didn't say a single word, everything had to be on her face and in her eyes.

The casting agency sent him five or six girls and Hamish insisted that none of them were right. Too tall, too strong, too young, too athletic. He had a definite idea in mind and wouldn't let go of it. Margaret and Brigid knew how emphatic he was when he got like that. Nothing would sway him from his creative idea, and his own personal vision.

He was looking at a casting sheet with a hundred photos on it, when Brigid sent Antonia in with a thick envelope of photos of additional models. Antonia held the envelope toward him, and he was distracted, and then looked up at her and stared.

"Oh my God . . . who are you?"

"Your gofer, Mr. Quist," she said in a trembling voice. She thought she'd done something wrong.

"That's right, now I remember. Sorry, I wasn't thinking. Walk away from me, as far as you can go," he said, pointing across the set, "then turn slowly, and come back to me. How old are you, by the way?"

"I'll be twenty in August." He nodded.

"I don't want a precocious ten-year-old in a shot like that," he said. Antonia did as she was told and he watched her intently, and then had her do it again. As she walked toward him, their eyes met, and he wouldn't let go of her gaze. "That's it, oh my God, that's it," he shouted, and looked at his two British assistants. "We've got her." He turned to Antonia then with a pleading look. "Will you do a walk-on for me? I've seen hundreds of girls, you're the only one that'll work. You're perfect."

"I'm not an actress, sir," Antonia said, acutely nervous.

"You don't need to be. All you have to do is walk and look at the camera. No lines. I promise. It will only be a few minutes. I can't do this without you." He seemed so upset and so desperate that she didn't want to deny him. She nodded agreement, wondering what she was doing. "I want her in a shroud," he said to Margaret. "I want to shoot it right now, the light is perfect." The set they were using was a forest, with an eerie mist drifting through it. Brigid and Margaret hustled Antonia away, then helped her undress in a tent, down to her underpants, and wrapped her in a sheet like a shroud. Brigid thought to put part of it over her head, which made her appear even more mystical. They had one of the makeup artists come to dust her down. She looked ethereal and ghostly pale, like an exquisite creature from another world. They dusted her chest, arms, and throat with powder too, and they brought her back to Hamish barefoot, with her wide blue eyes frightened because she was. He looked straight at Antonia and spoke softly.

"My God, I want to cry you're so perfect. Thank you for doing this for me. It's the greatest gift you can give me. Rolling in one minute," he shouted to the crew, and got on a dolly with a camera mounted on it, and told her where to stand. He followed her, and gave her the cue when he was ready to start, and told her to walk as gracefully as she could, with her feet barely touching the ground. "Stay looking frightened, it's magical. Follow me," he said, as he moved backward with the camera rolling. There was not a sound on the set, and Antonia was incredibly beautiful with just a dusting of powder and the sheet and nothing else.

They did it three times with her eyes never leaving his, and he went to her and thanked her for doing it. "You saved my picture," he said. He was deeply emotional about it, and Brigid and Margaret came to lead her away, and help her dress. Brigid held out a release to her that said she had agreed to be in the film for a walk-on part.

"You'll be paid union scale," Margaret told her. "It's hardly anything."

"This really meant a lot to him," Brigid explained. "When he gets an idea like that and he can't make it happen it really upsets him." Antonia had seen that, and it didn't seem like a lot to do. It wasn't a part in a movie, it was just a minute, but for him it was a work of art.

She followed the others back to the set, and a few minutes later, she was sent to the main office to pick up some insurance papers Hamish had asked for, and Antonia forgot about what she'd done. The look in his eyes was so intense as she followed him. No one had ever looked at her like that. She had felt invisible, but as though he were the only human in the world who could see her. It had been an extraordinary feeling.

He watched the dailies that night with the cameramen, after they finished shooting and everyone else had gone home. He held his breath as he watched Antonia. They had three brief segments of her, and he ran all three again and again.

"Oh my God. She's like an angel, or a ghost," he said almost to himself as he watched her. "She's exquisite. I want to cry when I look at her." The cameramen agreed that she was unusual and beautiful, and the piece of her coming out of the forest was exactly what he had wanted. She moved almost as though she were floating above the ground, with perfect grace.

Hamish noticed Antonia on set the next day, and stopped to talk to her, in his gentle velvet voice.

"You were amazing yesterday," he said so no one else could hear him. "I saw the dailies last night. You were the most beautiful woman I've ever seen. You're a natural, the way you move, the look in your eyes, your expression. The camera adores you. You could have a major career on the screen." He barely spoke above a whisper, but she heard him clearly, and felt afraid.

"I can't do that, Mr. Quist. It's not me. I want to write screenplays one day. I want to work behind the camera, like you do, not in front of it. I want to be invisible, not have everyone seeing me." There were tears in her eyes and he reached out and touched her arm ever so gently, almost like a feather, but she felt his strength passing through her.

"Don't be afraid, Antonia. You can't hide. Your beauty is begging to be seen. Don't deprive others of it."

"I'm not beautiful," she said, her lip trembling, and she didn't want to be like her mother, but she couldn't tell him that. He wouldn't understand.

"You're very, very beautiful, and you can be a great actress one day, if you want to be. You can learn the rest. You understood exactly what I needed yesterday and gave it to me. We were one person while you were moving toward me." She had felt it too, and had been mesmerized by him, but she didn't want to be. "Think about it. And thank you for giving me yesterday," he said, and went back to the others. She was haunted by what he said and tried to forget it, but she couldn't.

The rest of the filming went smoothly, and the three months she spent in L.A. were a magical experience. She loved working with the three women, and watching Hamish on the set. He truly was a genius. He brought out the best in everyone.

They gave her a small birthday party on the set, and she went to say goodbye to him and thank him when she left at the end of August, to go back to New York.

"I will never forget you coming out of the forest toward me," he said to her. "I will keep that little piece of film forever, and watch you again and again. It was perfection, and so are you. Don't forget that, and don't let anyone tell you something different. If they don't see the magic that is in you, then they're blind." He was a very dramatic person, and she had loved working for him, and had learned a great many things about filmmaking. He was an extraordinary director, and got the best performances out of everyone, not just her.

She was sad to leave the women she had worked for. They were staying for another month of shooting, and then post-production. They all felt like mother hens as they said goodbye to her, and told her to be good at school. She had had three mothers while she was working there, and she hadn't tried to find Fabienne this time. She didn't need her.

She was thinking of all of them as her plane took off and how sad she was to leave. It had been an incredible summer, which more than made up for the year before.

Chapter 10

Antonia never told her father about her walk-on part in Hamish Quist's film. It only lasted for a minute or two and her father would never see it, so it didn't matter.

She told Jake every detail of the summer, and he hung on her every word. He couldn't believe how lucky she was to work on a Hamish Quist film, and even to be in it, when she told him about the walk-on part.

"I'll never be in a movie again, it was a one-off," she said firmly. "I was terrified the whole time. Fortunately, it didn't last long."

"You're crazy. I would do anything to be in one of his films. I want to see it when it comes out," Jake said fervently, and she promised to go with him. She had never seen the dailies of the clip, and didn't care.

* * *

Six weeks after school started, there was a wave of excitement at the Tisch School of the Arts. Brian Kelly, the major Hollywood producer, was coming to give a lecture on filmmaking, and creating block-buster movies in particular. Everyone wanted to attend, even the purists who wanted to make independent films when they graduated were curious.

Hundreds of students crowded into the auditorium to hear him. Jake and Antonia went together, but they couldn't find seats together. She wound up in the only seat left in the front row, and Jake was fifteen rows behind her. Kelly was a powerfully built man of medium height with broad shoulders in his early fifties, with about five Oscars to his credit. No one could deny his success.

His lecture was powerful too. He was a bulldog of a man, and one could easily sense that nothing could stop him in the creative process. He didn't have the finesse of Hamish Quist, but he was impressive nonetheless. He was emphatic in his speech and told them to let nothing stop them, to fight for everything they believed in, and to never sacrifice the integrity of their films. They gave him a standing ovation, and before he left the stage, he randomly picked ten students to come backstage and meet him. He apologized that he didn't have time for Q and A from the whole audience. Antonia was startled when he picked her, and she hurried onstage with the other nine students to go backstage to meet him personally. It was an exciting moment and one of the appealing things about Tisch was that they got to meet some very important directors, producers, screenwriters, playwrights, and actors. Brian Kelly was a huge deal in Hollywood.

Antonia wound up at the end of the line of students, as the others shoved her and pushed her away. They left as soon as they had spoken to him. They were meeting him in a dressing room used for their school plays. By the time it was her turn, they were alone in the dressing room. Since he said he was in a hurry, she phrased her question to him quickly.

"How can you tell when the material is right for a successful film? What determines that? What criteria do you use?" It was a valid question and she was startled when he laughed at her, in a raucous, derisive way. He had a rough voice, and a blunt style of delivery, but he got his points across.

"It's a crapshoot. How can I tell when a pretty woman is going to give me a blow job or not when I ask her to? You're a beautiful girl, so what do you say? How about it, sweetheart? If you do it right, I come pretty fast." As he said it, he locked the dressing room door behind him, and made a swift move toward her. He cupped her breasts for an instant, and then grabbed her crotch hard, and then with surprising strength, he forced her down on her knees with both his hands on her shoulders, then unzipped his fly, and released his erect penis in her face. It all happened so fast, Antonia didn't know what had hit her. He gave himself a quick rub to keep it hard, as she stood up and backed away from him, staying near the door as she did. She hadn't expected anything like this, and he was so crude about it. He made no attempt to put it back in when he saw the shocked look on her face.

"Look, I can make things easy for you. You want to struggle here for four years with a lot of boring half-assed professors who've never succeeded at anything, or do you want the fast track to success?

Make me happy and I'll get you a part in any movie you want. You'll be in Hollywood by next week for a screen test, and with your looks, you'll be a star in no time. I can make that happen for you with one phone call. So what's a little blow job between friends?"

"I don't want a part in a movie," she said with the strongest voice she could muster. She was shaking in fear and anger. What if this was like Jeff and he tried to rape her, and no one would believe her if she said Brian Kelly tried to rape her.

"What are you doing here if you don't want to be an actress?" He looked startled, his offer to her was not going well, and he didn't have time to waste here. He thought he'd have a little fun with one of the students before he left.

"I want to be a screenwriter, and *earn* it, not give blow jobs to be successful," she said, and with that, before he could stop her, she unlocked the dressing room door, and ran out, leaving the door open, as he hurriedly manipulated his penis back into his pants. It was already soft by then. He walked into the hallway and glanced around, looking for the exit. The tactic worked well for him in Hollywood and rarely failed. These young intellectual idealists were idiots, and he had no time to waste on them. He was frowning when he found his guide provided by the university, along with two professors who were honored to meet him.

"How did the meet and greet go?" one of them asked him. He'd been in the dressing room with them for longer than expected.

"Kids aren't what they used to be," he said, frowning, "or you're feeding them a lot of crap here. They all want to make indie films. They'll never amount to a hill of shit with them. They don't know what success is or what you have to do to get it. They'll end up a bunch of car parkers and waiters, and they won't be making movies or winning Oscars." He glanced at his watch then, and stepped up his pace. "Come on, I'll be late for my plane."

He left in a limo a few minutes later, and the two professors seemed unnerved. They were teaching their students to be creative and not just sell out for commercial success. By then, Antonia had run all the way back to her dorm in tears, and was running up the stairs to her room. No man had ever done to her what Kelly did, or said things like that to her. Jeff had been frightening, but Brian Kelly had been crude and demeaning. She wanted to take a shower, and she kept thinking about his penis sticking straight out of his pants, waiting for her to suck it. He hadn't tried to stop her or hold her down the way Jeff had, and he wasn't going to rape her. He didn't care about her, he had pushed her to her knees on the dressing room floor so she would give him the blow job he wanted. She felt dirty just having met him. He was a disgusting human being. She wondered how many women gave him one, just for the promise of a screen test. Even if she wanted to be an actress, she would never have done it that way.

She was shaking when she sat down on her bed, and was still sitting there when Jake came by half an hour later.

"Where have you been? I've been looking for you everywhere." She didn't answer as tears rolled down her cheeks, and he came to sit next to her on her bed. "What happened?"

"He's a pig!" She choked on a sob, and told him what Kelly had done. Jake stared at her in horror.

"He did *that*? You have to report it to the university. I'm so sorry,

Antonia. The guy is sick. I should have gone in with you. I'm not letting you go anywhere alone from now on."

"He didn't pick you," she hiccupped, "he wouldn't have let me take you in." They both wondered how often he did that, and also how often it worked on gullible girls who thought it was the only way to get ahead. "I'd rather scrub toilets in an airport than get work like that."

Jake wanted her to report the incident to the school authorities, but she wouldn't do it. "He'll say it isn't true, and I'll get in trouble. I can't prove it."

"I'm sure this isn't the first time he's done it," Jake said angrily. "Maybe it's the only reason he did the lecture. To pick up young women and get blow jobs. Jesus, what a son of a bitch."

She was shaken for the rest of the day and for several days after. She didn't even tell Lara about it. It was too disgusting. This was the second lesson she'd had about not trusting male strangers, but she had never thought that a famous producer like Brian Kelly would take out his dick, stick it in her face, and tell her to give him a blow job. She knew she'd remember it forever. And so would Jake.

Halfway through spring semester, Hamish Quist called her on her new cell phone. She was amazed to hear him, and recognized his voice immediately. He had a very distinctive smooth voice.

"I have a project I want to discuss with you," he said, after they exchanged niceties. "I'm making another movie. We're casting right now. That little strip of film of you coming out of the forest like a ghost is one of the most beautiful moments I've ever shot, and the camera loves you. I have a tiny part for you in the next movie. It's less than one scene. We could do it in three takes like the last one. I desperately want you to do it. You have exactly the look I want." She hesitated before she answered. The vision of Brian Kelly crossed her mind, but Hamish Quist wasn't like that. He was a gentleman and she had worked for him for three months last summer with no problem.

"I'm not an actress, Mr. Quist, and I don't want to be. I don't want to be in front of the camera. I only want to write, and one day direct like you do. I have no desire to be an actress. I like being invisible, so no one can see me."

"Well, God didn't grant your wish on that one," he said gently. "You're a beautiful woman. The world deserves to see you. You look a lot like Audrey Hepburn, or that same feeling, with pale blond hair. You look like an angel, please let me shoot you in one scene." He was almost pleading with her. "You've become my muse since the last time."

"I can't. I don't know how. Is it a speaking part?"

"Yes, but a very short one, just a tiny vignette. I can get a drama coach to get you through it. And I can shoot around your school schedule, whatever it is." He was willing to do anything to have her in the film.

"Honestly, I'd be terrible in the part. You'd be disappointed."

"You could never disappoint me, except if you say no. Could we have a cup of coffee to talk about it? I'll show you the scene in the script. It's two pages with all one-line dialogue. We can cut it down if you like. I just want the audience to see you, you really do have the face of an angel. It will make the whole movie. Can I see you for a few minutes?" He was begging and she didn't like turning him down, but she wasn't going to do it. But she had liked him when she worked for him.

"Okay, for a few minutes. Are you in New York?"

"I am." He wasn't trying to force her. He was trying to convince her by being as gentle as he could. He believed that the success of his new movie rested on it, just like the scene in the forest in the last one. The scenes with her were like little hidden gifts. And introducing an unknown ingénue, especially with her beauty and very distinct looks, would make the movie a smash hit. He'd been thinking about it for weeks.

She gave him the name of a café where she and Jake went for espressos. It was two blocks from her dorm.

"Do you have time today?" he asked her.

"My last class is at three-thirty. I could meet you there at five." She wanted to be respectful of him. He was an enormously talented, successful man. But she didn't want to be in his movie. She didn't want to be like her mother and become an actress.

"I'll see you there, Antonia," he promised in a gentle voice. He was everything that Brian Kelly wasn't. She hadn't had a date since the Kelly incident. And sophomore year, she had avoided dating too because of Jeff.

She met Hamish at the café as promised that afternoon. He was waiting when she got there. He was wearing a black leather jacket, a T-shirt, jeans, and cowboy boots. She looked like a kid, in jeans and a pink sweatshirt and high-top pink sneakers, with her hair in pigtails. He smiled when he saw her. He liked her, he had the summer before too, and she was so heartbreakingly beautiful, but in a different, unusual way, like Hepburn, just as he had told her. She was very distinguished looking, with a natural grace.

There was something very protective and fatherly about him, which she sensed immediately. She knew he wasn't going to threaten her, or get angry with her. He used all the gentlest arguments to convince her.

"You can't be invisible, Antonia. You're too beautiful. That's a gift. You need to share it. Otherwise it's like locking a jewel in a dark closet where no one can see it."

"I feel safe that way." Tears filled her eyes.

"What have people done to you that you don't feel safe?" She didn't answer and he reached out and gently touched her hand. "I won't let anybody hurt you. Ever. I want to protect you." She believed him. And then, because she did, she nodded.

"Okay, I'll do it," she said in a whisper. "But it's only one small scene, right?"

"It's five minutes in the film. We can shoot it in three takes when you get out of school in June. We're shooting it in England this time. In a studio near London. And there's something else I want to ask you. Brigid and Margaret love you so much. Would you be willing to do a summer job with us, like last year, except in London this time, working for me, not the studio?"

She beamed the moment he asked her. "I'd love it."

He smiled broadly too. "Fantastic! The girls are going to be so happy. And thank you for doing the scene for me, Antonia. I really appreciate it. And I promise I'll make it as easy and painless as possible." Because he was who he was and she knew him, she believed him, and she knew he wouldn't let her down. She was really excited about working for him in the summer in London, and couldn't wait to tell Jake.

She and Hamish left the café together. He stood on the sidewalk, smiling. She looked like a little girl, and she was in a way, at twenty. There was a wonderful innocence about her, which was why he wanted her in his movie. You couldn't fake that.

They shook hands standing on the sidewalk, and then he gently bent down and lightly kissed her cheek.

"Take care of yourself, Antonia. And remember we'll take good care of you. I'll have the girls call you to set up your plane tickets. See you in June." He smiled at her and walked away. He turned back once to wave, and Antonia was smiling too when she walked back to her dorm. And she did feel safe when she was with him. The only two men she trusted in the world were Hamish and Jake.

Antonia never lied to her father, so she decided to be honest with him before she left for the summer. She went to the apartment to have dinner with him and Lara. She was nervous. She told him about the scene she was going to do for Hamish. She told him at the end of the meal, and Lara looked surprised. Antonia hadn't told her about it.

"It's a five-minute scene, a bit part. I've read it. It's perfectly respectable, like a cameo appearance. I just wanted you to know."

Her father exploded immediately. "You're just like your mother.

You hang around with all those slobs in the movies like a groupie, and you'll wind up a tramp like her. Maybe you already are. What comes next? Cocaine? You always said you don't want to be an actress, just a writer, and now you're doing a part in a movie." He shoved his chair back so hard, it fell over, and he left it there. His face was red when he stood in the doorway of the kitchen bellowing at her. "I've had one slut actress in my life, Antonia. I don't need another one."

She spoke firmly and clearly. "I'm not a slut, or a groupie. Hamish Quist is the most respectable producer in the business. I worked for him last summer, and I'm going to work for him again, doing errands. It doesn't make me a slut or a tramp because I do a five-minute scene in a movie, with all my clothes on. He says I remind him of Audrey Hepburn. She isn't a tramp, Dad, and neither am I. I can't help what my mother did to you, but I'm tired of paying for it, and being punished for it, because you never got over being mad at her. You've held it against me for my whole life. I'm not my mother." She was speaking loudly by the end of it, and he didn't answer. He stormed out of the kitchen and slammed the door behind him.

Lara gazed at her sorrowfully. "I'm so sorry, Antonia. You're right in what you said. He's still angry at your mother, and he takes it out on you. He can't blame you. And Hamish Quist is right, you do look like Audrey Hepburn. You're very beautiful." Antonia smiled sadly at her. She knew now that her father was never going to forgive her for who her mother was, and he was never going to love her. He never had, or not in a very long time since she was a young child, or a baby. Fabienne had escaped him, so he had punished Antonia all her life instead.

She got up from the table, kissed Lara, and left a few minutes later. This wasn't her home anymore.

Lara found Brandon in their bedroom after Antonia left, and looked at him angrily.

"It was terrible of you to take it out on her because Fabienne hurt you. Antonia is a wonderful girl and I hate what you do and say to her. It's so wrong and it's not fair. She doesn't deserve it."

"I didn't deserve what Fabienne did to me either." There were tears in his eyes.

"That's between you and Fabienne, not you and your daughter. It's not her fault. You have to stop punishing her. I can't stay with you if you don't. It makes me feel sick to see it."

"Are you leaving me?" he asked her, shocked.

"I might. I can't stand it anymore." He didn't answer his wife. He lay on the bed thinking about what she'd said, and about Antonia. He hated Fabienne more than ever because she had made him hate his own daughter, and he knew that Lara was right. But he couldn't turn the tides. For him, it was too late. He couldn't find his way back to Antonia. He hated her mother too much, and he couldn't tell them apart. They were one person in his mind.

Chapter 11

Jennifer Stratton, the drama coach Hamish had hired to work with Antonia, had perfect diction. She had an aristocratic accent that wasn't exaggerated, but identified her instantly as upper class. But she wasn't there to teach Antonia diction. She was an excellent drama coach, and she was there only to help Antonia learn her lines impeccably and deliver them flawlessly in her one scene.

"Think of it as one exquisite little painting," she told her, "a tiny Degas or Renoir. Every stroke, every mark of the pen, every color must be perfect. It will be the smallest scene in the movie, but it must be beautiful, because of the way you deliver those lines, and your expression must be in harmony with those words."

Jennifer made Antonia repeat the scene endlessly until she could have said it in her sleep. They tried it different ways with different inflections, until they found the one they liked best. Jennifer recorded Antonia speaking the lines so she could hear herself and decide which nuances she preferred.

Antonia spent two intense weeks learning the scene until it felt totally natural to her, like part of her. Hamish stayed away while she was working with the drama coach. It was a scene between a man and a woman. She tells him she loves him, and it changes the rest of his life. She is in an accident and dies minutes later and the words she says to him will haunt him forever. She is an innocent in the movie, and he never knew until then that she loved him. He has only minutes to savor it, to understand what she means to him, and then she is gone. It was a short but powerful scene, about the profound effect people have on one another, even in a short time. Each moment is precious. It was the crux of the movie, deep in the soul of it.

When they finally shot the scene, Antonia looked incredibly beautiful, in a soft, natural way, and the words came out of her mouth as though she had waited her entire lifetime to say them. She made each one a gift. There were tears in people's eyes on the set when they shot the scene. She was so gentle and so loving. The entire scene was like a caress. She had learned her lessons well. Hamish had tears sliding down his cheeks when the scene ended, and they only shot it twice. Both times were perfect, and even Jennifer was smiling when they were finished.

"You're an excellent pupil, my dear. If you ever want to become an actress, you would be an immense success."

Hamish told her precisely the same thing. "You could be a great actress if you wanted to be. You should think about it. It's a crime to waste a talent like that."

"I want to put it in writing for others to say, not say it myself," she explained to him again.

"You could be a very big star," he said quietly. He knew true star-dom when he saw it. He had worked with the best.

He took her to dinner that night to celebrate and thank her. They had an elegant dinner at Harry's Bar.

"Now explain to me about why you want to be invisible," he said as they ate dinner. "What's that about?"

She told him about her mother and her father, her father's bitter-ness, and how unwelcome she had felt in her own home all her life, and how terrified she had been, and terrorized by her mother before she left.

"I was always afraid that they would get mad at me, and they usually did. It got to be much easier to disappear, and become invis-ible. It worked for me, and it still does. I was always the intruder in their home, the unwelcome guest. My life went much more smoothly when they didn't even remember that I was there."

"How sad," he said, and she could see that he meant it. He took her hand and kissed it.

"I told my father about the scene I was going to do in the movie, and he called me a tramp and a slut. He hated my mother with a passion by the time she left. I do remember that, and she hated him. They fought constantly. I lived in a war zone, so I used every kind of camouflage to hide from them. Being invisible was the best one."

"You're grown up now," he reminded her. "They can't hurt you. Your mother is gone, and your father sounds like a bully and a cruel man, but he can't do anything to you now. They have no power. I don't want anyone to hurt you," he said. He had been watching her since she arrived. There was something so enchanting about her, so innocent and pure, that it tore at his heart. She was like a little bird that needed protection, but she was strong too, stronger than he knew, but he could sense that in her as well. She had endured a great deal of silent abuse and deprivation for her entire life, and had been punished for her mother's crimes.

They talked about the movie then, and other things. His travels, and hers. He explained that he came from a simple background, in an industrial part of England. His grandfather had been a coal miner and died young, and his father had worked hard to provide for his son as a teacher and taking on odd jobs, and had died young as well. He said his mother was a remarkable woman who kept the family together as a nurse when they had no money, and managed to feed and clothe him and his two brothers. She made everything. She had provided all her children with a good education, and she had lived long enough for him to spoil her. She had worked as a private nurse for a wealthy old lady, a countess, who had left his mother some money when she died. His mother had turned it over to him immediately, so he could make the movies that he dreamed of. She had made his career possible. And now he could afford whatever he wanted, and had bought his mother a beautiful home before she died. Her final days were her happiest, decked out like a lady, living in a home with beautiful things.

Antonia said that she had been well provided for. Thanks to her father's success in business, she had lacked nothing materially and was grateful for it. But there was no love in their home. Her father was a bitter man, filled with rancor and hatred for her mother. Lara had done all she could to turn Brandon around, Antonia knew that now. But Antonia had come to believe that it was impossible. Brandon would never forgive Fabienne, or Antonia by association. She had finally given up. She hadn't said goodbye to him when she left, or even sent a message to him. She wasn't sure when she would see him again, but she was in no hurry to. Her visits with him were too painful, the results too far reaching. It sounded tragic to Hamish that a girl with so much beauty, brains, charm, and love in her, should be striving to disappear to avoid her loveless home and angry parents.

She told him about trying to find her mother, with no success.

"Why would you even want to?" he questioned her. "She abandoned you, what is there left to say?"

"Maybe I just want to know why, and hear it from her, not my father's version, and know if she's dead or alive. As long as she's living, I'll keep hoping that I'll see her again someday. I need to put that hope to bed for good, and throw it away. I have a good life without her, and I need to give up on my father too. We'll never have a decent relationship, he won't allow it. The deck is always stacked against me with him, so I'm done."

What resulted from Hamish's conversation with Antonia was that he wanted to take care of her and protect her, but he was more than twice her age. He was almost forty-four, and she was not quite twenty-one. He couldn't see a way to shield her from harm if they were not together as a couple, and he didn't think that was fair to her. He had feelings for her he hadn't expressed and didn't want to admit, and he was trying to keep them to himself. It was getting harder and harder to conceal. He didn't want to burden her with his feelings, so he was staying at close range but not crossing any lines or bridges, yet. He was a perfect gentleman, particularly with her.

He took her home to the apartment he used for guests, and additional crew when they were filming. She was staying there for the summer. It was down the street from his home. He dropped her off as he would a daughter or a niece, or a friend. She thanked him for dinner, and he watched her go into the house. He was happy that she would be there for three months, and he would see her every day on the set, or in his office. He loved being close to her, and he knew that his two assistants would take good care of her too. Her home life for all of her twenty years sounded like a loveless nightmare thanks to her selfish, narcissistic parents.

Antonia loved being in London, and working for Hamish. Brigid and Margaret took her around London when they had time off, and she had fun being with them. It was a beautiful city, and she loved discovering its history.

One of the young actors in the movie had asked Antonia out several times. He wanted to take her out to dinner, or to the nightclubs, but Antonia refused each time he asked. She could already see what he was, and knew where it would lead. He was only interested in himself, having a good time, and getting laid. She didn't want to be a toy for him. She thought it would just end up in another scene like the one with Jeff, or maybe even Brian Kelly, or a shallow relationship she didn't want. He was easy to turn down. Eventually, he made fun of her and called her the Virgin Queen, which she thought proved her point. She was happier keeping her social activities limited to the assistants who worked for Hamish.

* * *

It was the most exciting summer of her life, watching the film develop, and studying the scripts, and learning from them. Hamish taught her many things about the industry, intentionally and by example. And London was a fabulous city. She didn't want to leave. Hamish took her to dinner from time to time, and she loved the women she worked with. She didn't want to go back to New York, but she had to complete her senior year and graduate.

On her birthday, Hamish organized a party for her at San Lorenzo, and a large group of them went dancing at Annabel's afterward with some of the cast, since he was a member there. She was twenty-one now, and had come of age. She felt very adult, which made him smile. Twenty-one was still a baby to him, and to most of them. But after her London summer, Antonia felt very sophisticated and grown-up.

She hadn't heard from her father all summer. He was still angry about the movie she would be in. But Lara called her from time to time. They had rented a different, smaller house in the Hamptons, went there on weekends, and for the month of August. Things were tense between Lara and Brandon, ever since she had confronted him about his treatment of Antonia. He couldn't tolerate being criticized and challenged, particularly by his wife. And she couldn't stand the heartless way he treated his daughter. Lara felt guilty being the object of his affection, when his daughter got none.

There were tears when Antonia said goodbye to the crew in London, and she had promised to come back. Hamish had cleverly gotten around her needing a work permit, by depositing a "gift" for her in her bank in the States. It was more than she'd expected, and she was surprised by how generous he was.

Senior year took off in a rush. She and Jake had been given rooms in the same dorm again, and they hung out together more than ever, and worked side by side doing their homework assignments.

He had met a sophomore he liked in October, so he had a little less free time for Antonia, but he had dinner with her regularly, so she didn't feel abandoned. It was the first serious relationship he'd had since he was there, and he was enjoying it. Antonia was happy for him, and focused on her schoolwork.

She was in her dorm room when Hamish called her in December. It was snowing outside, and she was happy not to be out. She was surprised to hear his voice. She hadn't heard from him since she left London three months before. He had no reason to call her. The movie was finished, and due to open before Christmas. She couldn't wait to see it.

He asked her how she was, and then switched to the reason for his call, as soon as she said she was fine.

"What are you doing day after tomorrow?" he asked her.

"My laundry," she said with a laugh, but it was true.

"No, you're not. You're coming to the premiere of *Summer Snow* with me." It was the movie she was in. "I flew in for it, but I need a date, and I'd like you to be it. I hate going to those events alone, and this is your debut," he teased her, but it was true. And it was a good excuse to see her. The premiere was at a new theater, and there would be a party at the Plaza afterward. "Those events are always a zoo, but I have to go, and you really should too." There would be a red carpet for press interviews, and the two stars of the picture were going. The media would corner any big star who came to the event. And there would be plenty of photo ops. It sounded overwhelming to Antonia.

"Do I have to go?" she asked, sounding skittish.

"Do you know how many women would give their right arm, left leg, and several other body parts to go with me?" he said, teasing her. She laughed. "Come with me. If it's too big a mess, we'll leave. I promise." He had always kept his promises to her so far.

"I have nothing to wear." The time-honored, all-purpose excuse.

"Then go shopping. That's easily remedied."

"I have a paper due." Another excellent excuse, and he knew it.

"I'll write it for you. Now go buy something to wear. If this is a once-in-a-lifetime appearance in a film, you *have* to go!"

She followed his advice and went to Bergdorf the next day, and found a simple black velvet evening gown with a rhinestone jacket that made her look like a czarina. She bought rhinestone earrings too, and she had a small black velvet clutch. All she was missing were the shoes, and she found those at Bergdorf too. She had everything she needed. She'd used some of her money from her summer job to pay for it. She liked the simplicity and clean lines of what she'd chosen, and her figure was sensational, and the dress showed off her tiny waist.

He picked her up the next day at five-thirty. She had put her school assignments aside. He had allowed half an hour to get uptown to the theater, and he felt a little odd picking up a schoolgirl to go to the premiere. He was wearing an impeccably cut tuxedo and looked like a movie star himself.

When they got to the theater, there were banks of photographers outside held back by red velvet ropes with security guards to keep them in line. Inside, there were even more photographers, and waiters were serving champagne and caviar hors d'oeuvres. There was a long area roped off as the red carpet, with a backdrop that would work well in photos. Assorted stars were lined up to be interviewed by newspapers, magazines, and TV.

Hamish and Antonia made their way decorously down the expanse of red carpet, and had almost reached the theater itself, where they would view the movie, when the press realized who she was and started shouting her name. She felt foolish posing for photographs with such a small part in the film. But the press didn't care. They wanted her. Antonia and Hamish posed for a few shots and then walked into the theater to claim their reserved seats. Hamish could feel her shaking as she held his arm, and she looked spectacular in the black velvet dress and rhinestone bolero. A hundred flashes went off in their faces as they walked into the theater, and he could feel her flinch.

"Can we go now?" she whispered, looking terrified.

"No, we have to see the movie first," he said gently. "You're safe. You're with me." She nodded, too nervous to speak, and they found their seats quickly and sat down. It took another half hour for the theater to fill. Several members of the cast came to say hello to them. And then the movie started.

She could see that Hamish was right about the scene she was in. The brief moment was crucial in the film.

"You're great in it," Hamish reassured her, and they sat back to enjoy the movie. He was very happy with it. It was a beautiful film, with major stars in it. On the way out, the press was even more excited about Antonia, once they all realized that she was the ingénue in the film. It took them half an hour to escape into the limousine, to drive to the Plaza, where the photographers kept shooting them every step of the way. They'd been photographed enough, and only stayed twenty minutes, and left, and the limo drove them back downtown. Antonia let out a huge sigh once they escaped the press.

"How do people stand that?" she said, leaning her head back against the seat. It placed her throat in a graceful white arch, and Hamish had to pretend not to notice, in order to keep his hands off her.

"Some people actually like it." He smiled at her. "I don't enjoy it either, but that's what premieres are for, to get lots of press for the movie."

"I love the film," she said, smiling at him, and he couldn't resist teasing her.

"I've never taken a date back to her school dormitory before. I feel like a cradle snatcher." And in a sense, he was.

"I'm not a date, I'm an employee," she corrected him comfortably. She felt surprisingly at ease with him.

"No, you're not. You were an employee last summer. Tonight you're a date, and a star."

"Oh. How soon will the reviews be out?"

"By tomorrow morning."

He wanted to take her out for another glass of champagne somewhere, but she said she had an early class in the morning.

She thanked him when she got out of the car, and she looked like a movie star, even though he was dropping her off at a college dorm.

"Thank you, Hamish, I had a wonderful time," she said politely, and he laughed.

"No, you didn't. You were scared to death on the red carpet. I could feel you shaking."

"I loved the film," she said. "And being with you." She said it so softly he could barely hear her, and she gazed at him with big shy eyes.

"You can't be invisible *all* the time," he said, and she nodded. She looked so beautiful and so vulnerable that he couldn't stop himself. As the snow began to fall again, he bent down and kissed her. It really had been a beautiful evening, despite the collegiate setting now, and the stress the press had caused her. She hadn't expected him to kiss her, but there was something wonderfully romantic about it. She wondered if he had meant it, or he just got carried away on the high of the evening. But she wasn't going to ask him. She enjoyed the moment, thanked him, and floated into her dorm as he watched her go.

The reviews the next day were fabulous and well deserved. The film was a total victory for Hamish, and the cast. And they raved about Antonia's performance, and said she was the most exciting young face to hit the screen in years. And one of the reviewers saw the resemblance to Audrey Hepburn too, so he wasn't wrong.

Antonia called Hamish at his hotel as soon as she read them.

"Bravo!" she said when he answered the phone in his suite. His phone had been ringing constantly since early that morning. "And thank you for last night."

"Thank you for giving me that scene. It gave the picture an extra push." Even she could see now that it did.

"They want more of you, Antonia," he said gently.

"They can't have me. I'm not an actress."

"You could be, a great one."

"It's not what I want to do," she told him for the hundredth time.

"When am I going to see you again?" He changed the subject.

"How long are you here for?" She had forgotten to ask him.

"Two more days. Let's have dinner tomorrow night." He had press interviews lined up all day and evening.

"That's perfect. I have to turn a paper in tomorrow, so I have to finish it tonight." He felt like he was dating a schoolgirl, but it amused him.

"How much longer do you have here?" he asked her.

"I graduate at the end of May," she said proudly. It was only five months away, and he knew he could wait.

When he took her to dinner the following night at Majorelle uptown, the subject of his next movie came up. He was working on the deal now, and the casting. It was a juggling act to find a time when everyone was available, particularly the cast. He almost had it nailed down but not quite.

"There's a supporting role for you in that movie, Antonia, if you'll do it. And I have a confession to make. I'm offering it to you for two reasons. One, I think you would be extraordinary in it, and I know you can do it, if you're willing. And two"—he looked at her tenderly and felt young again when he did—"I'm in love with you," he said softly. "I want to work with you, and I want to find a way to keep you with me all the time." She didn't answer him for a minute, and he kissed her. She hadn't expected this to happen. She had loved working for him for two summers, and what he had taught her, but she never expected to fall in love with him.

"I want to be with you too," she whispered back. She felt safe with him. She didn't need to hide when she was with him, and she wanted to make him happy. "I'll do the movie," she said bravely. "And maybe one day you'll let me write a screenplay, and we can work on a movie together that I write and you direct. Is that a deal?"

He smiled broadly at her in answer. "You're a stubborn woman, which is part of why I love you. I promise we'll write and direct a movie together one day. And in the meantime, I'm going to make you a star." He was certain she would be. The public would love her, but not nearly as much as he did. He was crazy about her.

"You make me happy," she said peacefully. "That's all I need." She didn't want to be a star. It had never been her dream.

"You make me happy too. We'll be ready to start shooting in June. You'll have graduated by then, so that should work perfectly. And I want you to stay with me after we finish the film. I have an idea of how to do it," he said mysteriously, "but there's plenty of time to talk about that. What are you doing over Christmas?" he asked her, and she wasn't sure.

"My father and I haven't spoken since June. I could go to San Francisco with my friend Jake. I had a great time there three years ago. I haven't decided yet."

"I have a better idea. Let's go someplace warm together, the Turks and Caicos or Saint Bart's maybe. Would you like that?" She was smiling at him. Doors were opening into a new world, with a whole new view. He was offering her another life. "Let's do it," he said quietly.

"I'd love to." She was going to call Lara and tell her. She knew Lara would be disappointed, but after what her father had said, Antonia didn't feel ready to see him yet, even after six months, or spend Christmas with him. He had been cruel about her small part in the movie, and he would be even angrier now. He had continued to pay for school and her expenses, but he had no other contact with her. It was typical of him to withhold love and approval. But Brandon considered supporting her financially his duty.

The war he was waging with Antonia had put a strain on his marriage. Lara had told him point-blank that he was abusive to Antonia. And he refused to back down about her being in a movie. He would be even worse now, if she got good reviews and attention in the press, but she didn't care. She had Hamish, who was so gentle and kind to her, and wanted to protect her.

They made plans for their trip all through dinner, and he said he'd have the girls in his office set it up the next day.

"I'll pick you up with the plane, and we can fly down there together. I have to go back to London first for a few days to meet with some of the investors."

It all sounded like a dream to her, and to him too. She was young, but the age difference didn't matter to either of them. The years melted between them. They talked about spending Christmas together, and the movie that he'd start in June, with her in a supporting role. She was still uneasy about it, but he had convinced her, and she was going to do it for him. He was like the father she never had.

"It'll help you write a screenplay one day. It's good for you to have some experience in front of the camera, especially if you want to direct too," he reassured her. It justified acting in a movie, which she had never wanted to do.

"You're not invisible anymore, Antonia, and you don't need to be. I see you, and I love what I see. You don't need to hide. I won't let anyone hurt you." She believed him. Hamish Quist was an honest man, and he loved her, and she loved him. And she wasn't an intruder anymore. She belonged with him.

Chapter 12

Antonia called Lara to tell her she wouldn't be home for Christmas. Lara had suspected that would happen, since there had been no contact between father and daughter for six months. Antonia had retreated after his vicious attack on her about the movie, and the cruel things he had said to her, none of which were true. She was nothing like her mother. He refused to back down, no matter how many times Lara talked to him. He said he wanted nothing to do with her if she was going to become an actress like her mother. He was paying for her education, which he considered his obligation, and she was graduating soon, but if she was going to embark on an acting career, he said she'd end up a "whore" like her mother. It made Lara shudder when he said it.

"You can't just reject her, Brandon. She's your daughter."

"I can and I will," he said stubbornly.

"She's grown up without a mother, and she has barely had you. Now she won't even have you." She already didn't. It made Lara's heart ache thinking about it. She saw him in another light now. She couldn't feel warm toward him, knowing how unkind he was to his daughter. He was emotionally abandoning her, after years of punishing her. And Antonia realized it too. She had told Lara that she couldn't make excuses for him anymore. When she thought of the solitude and loneliness of her childhood, it made her shudder. She had always believed she deserved it, but now she knew she didn't. She was an adult and her eyes were open.

And nothing Lara did or said softened him. He didn't want to lose his wife, but he couldn't reach out to his daughter. She had always been an upsetting reminder of her mother, just by her very existence, despite the fact that she looked nothing like her and had never behaved like her. In his mind, she was always Fabienne's daughter, and he couldn't see beyond that.

"Are you going to San Francisco with Jake for the holidays?" Lara asked Antonia when she said she wasn't coming home. Lara had met Jake several times when she came downtown to meet Antonia for lunch, and she was grateful that they had found each other and were good friends. She thought he was a lovely boy, and she knew Antonia had had a great time when she went to San Francisco with him.

"No, I'm planning to do something else," she said vaguely. She wasn't ready to tell her about Hamish yet. She thought Lara might object to the age difference, or think it was happening too quickly. But she felt right about it, and didn't want to have to justify it to her.

"I'm sorry your father is being so unreasonable."

"So am I, but that's not new. He's never been able to separate me from my mother in his mind. I realize that now. I never had a chance with him. Being in a movie is just another excuse. And Hamish just offered me a supporting role in his next movie. He thinks I have talent." She sounded tired. It depressed her to think about her father, and how viciously he had rejected her. Before he had been indifferent and cold. Now he was aggressively hostile to her.

"Is that what *you* want?" Lara asked her. She knew how much Antonia had never wanted an acting career, and only wanted to write screenplays. This was a radical departure for her.

"He says I'll be a better writer and director one day if I've had some experience in front of the cameras too. I won't do it again if I don't like it. He's a brilliant director and maybe I'll learn something from it. But my long-term goals haven't changed." Lara was happy to hear it and thought she had real writing talent. "What about you? Are you okay with my dad?" He was much kinder to his wife than he was to his daughter, but there was a hardness to him that they both recognized. Antonia didn't see how Lara could love him anyway.

"He's not easy, and he's getting harder as he gets older. He's still so bitter about your mother."

"He'll carry that torch forever," Antonia said coldly. It had burned them all. Even Lara, and she didn't deserve it either.

"We're trying to work things out," Lara said quietly, but she didn't feel the same way about him that she used to, ever since he had lowered the boom on Antonia and shut the door on her. Antonia wondered if Lara would ever leave him, but didn't want to ask, maybe she didn't even know herself, but she'd had ample proof now of just how unkind and unfeeling he could be, and it was not unique to his relationship with his daughter. There were times when he was harsh with Lara too. She was sorry that Antonia had to go through it, and she did her best to make up for it. But you couldn't replace a mother and a father, and Antonia had been unlucky with both. Lara understood now that it was why she had been so shy as a child, always hiding, fearful, desperate to remain unseen and unnoticed. She had been damaged by them, and nothing could make up for it, not even a loving stepmother, although she had tried.

They had lunch before her school vacation started, and exchanged Christmas gifts. Lara was always generous with her. Antonia had bought Lara a leather varsity jacket in the NYU colors of violet and white, since Lara loved purple. She said she'd wear it proudly, and she'd gotten her a fun sweater to go with it. Lara had bought Antonia a short black Alaia dress she loved that fit her perfectly. She still didn't mention Hamish. She wanted to keep it to herself for a while. Their relationship was something very precious and fragile that she wanted to protect for as long as she could. She had only told Jake about it, and he was happy for her, although he didn't like the age difference. He realized that she was probably looking for a father, and Hamish was good to her. Jake had gotten serious about the girl he was seeing too. He was planning to stay in New York to audition for acting jobs after he graduated. Their plans for the future were taking shape. And now all of hers included Hamish, and there was no doubt that he would further her film career, which wasn't why she loved him, but it couldn't hurt, and he had promised to help her, whatever direction she took.

The only thing Jake didn't like was that he thought she was agreeing to try acting in order to please Hamish, not from any desire of her own. Jake would have given anything for a part in one of his movies, but he never asked her. He didn't want to exploit their friendship. He hoped he'd get to meet Hamish, and was sure he would if their romance continued. He never pressed Antonia about it, he respected her too much to do that, and he wanted to protect her too, since no one ever had in her entire lifetime. He hoped that Hamish would now, and in that sense, maybe a father figure, and a man of his age, was the right thing for her. He hoped so. He hated the thought of her getting hurt again, and she was an innocent in matters of the heart. At twenty-one, she was still a virgin, which Hamish had realized too.

The vacation Hamish took Antonia on was like a fairy tale for her. After a brief trip back to London, he picked her up in his plane at Teterboro Airport in New Jersey, and stopped just long enough to refuel and take off again with her for Saint Bart's. He had rented a villa with a private pool from the best hotel on the island. They spent ten days there, on the beach and in their pool, in bed, where she lost her virginity to him. He was an exciting, adept, and gentle lover, wise and mature enough to be attentive to her as he introduced her to wonders she had never imagined before. Their lovemaking brought them even closer together, and they learned more about each other in the ten days they spent together night and day. She realized that his simple middle-class origins had given him a burning desire to become successful and not lead an ordinary life in an uninspiring job he didn't like. And he was blessed with enormous talent. As a boy, he had loved going to movies as much as she did. He remembered almost every detail of every film he'd ever seen, and said he had learned from all of them, as she had. He was fascinated by the human condition and the intricacy of relationships in real life, and on the screen.

She loved his handsome, strong masculine looks, the salt and pepper hair, his piercing electric blue eyes, and his long lean body. She thought he was the sexiest, most attractive man she'd ever seen, better than all the usual actors she'd now seen so many of, obsessed with their own looks. They seemed like cardboard figures to her compared to him. Hamish had a brilliant mind, a tender heart, and a soul.

When they flew back to New York, reluctant to leave their idyllic villa in Saint Bart's, Hamish checked in to a hotel in SoHo, to be near her for a few days, and she stayed with him. She came back from her classes straight to their hotel, where they made love. They ordered room service for their meals, and he worked on his computer while she did her homework. He smiled when he saw her pull her books out of her backpack.

"I don't think I've ever had a girlfriend who had to do homework." He grinned at her, and she curled up next to him on the couch in the suite to do one of her reading assignments. It was hard to concentrate with him in the same room. She wanted to talk to him, and make love with him. He had given her the script to read for his next movie while they were in Saint Bart's, and she loved it. And he was right. The supporting part was perfect for her. And if he got all the talent he wanted, she would be working with some major actors and actresses in the cast.

Before he returned to London, he had arranged to introduce her to an agent, as he thought it vital for her to have one. There would be many contracts in her future, and he felt that anyone involved in the film industry, in whatever guise, should have an agent. Fred Warner was one of the few he trusted, and he hoped she liked him. He had already discussed Antonia with Fred, and he was curious to meet her. He'd never heard Hamish speak of a woman like that. It was obviously a serious attachment. She wasn't just a talented young actress he wanted to help, or a passing fancy, or a diva like his two ex-wives. He said she was a real person, a woman of substance, and he had never known anyone like her, and warned Fred that she was very shy. He was sending her to the agent's office on her own, so she wouldn't feel pressured, and he didn't unduly influence her. If she hired him, Fred would be her agent, and she had to feel comfortable with him and trust him without Hamish there to make it work.

Antonia went to see Fred Warner on her second day of classes after they got back. She wanted to stop at the dorm to change, but she didn't have time, so she showed up in boots and jeans, with a heavy fisherman's sweater and hooded parka, and she was so small that she looked like a child going to the park to play in the snow. There was still snow on the ground, and her cheeks were flushed after she walked from the subway to his office, and took off her mittens to shake his hand when she was led into his handsome wood-paneled office, with extraordinary art on the walls. He represented some very big-name artists.

Fred was a tall, heavy-set, portly man. He was in his early fifties but looked older. He was wearing a well-cut tweed jacket made by his tailor in London, a blue shirt, and an Hermès tie, and smoking a

Cuban cigar. She wasn't at all what he had expected, as she took off the parka and sat down, with a shy smile. He smiled at how young and innocent she seemed, with a halo of soft blond curls framing her face. He was shocked to realize that Hamish Quist was in love with a baby.

"Hamish has been telling me about you," he said after his secretary brought in a cup of tea for her. It was freezing outside. "He tells me you want to be an actress."

"Actually, I don't," she said, and he was surprised. "I want to be a screenwriter. I've wanted to do that since I was seven or eight, and since meeting Hamish, I'd like to direct too, the way he does. Hamish wants me to be an actress, and I've only agreed to do this one picture, because it's important to him." She sounded very sweet as she said it, and very naive, but she appeared to know her mind, and expressed herself well.

"And is it important to you to do this picture?" he asked, curious about this elfin creature who had bewitched Hamish Quist, who was a man of the world and not easily captivated as he was with her, and was usually of sound mind. He had dated many beautiful and famous women, and none like her. She was entirely natural, quiet, and direct. She was shy, but not giddy, and appeared to have her feet on the ground, and she was obviously in love with Hamish, if she was willing to do a film with him, which wasn't on her career path or an important goal to her.

"I don't know yet if the film is important to me," she answered honestly. "It might be later, but it isn't right now, except so that I can be with him, and work together."

"Whatever happens, you'll learn a lot from him. He is one of the great directors of our time, and he has an incredible eye for the right script." Fred admired him immensely and liked him as a human being too.

"I'd love to write a screenplay that he could produce one day," she said softly. Fred smiled at the thought, and relit his cigar while they talked. He felt remarkably comfortable with her, which was unusual for him with someone her age, and she had none of the character traits of actresses. There was an amazing humility about her. She was clearly not a narcissist, which most actresses were. "Hamish thinks I need an agent," she said simply. "Do you?"

He didn't hesitate with the answer. "Yes, I do. The movie industry is complicated and there are a lot of sharks in it. Not Hamish, but a lot of others. Whether you act or write or direct, you'll need an agent to protect you. There are always contracts involved, and I'm an attorney too, which doesn't hurt." She nodded, it made sense to her, and she knew Hamish had a lot of faith in him. "There can be some very arduous negotiations at times. You can't fight those battles yourself. You should take care of the creative end, and I would do the rest."

"That's what Hamish said," she confirmed.

"He's right about that. You don't have to hire me, but you do need an agent, even working with Hamish on this film."

"He thinks so too. Would you take me on as a client, Mr. Warner?" she asked with wide blue eyes and he smiled. He loved her innocence and her openness. He could see why Hamish had fallen in love with her. She was totally transparent, and utterly beguiling. She made you want to put your arms around her and hug her like a child, but she was a woman too.

"I'd like that very much," he responded. "And call me Fred." They chatted for a little longer and shook hands. She was dwarfed by his size when he stood up, and as he walked her to the door of his office, she seemed even smaller next to him. And yet she was very much a woman, and extremely bright. Hamish had found an absolute gem, in his opinion, and Fred was delighted to represent her. He had a feeling that it was going to be fun, and she'd go far. Hamish had always had an eye for unusual talent, and he had done it again. This was no mistake for any of them. He didn't know yet if she would write, act, or direct, or all three, but whichever avenue she chose, he was absolutely sure she would be a star, and a very major one, one day.

Hamish was pleased when she told him how much she liked Fred Warner. She said they had mutually agreed that he would be her agent.

"You can't go wrong with Fred, Antonia. He's an honest man, and the best agent I know." Fred called Hamish himself the next day and raved about her.

"She's smart as a whip, but gentle and polite, and a sweet person. You've hit the jackpot there," he complimented him, and Hamish smiled on the phone.

"I think so too. She's very discreet and modest and self-effacing."

"But I think she knows her mind too," Fred added. "She's not convinced that acting is the direction for her long-term. She's very determined to be a screenwriter, and direct like you. You make it look easy, Hamish, although I don't think Antonia is looking for the easy road, but she finds it more interesting than being on-screen. There's nothing narcissistic about her."

"For once, I wish she had a little more of that," Hamish said, and they both laughed. "She's incredible on-screen, and she has no idea that she is, which makes it even better." They both agreed that she had the makings of a major star, in whichever discipline she chose. Hamish hoped it would be acting, but Antonia wasn't convinced yet, and he was well aware that she was doing the next film just for him, and had no great desire of her own. She wanted to write, which was another way for her to hide and be retiring. All her emotion would go into her writing, and not her face, which felt much more naked to her, and somewhat frightening. If the audiences or the critics hated her acting, they would be rejecting her as a person. And she had endured that all her life, from her parents. She didn't want more of that even with Hamish's protection. But whatever direction she chose, Hamish knew she had talent.

Hamish hired a drama coach for her before he left New York. He wanted Antonia to work with the script. There would be many changes before the final version they shot with, but he wanted the character to become part of her, so that her performance would be seamless when they started shooting in June. She had five months to work on it until she felt more like the character than herself. Great actors spent months preparing for a film, until they had absorbed the character they would be playing. It was part of the skill she'd have to learn, and Hamish was confident she would.

Once Hamish went back to England, he called her every day, and she had all her senior projects to complete and classes to finish successfully before she graduated in May. She and Jake spent long hours in the library studying together, and she stayed well below the radar and avoided the press. The paparazzi were on the lookout for her, and she slipped right through their fingers.

She and Jake were both already sad thinking about not being together on a daily basis anymore after graduation. He had become like a brother to her. But she was going to England to make the movie, and planned to stay in London afterward to be with Hamish. Jake had promised to come visit her, but that wasn't the same thing as seeing each other every day. They were moving on to grown-up lives and the next step in their budding careers.

She broke the silence with her father to tell him about the movie she would be filming in June. It seemed only right to advise him, and it was a respectable production and an important role. Hamish even thought she could win an Oscar for it.

Antonia met her father at the apartment to tell him, and Lara was there, hoping to soften things if he didn't take it well. Antonia's admission unleashed a torrent of insults, abuse, and accusations yet again. In essence, he told her that if he'd known she was going to pursue a career as an actress, which she had promised not to, he would never have paid for her to go to NYU, and he didn't want to see her again. He told her again that she was well on the way to becoming a tramp like her mother and it was obviously in her genes. Unlike Fabienne, Antonia had been moderate, proper, moral, honest, and well-behaved all her life. She had never been involved in drug use, been casual or promiscuous about sex, although Fabienne was older when she fell into those bad behaviors, but Antonia had never given him a moment of concern right through college, and that hadn't changed. She now had a serious relationship, with a highly acclaimed and decent man, and Brandon accused her of sleeping with him to get the part.

There were tears in her eyes when she left the apartment, and she felt sick to her stomach, and so did Lara. They both could see that her father was incapable of being fair to her wherever an acting career was involved, or anything that reminded him of Antonia's mother. He was obsessed with his own visions of immorality and drug abuse, and promiscuity. He could not conceive, or believe, that Antonia could still be a decent person and work as an actress. There was no point even talking to him about it.

She went back to the apartment when she knew he wouldn't be there, and packed some things she wanted to send to London. Lara met her there and helped her. She left only a few mementos of her childhood at her father's apartment. She couldn't imagine going there again, nor could Lara. They continued to meet for lunch downtown near school, and went to the movies together once in a while, but Antonia didn't have much time in her last months of school.

Hamish flew in roughly once a month for a weekend with her, when she wasn't overwhelmed with writing assignments, senior projects, or exams. She wanted to graduate with honors, and kept her grades up till the end.

She debated about inviting her father to her graduation, and finally decided that she should since he had paid for her education, no matter what he thought of it, and of her, now. In the end she sent the invitation, and Lara accepted with joy. Brandon threw it in the wastebasket when he saw it.

"Brandon, you have to go. She doesn't have a mother. You're the only parent she has."

"She has you, and you're a hell of a lot better than her mother. She broke her word, Lara. She promised me she'd never become an actress, and look what she's doing. She lied to me. This is going to be the third movie she'll be in, because of that sleazebag producer she's sleeping with to get the part." It turned Lara's stomach to hear him say it.

"He's not a sleazebag. He's an Oscar-winning producer and director, a very famous one. And she says he's wonderful to her. And he has an impeccable reputation."

"Those guys are all the same," he said with obvious disgust, "and he's old enough to be her father. What do you think that's about? It's all about sex, drugs, and rock and roll, and when he gets tired of her, what do you think will happen? She'll end up in the gutter like her mother. Fabienne belonged there all along. I just wasn't smart enough to see it."

"Antonia's not like that and you know it. And what if you're wrong? What if she becomes a famous actress, or a filmmaker of some kind?"

"She doesn't need me, if that's what she does."

"Parents are supposed to give their children unconditional love. You're telling Antonia that you only love her if she's not an actress."

"That's right, I am. She knew how I feel about it, and she did it anyway."

"You've blamed her all her life for her mother's sins." It was no longer a secret.

"I know I have. Can you blame me? She walked out on both of us, with her sleazy little druggie friends from Studio 54, to run away to Hollywood."

"She was an idiot, a bad wife, and a terrible mother. Antonia is a wonderful girl, she's never given you a minute of trouble. How can you abandon her now? It's as bad as what her mother did to her when she was seven. And you're bigger and smarter than that. You have no excuse."

"I don't need an excuse," he said with a hard look on his face.

"Don't you miss her? I do, I hardly see her anymore."

"I don't miss what she's turning into, and will become in that world."

Lara walked out of the room then. There was no point talking to him. It was like talking to a wall.

Lara attended Antonia's graduation, and Hamish had flown in the night before. Lara met him for the first time, and was bowled over by him. Despite his fame and enormous success, she thought he was a very gentle, modest man, and his eyes lit up every time he looked at Antonia. Lara was relieved to see it, given the harsh treatment by her father. Brandon had had very impressive financial success, and had lost his soul somewhere along the way. And as time went on, Lara had realized that the only things he liked spending money on were what he considered investments. For comfort or for fun or even a special occasion, he did not spend a penny. All that mattered to him was his business and his money, and he was willing to sacrifice his daughter because she was choosing a career path he didn't like or approve of. And he refused to see the difference between Antonia and Fabienne.

Lara had lunch with Antonia and Hamish after the graduation at the Gramercy Park Hotel, and Antonia had her diploma displayed proudly on the table. She had graduated magna cum laude. Both Lara and Hamish thought it was a crime that her father wasn't there. But Lara was happy to know now that Antonia was in good hands. Hamish had taken on the role of father as well as lover, and Lara could see why Antonia was so comfortable with him. He wanted to shield her from all the hardships of the world, including her heartless, emotionally abusive father, who had starved her of love all her life. Hamish saw no reason why Antonia should see him again, and urged her not to. Lara felt that way herself, and thought that Antonia was better off without him. Lara had tried so hard to soften him, but Fabienne had left him bitter and damaged beyond redemption. She was sorry she hadn't understood it better herself before she married him. His anger and bitterness tainted everything, and he was unpleasant to be around. But he was the loser in the end. Antonia was on her way to a better life without him, and Lara was happy for her.

Hamish was staying at the Waldorf Astoria for the graduation and went back to his hotel to return some calls, while Antonia packed up the rest of her things in the dorm, and said goodbye to Lara. They were leaving the next day for London. She had sold her stereo and her fridge to a sophomore. She had given her bike to Lara, and she was shipping her computer and some clothes to London.

She and Lara both shed tears when she said goodbye, and they promised to talk often. Lara said she'd come to London to visit and wished her luck with the film.

"Say goodbye to Dad for me," Antonia said softly, as Lara's eyes filled with tears and she nodded, sorry for her not to have her father's approval, which she so deserved.

Antonia said goodbye to some girls in her dorm that afternoon, and met Jake for a fast hug in her room. It was already stripped bare, and he had been running around New York for three days with his family. They had all come from San Francisco to see him graduate. Antonia had seen them at the ceremony, and they were thrilled to see her. And now, it really was over. She and Jake stood looking at each other, smiling through tears, as he pulled her into a fierce hug and held her.

"If he doesn't treat you right, you come back to New York and stay with me," he said in a gruff voice, his tears falling into her long blond hair.

"I'll be fine," she promised, drenching his T-shirt with her own tears. "You take care too."

"Don't forget me when you're famous," he said sadly, and she gave him a sisterly shove.

"Oh shut up. That's not going to happen. I'll probably get crap reviews and then he'll let me write a screenplay."

"More like you'll win an Oscar and forget who I am."

"Or you'll be the hottest actor in the world and we'll be in a movie together." They teased each other with their fears and fantasies. It was going to be hard for Antonia to leave Jake. She loved him so much. He wanted her to be happy and lead a charmed life, and she wanted much the same for him. It was hard growing up and leaving this final nest. They were on real time now.

"Shit, Jake, we're grown-ups." She still couldn't believe that college was over and they'd graduated. It had gone by in a flash.

"Speak for yourself, I'm Peter Pan. I refuse to grow up." But that was easier said than done, and sooner or later, life would force their hands.

He helped her down the stairs with all her bags and suitcases and shopping bags. She was taking all of it on Hamish's plane, so he told her she could bring as much as she wanted. And when she arrived in his suite at the Waldorf after her last tearful hug with Jake, Hamish realized that she had taken him at his word. She looked like a kid returning from camp. She even had a duffel bag.

"You're bringing all that?" He looked surprised and she was instantly sheepish.

"Is that okay?"

"It's fine." He laughed at the sudden mess in the suite. It looked like a gypsy camp, and he loved it, and her.

"I'd forgotten a few things," she said apologetically. He got up and walked over to her and put his arms around her.

"Come here, Miss Magna Cum Laude. I'm so proud of you. Have I told you lately how fantastic you are?"

"Not since yesterday." She grinned at him, as he kissed her. He felt as though he had half adopted her and half fallen in love with her, and he didn't mind the feeling at all. All he wanted to do now was protect her, make her happy, and make her life easier in a thousand ways, as no one had ever done for her. He didn't ever want her to feel sad, or unloved, or invisible again.

Chapter 13

Antonia's hard work with the drama coach in New York showed when they got to work on the film. She learned her lines with ease, and was the consummate professional. She followed Hamish's direction, and trusted his vision of every scene. Only once or twice did she make alternate suggestions, and he liked them, and they worked when he tried them. They proved to be an efficient, collaborative team, with a sixth sense for each other. Hamish was respectful of her and the other actors, and brought out the best in everyone. He had hired her a new drama coach, but with his meticulous and very clear direction, she didn't need the coach.

They ran into surprisingly few problems on the set, and much to everyone's surprise, they wrapped at the end of September. Antonia and Hamish went to Italy for two weeks, and then he moved on to post-production, but her part in the film was over, except for a few B shots and voice-overs.

Antonia did some writing while he was busy, and she called Jake and Lara from time to time. Jake had gotten a part in a low-budget indie film, and Lara was busy with a real estate boom in New York.

Antonia's life with Hamish felt like a fairy tale. Whether working or at home, they got along. The press had decided that they were the new golden couple and followed them everywhere, which she hated, but Hamish was good at eluding them, and knew places where they could go to avoid them.

She had hated being fussed over on the set too, while they were making the movie. She liked to do her part, and then leave the set and keep to herself in her dressing room while she studied the next scene. She never blew her lines and all the other actors loved working with her, because she was so undemanding, supportive, professional, and easygoing. And she never traded on her relationship with Hamish to get special favors.

Fred Warner had come from New York for a few days to watch the shooting of the film, and was happy with the way it was going. Antonia had no complaints, she was the most un-diva-like actress he had ever met.

"That's because I'm not an actress," she teased him when he complimented her. "I'm a screenwriter trapped in the life of an actress." He laughed. She never let him or Hamish forget that she had other aspirations, and acting wasn't her dream. But she was good at it nonetheless, and Fred was impressed by the time he left.

When they wrapped in September, Fred asked her what her plans were, and she said she was going to do some writing while Hamish was involved in post-production.

The night he finished post-production in November, he came home with a boyish grin and put a package on the table. The box was about the size of a shoebox, and she was excited to open it, and found another box inside the first one. She kept opening until the fifth box, and had a small black velvet box in her hand. She looked up at him with wide eyes. She hadn't expected anything from him. He dropped to one knee next to her as she opened it and saw a beautiful antique oval fifteen-carat diamond ring nestled in the box. She looked at him with tears in her eyes.

"Antonia, will you marry me?" There had been no one to ask except Antonia herself. She'd had no further contact with her father and doubted she would again. So he asked her, and she whispered "Yes," and put her arms around him and pressed him to her, as he stood up and held her tightly in his arms, and then put the ring on her finger. It fit perfectly, as though it had been made for her. It was an exceptionally pretty stone, with lovely lights in it despite the antique cut. It was French, made by Cartier at the turn of the last century.

Hamish was double her age now, she was twenty-two, and he was turning forty-five. The press rapidly caught on when they saw the ring, the next time they went out together, and their engagement was announced. She had called Jake and Lara to tell them as soon as he gave her the ring. And when she saw news of it in the papers, she wondered at times if her mother read about her in the press and if she was proud of her. She had no way of knowing.

Lara told Brandon when she got the call, and he made no comment. His heart was hardened against Antonia, and took no pleasure in the news of her engagement.

Hamish and Antonia got married in a tiny chapel in London, in secret with twenty close friends around them, and they had their simple wedding dinner at a friend's home, in order to avoid the press. She would have liked to have Lara and Jake there, but it would have created a problem with her father if Lara came. And Antonia didn't want him there. And Jake had a small part on a day-time soap on TV, and couldn't get away. It all went off beautifully, and they went to Paris for their honeymoon and stayed at the Ritz.

Her wedding ring was a plain, narrow gold band. She loved the simplicity of it, sometimes she just stared at it. She was still stunned by the turns her life had taken, and in each case what had led her to the next step. She felt at peace and no longer worried about the future, and wasn't haunted by the past. Hamish had made up for everything that had happened to her. She tried not to think about her father. His bitterness had poisoned him, and she felt sorry for Lara, living with him.

Hamish dove into a stack of scripts when they got home from Paris. He was looking for something for her. He was thrilled with the way the film with her supporting role had turned out, and hoped she'd win an award for it. But he was hungry to start a new project, and finally found one in January. It was a screenplay that had been adapted from a book he had read and loved, and he thought the adaptation had been well done.

He contacted the author's agent, and found that it was available to option, and he had Antonia read both the book and the screenplay while he negotiated a price. There was a wonderful role in it for her as a young wife in Victorian times, struggling for a voice of her own, which she achieves by writing a book in secret under a pseudonym. The book becomes a bestseller and her husband leaves her at the end of the novel. The movie was full of her conflicts and struggles, and it spoke to Antonia. She was excited at the prospect of playing the part, which was why Hamish had picked it among all the others. He thought Antonia would play the young wife brilliantly. It was a character she understood. The young woman in it was from an aristocratic family and under tremendous pressure to follow tradition, stay in her place, and remain silent. In a way, not so different from Antonia's struggles with her father, although for different reasons.

He was able to buy the option for the screenplay, and began putting together a cast. The project moved quickly, and was scheduled to begin shooting in August. Antonia kept busy writing until then. Jake had just gotten a small part in a Broadway play, and she was excited for him too.

She worked with her drama coach again to prepare for the part, and put a great deal of thought and historical research into it. She was enjoying acting more than she had thought she would, and her writing meant a great deal to her too.

By the time they began shooting the film at a chateau in France in the countryside, Antonia knew the main character like her own heart and soul, and Hamish and the other characters brought out a depth of feeling that she didn't know was in her. Only Hamish wasn't surprised. He still said that she was a born actress with a special gift.

And when Jake's play folded in September after a short run, he flew over for a few days to visit and watch her on the set. He was enormously impressed too, and when they ate a dinner of bread and cheese and pâté one night, while Hamish was checking the dailies, he questioned her about the direction her career was taking. She had been so adamant about not being an actress and now it was the whole thrust of her work.

"Do you do it for you, or for him?" he asked her after a glass of wine. He was disappointed about his play, but happy for her. Her career was taking off like lightning, in part because of Hamish and the opportunities he created for her.

She thought about it before she answered. She was always honest with him, and tried to be with herself. "For both. But mostly for him. It means so much to him. I'm still writing, and I'll do a screenplay one day. And I do love the roles he finds for me. He says I'll write better and be a better director if I've done some acting first."

"You can't just do what he wants, though, no matter how good he is to you," and there was no denying that. "You have to follow what you want too," Jake reminded her.

"I do, and I will, but the acting is working for now. It probably won't be forever."

"It might be, if you're good at it, and have some big hits. You won't be able to get out of it then."

"I'm not his prisoner," she corrected him. "I'm doing it willingly. And it's fun."

"Don't give up your writing!" he scolded her.

"I won't," she promised.

"Have you heard from your father?" He was almost afraid to ask. She'd been in England for fifteen months by then.

"No, and I won't," she said simply. "He's written me off. He won't back down. He never does. And I think he waited years to 'divorce' me, like he did my mother. He can't tell us apart, especially now that

I'm acting." She seemed at peace about it. "I actually don't miss him. Hamish is almost like a father to me at times." Jake looked worried when she said that.

"You don't need a father anymore, Antonia. All you need is yourself."

"He's a father, a partner, a lover, a teacher. There are a lot of facets to him and our relationship." She smiled at Jake, and he could see how happy she was. He hadn't found anything like it yet himself, and so far, all his romantic relationships had been short-term. For now, his career came first, which every one of his girlfriends had objected to.

"Maybe you're right. God knows, I haven't gotten that part of my life right yet. I went out with two gorgeous young actresses during my brief disastrous Broadway run. One turned out to be sleeping with half the cast and I didn't know it. Possibly the entire cast. And the other one had a girlfriend she was madly in love with, and she only went out with me to see if she still liked men, and realized she didn't. I think I need some nice girl from the Midwest with a normal job. Actresses are too complicated for me." He smiled ruefully and she laughed.

"Hamish saved me from all the creeps I kept meeting, like Jeff in L.A., and all the narcissistic young actors who are madly in love with themselves." Hamish adored her and she loved him, and their relationship was passionate and worked for both of them. Jake was still too young to find a serious woman and settle down. She couldn't see him marrying for years. Hamish was older, which was different.

He joined them when he came back from seeing the dailies. He told her how great her performance had been that day. Jake had seen it in person and agreed. Hamish poured himself a glass of wine, and another for Jake, and eventually she went to bed and left them to each other. Hamish was advising him on his career and which producers to avoid. She loved that they got along.

Jake stayed after that for a few more days, and noticed how attentive everyone was to Antonia. They were treating her like a star, she was learning her trade with great thought and preparation, and he thought Hamish was right and she would be a big star one day. He said it to Antonia that night.

"Ugh, don't talk to me about it. I hate it when they fuss over me on the set. It makes me feel like a fraud. I'm not a big star, not yet. I haven't earned it. Hamish has opened some doors for me, now I need to prove I'm worthy of it, but bowing and scraping and kissing my ass," she said bluntly, which Jake loved about her, "doesn't make it true. I have to earn it or it isn't worth a damn. I hate that anyway. I'm a normal person. I want to be treated like one."

"You're in the wrong business for that. It's all about being a star. Or pretending to be one, if you aren't."

"It's all fraudulent," she said. "That's why I like the other side of the camera better. It's real. From that side, you're looking out at the world. From the other side, the world is looking at you. I hate that," she said with feeling, and he knew it was true. She hated being the center of attention.

"Still hiding and trying to be invisible?"

She hesitated and then nodded.

"I'll probably always try to be invisible," she said honestly. "It's who I am. You can hide in the characters you play as an actor or actress, but when you're invisible, no one can see you at all."

"You're too wonderful to hide," he said gently.

"Sometimes all the attention is just too much. I'm not good at it. If I didn't have Hamish to hide behind, I'd be miserable."

They spent some really nice moments together before he left. They could say anything to each other, and she was sad to see him leave. Hamish took her out to dinner that night, to cheer her up, and they had a fun evening at a small lively local neighborhood bistro in the village next to the chateau. They both loved France, and Hamish spoke fluent French, which made it easier.

They were sorry when the shoot moved back to London to a studio, and they wrapped a few days before Christmas. They were tired, and really happy with how the film had gone. It had been a great part for Antonia, and she had played it well.

They had thought about going somewhere for Christmas, but decided to spend it lounging around at home, and celebrated their first anniversary on Christmas Eve, and went to a friend's party on Christmas Day. They lay in bed afterward and Antonia smiled at him.

"I have a present for you," she whispered, teasing him.

"Where is it?" He felt under her pillow, and there was nothing there. She giggled at him, and he grinned. "Where did you hide it?"

"You have to find it," she said, and he started to get out of bed, and she pulled him back. "It's here in the bed." He looked under the covers and saw nothing, and then she gently took his hand, and put it on her belly, and he could feel the slightest roundness swelling under his hand, and looked at her in amazement.

"Oh my God! Antonia! Why didn't you tell me?"

"I didn't want you to worry about me while we were shooting.

I've been feeling fine. But my corsets have been getting damn tight for the last few weeks." He pulled her close to him and held her. She was sharing miracles with him that he hadn't even hoped for. Marriage to her had been like a fairy tale, and now they were having a baby. He had given up the idea of children years before, although when he married Antonia, at her age, he thought it might happen, but they hadn't talked much about it. They had so much going on, from one film to the next.

"When is it for?"

"June," she answered, as he gently ran his hand over her belly again.

"Oh my God," he said, thunderstruck by the news. "Can we tell people yet?"

"I think it's safe, I'm three months pregnant, and it's been easy-peasy so far. I haven't had any problems or felt sick."

"You'll probably have it in a field and go right back to work," he teased her.

"I want to have it at home," she said simply, and he frowned.

"That sounds risky to me. And I'm not going to deliver a baby. Let's go to Paris and have it at the Ritz. We can call room service for champagne when it's born." He couldn't believe they were talking about a baby of their own. He couldn't imagine it yet.

"We'll see," she said, with a Mona Lisa smile.

"I assume you don't want to work now?" he questioned her.

"Well, you've got post-production now, so you'll be busy till February, and we don't have a new screenplay. The baby will come in June, and I could go back to work pretty soon after that," she said, and he nodded. "And you're not going to want me in every picture anyway. You can do the next one without me, and I'll sit on the sidelines getting fat."

"Excellent idea. But I'll want you in the one after that, unless you get too fat of course." She swatted him then and he laughed. He thought she had never looked more beautiful. He felt again the tiny bump that was their baby. It was the most exciting news of his life, and he had never loved any woman more.

Antonia called to tell Lara about the baby after she told Hamish. She had wanted to tell Hamish first, but Lara was the closest thing she had to a mother, and Lara was ecstatic when she heard the news.

"Oh, darling, that's wonderful. How do you feel?" She had never had children, nor wanted them, but she always celebrated the news for others, particularly Antonia.

"I feel great. And Hamish is thrilled. I think he wants to have me carried around on a litter so nothing goes wrong." Antonia didn't tell her whether or not to tell her father. It was up to Lara. The subject of her father no longer came up when they talked. It was better that way, and there was nothing to say.

"I can't wait to see it. I hope it's a girl," Lara said excitedly, and when they hung up, she ran into Brandon in the kitchen. It was Sunday and he was reading the paper, and looked up when Lara walked in. She was smiling broadly.

"What's up?" He smiled back at her, in a good mood.

"Antonia's having a baby. She's three months pregnant. Isn't that great news?"

She beamed, and his face went cold immediately.

"For whom?" he said, picking up his paper again with a sour expression.

"For them of course, and for us. It's a new life, that's always a good thing and a blessing."

"I hope it's not a girl, or it'll be a tramp like her and her mother. It's in their blood."

Lara stared at him as though she couldn't believe what she'd heard. "Please tell me you don't mean that."

"Of course I mean it."

She was shaking as she looked at him. "Brandon, you lost your wife sixteen years ago, for whatever reason. I don't know if she was a good person, or as bad as you say. And in the last year and a half, and actually long before that, you've managed to lose your daughter, and pushed her away in every way that you could. And she's not a whore or a bitch or a tramp or a slut, or any of the things you call her and her mother. And my guess is that she's probably nothing like her mother. I do know one thing. Antonia is a fantastic person, and a lovely human being, and you've treated her badly ever since I've known you. I've made excuses for you for years, even to Antonia. I can't anymore. Watching you try to systematically destroy your own child makes me sick, for you and for her. You're so full of poison, you don't even know what you're seeing or who she is. I'm not going to sit here and listen to you vilify her baby too. If you can't even be warmed by that and be happy for her, and your own grandchild, then you're even sicker than I thought." She walked out of the kitchen then and didn't say another word. She went to her closet and pulled out a suitcase, and laid it on the bed.

He came in a few minutes later to see what she was doing, and was startled to see the suitcase. She was packing.

"What are you doing?"

"I'm leaving. I can't do this anymore. You're a sick man."

"Oh come on, you're not going to let Antonia ruin things for us, are you? She destroyed my marriage to Fabienne when she was born. We can't let her ruin ours too."

Lara turned to face him squarely after she closed her bag. She was only taking basics for now. "Antonia didn't ruin anything, then or now. You did. I have no respect for you after the way you've treated her. And I'm sure Fabienne didn't help. I'm leaving you, Brandon. I want a divorce." His eyes opened wide. "And you can relax, I don't want a penny from you. I have everything I need. I'll pick up the rest of my things when I find an apartment." And with that, she picked up her suitcase, walked out of the apartment, and rang for the elevator. He didn't follow her or try to stop her. He stood rooted to the floor, and stared at the door. He never thought Lara would do something like that to him. But he hadn't expected Fabienne to leave him either, and she had. Lara was a good woman, and he knew it. He sat down in a chair in their bedroom and started to cry. As he saw it, all the women in his life had betrayed him, starting with his mother, by dying or leaving, or changing into something they hadn't been before. And now Lara was one of them too, and was leaving him alone.

Chapter 14

Antonia was shocked when she got a note from Lara saying that she had left her father. She didn't say why, but Antonia knew it had to be something serious for Lara to do something so extreme. She was a kind, loyal, loving woman, and had genuinely loved him in the beginning. Antonia knew that. She mentioned it to Hamish, and his only comment was that it seemed like she'd be better off. He had no love lost for Antonia's father, whom he'd never met, but he had heard enough stories of her childhood to convince him that Brandon was a selfish son of a bitch.

Antonia called Lara but didn't reach her, and a few weeks later, she got another letter saying that she'd found an apartment she loved in the East Sixties, she had just moved in. She sounded happy. Antonia wondered how her father was doing, and assumed probably not so well. She didn't write to him or call him, but she wrote to Lara and told her she was happy for her if it was what she wanted. She still had no idea what had gone wrong. They had been married for eight years, and Lara had been good to her. She was sure they would stay close.

Antonia's pregnancy went easily. She was young and healthy. She got lots of exercise, ate well, and did a lot of writing, while Hamish spent months looking for a new project.

They went to Paris several times for romantic weekends, and Venice in May as their last trip before the baby. Hamish helped her get the nursery ready. They gave up a guest room they never used, and Antonia decided she didn't want a baby nurse. She wanted to take care of the baby herself, which surprised Hamish. All of his friends had baby nurses from the fancy nanny schools around England, particularly Norland, which was the Harvard of nanny schools, but Antonia told him she wanted to enjoy this special time with him and the baby. And since she wasn't starting a movie, she wanted to take advantage of it. The film that she had starred in about the Victorian wife was due to come out in September. And the one that she had played a supporting role in was due out at the end of May.

She went to the premiere with Hamish, and was hugely pregnant, but she looked beautiful in a filmy evening gown that floated around her. The press went crazy when they saw her, and wanted photos of her pregnant. She smiled up at Hamish, and he gently shepherded her out of the crowd and into the dark theater. By June, it was breaking box office records, and critics gave rave reviews of her performance. But the baby was the focus of her attention now.

* * *

They were sitting in bed watching a movie when the first labor pains hit her. He had talked her out of giving birth at home, which he thought was dangerous, but she wanted it to be as natural as possible. She'd agreed to go to a hospital and have a midwife deliver her, which was common in England. She'd met her several weeks before, and had been followed by a doctor before that. Everything was ready, and labor started two days before her due date. She was a textbook case for young motherhood, but Hamish was nervous anyway. It was his first child at forty-six, nearly forty-seven. Antonia was almost twenty-four, which seemed like an ideal age to have a baby. She was healthy and young, and had gone to exercise classes until a few days before.

They called the midwife, and at midnight when the pains were five minutes apart, the midwife told them to come to the hospital. Antonia was smiling when they got there. They examined her, which was uncomfortable, and a nurse suggested a warm shower to help her relax. It helped as the contractions got more intense. Things seemed to be moving along quickly, which the midwife said was unusual for a first baby.

An hour later, Antonia was panting and blowing the way they told her to, in serious pain, and had a death grip on Hamish's arm.

"Don't you want drugs?" he whispered to her. She shook her head, trying not to push because the midwife told her not to. She wasn't fully dilated yet, at four A.M. Half an hour later, the pain was so intense that Antonia was screaming. Hamish was in tears watching her. He had never seen any human in such agony and he couldn't bear it for her. It was a full hour of the midwife telling her not to push as the pains ripped through her. The midwife said she was doing wonderfully, which seemed unlikely to Hamish, and then finally they told Antonia to push, which was even more of an ordeal with each contraction than trying not to. He wanted to take her in his arms and run home with her, but there was no escaping what was happening. And at one point, after several fruitless pushes, the midwife reached in and turned the baby slightly, while Antonia screamed in agony and then everything started moving quickly.

She knelt on the bed while Hamish held her, and then lay down again, in tears, while he stroked her face and kissed her between pains. The midwife stepped up the pace then, and said the baby was starting to show signs of distress, and they wanted to get it out quickly. Two nurses held her legs, the screaming continued, and on the last huge, horrendous push, there was a wail in the room mingled with Antonia's, and suddenly it was the only sound in the room, as Hamish saw a baby boy lying between her legs and Antonia was crying and smiling, and as he looked up with tears pouring down his cheeks, he saw that the sun had come up and had streaked the sky with brilliant orange and pastel colors.

A new day had dawned and a new life with it. Their son had been born, and Antonia looked like a Madonna as he gazed proudly at them both, and kissed her, as they put the baby to her breast, and they lay there as one. It all seemed like a miracle to him, and Antonia was stroking the baby's face with a trembling finger, the agony almost forgotten. They took the baby away to clean and weigh him, as Antonia lay in bed peacefully, and Hamish looked down at her adoringly.

"You're amazing," he whispered to her. "I'm so proud of you. . . . I'm sorry it was so hard." She was completely at peace, as though the pain didn't matter. It had all been worth it when she saw their son.

It was a bright summer morning by then, and they brought the baby back shortly after and said he was perfect. He weighed nine pounds, four ounces, a healthy size for anyone, and startling for a woman the size of Antonia. He was a strapping boy. They named him Dashiell, Dash, because Hamish loved the writings of Dashiell Hammett as a young man, and they both liked the name.

They rolled Antonia into her room an hour later, with the baby tucked in beside her on the gurney, and Hamish following, still astounded by the miracle he had seen, when his son appeared, and how quickly everything had returned to normal, and their little family had been formed.

Antonia spent three days in the hospital and Dash was nursing well by the time they went home. Lara was the first to congratulate them, and Fred Warner, when Hamish called him. Antonia left a message for Jake too. She wanted Lara to be the baby's godmother, and Lara promised to come to London soon to see him. They had a whole new life to look forward to, and a son to bond them even closer. When Antonia saw Dash, sleeping in the nursery, she wondered how she had been so lucky to be so blessed. She had everything she could ever have wanted, a son and a husband she adored.

They took turns taking care of the baby, and Hamish loved watching him nurse. It was such a peaceful scene, and Antonia looked so beautiful. They spent the summer enjoying him, and in August, someone sent Hamish a screenplay that he fell in love with. The same familiar process began, and after he secured the funding, they were set to start shooting in February. They had to wait several months for one of the stars to be available, but he was well worth waiting for and a big box office name. There was a good part in it for Antonia, a supporting role, in a star-studded cast.

Dash was eight months old when they started shooting. She was still nursing, and they arranged to have a baby nurse on the set. Antonia could nurse him in her dressing room. And she was excited about the actors she was going to work with.

Everything went smoothly as the production got underway, and then after six weeks, they had a problem with the insurers. Hamish had to go to London to see them. They were shooting in the north of England at the time, and Hamish didn't want to waste time taking the train. He arranged for a helicopter to pick him up for the meeting with the insurers and his lawyers. He told Antonia he'd be back by that evening. He left the assistant director in charge of the scenes they were shooting that day. The AD was experienced and Hamish felt comfortable leaving him to run the actors through the scenes of the day.

Hamish took a few minutes to stop and see Antonia and the baby in her dressing room before he left. The baby nurse was something of a dragon, and stood at the door like the palace guard at the gate as Hamish slipped in to kiss his wife. She was smiling and whispered to him when he bent to kiss her.

"I have something to tell you when you get back tonight." He looked at her questioningly and she giggled mischievously. He suddenly remembered the last time he had seen that look on her face.

"Wait a minute," he said, smiling too. "Tell me now, before I go, or I'm going to be distracted all day. You can't drop one shoe like that."

"Yes, I can," she said, playing with him. "It can wait."

"No, it can't. . . . I can't. . . ." He whispered to her then so the nurse wouldn't hear them. "Are you pregnant again?" She nodded with a jubilant look. They had agreed that they wanted another baby, but didn't know when, and they had decided to let it happen whenever it did. Dash was nine and a half months old, and a happy little boy. "That's fantastic! When?"

"I'm not sure. I'm about two months. It happened around the time we started shooting. So that would make it due in November." He beamed at her and kissed her again. He was thrilled at the news and so was she. "See you tonight. I love you. And good luck with the insurers." They were giving them trouble over one of the policies, since there were some dangerous stunts in the movie. They were on location to shoot them, which was costly, so the problem had to be resolved quickly. Hamish didn't want to fall behind in their shooting schedule while they waited for approval, so he wanted to get it taken care of as soon as he could. He was determined to be persuasive, or to get tough with the insurers if he had to.

He gave Antonia a last wave before he left her trailer, and the baby nurse handed her the baby to feed. The doctor had told her she would have to stop nursing soon, or it could cause cramps and even a miscarriage, since she was pregnant again. She was going to stop in a few days, when they got back from the north border. It was easier to nurse Dash while they were on the road than switching him to bottles and formula. She looked down at him, nursing happily, and wondered what the new baby would be like, and if it would be a boy or a girl. She was happy she had told Hamish about it and he was excited too.

The scenes they shot that day went smoothly. There were no problems or incidents, and Hamish had called the set when he left Gatwick in the helicopter. He had them tell Antonia he'd be back in an hour and the meeting had gone well.

An hour later, she had changed into street clothes, and went back to the hotel with the nurse and the baby to wait for Hamish there. The food in the town they were shooting in was abysmal, and she wasn't looking forward to another night of shepherd's pie, but it was the only decent thing on the menu. She was getting hungry, and Hamish was late. It was two hours since Hamish had left Gatwick. They had probably been delayed taking off. It was a busy airport, though not as busy as Heathrow.

She had just finished nursing the baby again and handed him to the nurse to put down in the next room in the crib they had brought with them, when the second assistant director knocked at her door.

"Hi, Tom." She smiled at him. "Hamish isn't back yet. Is there a problem?" He stared at her as though he had seen a ghost and took a moment to answer. He didn't know who else to tell what had happened.

"There's been an accident," he blurted out. He was deathly pale.

"Was there night shooting on the schedule for tonight?" She knew they weren't shooting the stunts yet, until the insurance issues were settled.

"No . . . Hamish . . . the helicopter . . . they hit a flock of birds," he said, as tears sprang to his eyes, and Antonia grabbed his arm with a look of terror.

"What are you saying?" she asked, out of breath. It reminded her of childbirth, but this was worse. "Hamish . . . is he okay? What happened?"

"The helicopter went down with a broken blade, they spun out and hit a cliff on the way down. Hamish and the pilot were killed. The police just called the office . . . oh God, I'm so sorry, Antonia." He was sobbing and so was she, as she clung to him. She felt as though she'd fall over if she didn't.

Word got out quickly and within minutes, the entire cast, both assistant directors, the sound and light men, and all the crew they had with them were pressing through the halls of the hotel. Somewhere in the distance, she heard her baby crying. People were hugging one another and sobbing. A few hours later one of the other producers flew up from London in another helicopter to give them the details and confirm the news.

The producer, who was one of Hamish's associates, flew Antonia and the baby back to London, and the rest of the crew remained on location until they decided what to do. They would lose time and money if they shut the location shoot down and had to reschedule it. And Antonia had to make the arrangements. Hamish's body had been recovered and was in a police morgue in the middle of England and had to be brought home.

Antonia felt as though she was moving underwater. She had no idea what to do. He had been smiling and happy that morning when he left, and excited about the new baby, and now tragedy had struck them. She kept thinking that it had to be a mistake. But it wasn't.

The producer stayed with her that night, and faces came and went. Some she knew and some she didn't. Policemen, people from the set, the baby nurse took care of the baby and Antonia didn't nurse him. It was all a jumble of people and faces through the night and into the next day. And then suddenly Fred Warner was with her with his arms around her and she was sobbing, he was telling her it was going to be okay, but how could it ever be okay again?

Somehow, Hamish's associates organized what had to be done. The location shoot had to continue or it would cost too much money to do again. The actors on location had to rally, and the crew. They'd gotten approval for the stunts, and the second director had taken charge of the scenes that remained to be shot.

Arrangements had to be made for Hamish's funeral. That was Antonia's job and Fred helped her. She called Lara, who flew over. Jake was in San Francisco because his father was sick after surgery, so he couldn't come. Somehow she muddled through, and four days later she was standing in a church she'd never been in before, wearing a black suit and a hat that Brigid and Margaret had bought for her. Hundreds of people came. People spoke about Hamish. His two brothers, whom she hardly knew, were there. A minister who didn't know him performed the service and gave a eulogy. The paparazzi were there, being held back by the police. It was all a blur, and afterward Antonia couldn't remember any of it, and wouldn't have wanted to anyway. They were the worst days of her life. Hamish was gone, and she still couldn't understand that he wasn't coming back. She was waiting for him to come home, and it just wasn't possible that he wasn't going to. The world had come to an end, and everything in it had come to an end for Antonia. They had had the perfect life for almost three years, and now it was over. He was forty-seven years old. It just wasn't possible that he was dead.

They buried him at Highgate Cemetery on Swain's Lane, and afterward hundreds of people came to the house to drink and cry and talk about him. Hamish's brothers went back to Amsterdam and Madrid, where they lived.

Lara took her upstairs to lie down after two hours of it. Antonia looked like she was going to collapse at any moment. She had confided to Lara that she was pregnant. It was another reason why he couldn't possibly be dead. He couldn't be dead if she was going to have his baby. And Dash needed him and so did she.

It took a week for it to sink in, and the decision the producers had made was that they had to finish shooting the movie. They were about halfway through by then.

Both assistant directors were talented, experienced professionals. They didn't have Hamish's touch, but they had worked with him for long enough that they knew what he would have wanted, and were capable of taking over for the rest of the film.

Antonia had to go back to the set a week after the funeral. They shot around her until then, to give her a few extra days at home. She didn't bring the baby back to the set, since she had stopped nursing him. Lara had to go back to New York to her office, and Fred stayed for another week to make sure she was all right. But she knew that she would never be all right again. How could she be without him? He had made everything right in her life.

The cast had to draw on all their acting abilities not to let the rest of the filming be too mournful. They had to dredge up laughter and smiles and sex scenes and passion. They had to look normal, and finish a film that would do Hamish honor. The producers had already said that the film would be dedicated to him, which was small consolation to Antonia. She didn't want a film as a monument to him. She wanted her husband, and Dash's father. Hamish was the only person who had ever taken care of her, and now he was gone.

She had no idea how she did it, but she finished the movie with the others. There was no celebration when they wrapped. They all quietly drifted away and were crying and subdued when they said goodbye to one another. It had been the saddest set they'd ever been on, and once it was over, and post-production was being handled by other people, Antonia's life stopped completely.

It was June by then. They celebrated Dash's first birthday, just Antonia, Hamish's assistants, and the nanny who had stayed to help her.

Her pregnancy was visible by then, and Hamish's assistants were handling all the paperwork involved with his estate. He had handled his affairs responsibly, and had left most of what he had to Antonia, with a large portion of his estate to their son, to be divided equally if there was another child or children in utero or alive by the time he died. So he had protected their unborn child too. He had protected everything and everyone, except himself from the flock of birds that had killed him, and a damn helicopter. Antonia was torn between rage, despair, and fury that fate had betrayed her and stolen her husband from her fifty years before his time. But rage did no good. It didn't change anything.

They finished the film and she knew she'd never see it. She couldn't. And when Fred came to see her again, to check on her, she told him what he was afraid she would, when he mentioned her doing another movie sometime. She looked him straight in the eye immediately.

"I'm not doing any more movies, Fred. Not as an actress. My acting career is over. I did it for Hamish. Maybe I really will write a screenplay, but I couldn't do this again. It was what he wanted. I did it for him. That movie was the last one you'll ever see me in. I hope you'll handle my work one day as a screenwriter or director too."

"Of course, but he was right about your acting, you know. You are phenomenal. You have real talent. It would be a shame to bury that with him."

"I can't do it. I couldn't. I have no reason to." He hoped she would change her mind later, but he didn't argue with her. It was much too soon to push her about the future. It would have been cruel. She was in no condition to think about her future or her career. And by then she was six months pregnant. She had survived the summer without Hamish. But she had a whole lifetime ahead of her. He had been gone for four months, the longest four months of her life. She couldn't imagine having another baby without him. It was a final gift from him, but she was going to be a widow with two children at the age of twenty-five.

* * *

When Lara got back from London, after being with Antonia for a couple weeks, Brandon called her at her office. She was surprised to hear from him. Their divorce papers had been filed, and it was due to be final in a few months. There was nothing left to discuss. From Lara's point of view, it was eight wasted years, with nothing to show for it except her warm relationship with Antonia, which was a bonus and the only thing of value to come from the marriage.

"I'm sorry to bother you," he said, sounding hesitant. "I wanted to know how Antonia is. I read about her husband. I was very sorry to hear it." He sounded genuinely sorry, and Lara was surprised. At least he had the decency not to make rude comments.

"She's about the way you'd expect. She's in shock, and in terrible shape. They were in the middle of shooting a movie. Hamish was wonderful to her. She's lost without him. Their son was nearly ten months old when his father died, and she's expecting another one."

"That's awful. She doesn't deserve that." He sounded very moved by what Lara said, which surprised her too.

"I'm happy to hear you say it," Lara said coldly. She would have hung up on him instantly if he made any vicious remarks. She had run out of patience, and had lost all respect for him.

"Is there anyone there with her?" He sounded concerned.

"Not really. Hamish had two brothers, but they live abroad and weren't close. Antonia hardly knows them, and she has no family either," she said pointedly. "You're out of the picture and I went over for as long as I could to help her. She has an agent, who is their friend, who's been very helpful. He's been very close to her and Hamish. Otherwise, it's just employees. She's going to be very much alone for a while, until the kids get older."

"Is there anything I can do to help?"

"At this point, I don't know. Maybe write her a nice letter, just so she knows you have some kind of compassion for her. It's late in the day for you to show up, after all you said to her."

"I know I did a lot of damage," he said remorsefully. "I've been thinking about it a lot. You were right. I never let go of my anger at Fabienne, and I took it out on Antonia." She wasn't sure, but she thought he might be crying.

"Well, at least you realize it." But it didn't change how she felt about him now.

"If you think about anything I can do, let me know."

"You can't bring her husband back," Lara said in an icy tone. She was utterly fed up with Brandon.

"I know, and obviously they don't need money." Hamish had left her a fortune, which didn't console her, and a huge inheritance for his children. But at least they weren't in financial need or starving, to make things even worse.

"I'm glad you're thinking about her," Lara said. "A letter might be a good idea, just so she knows you care."

"I'll do that. And, Lara, do you suppose I could see you sometime? I have a lot to apologize for to you too."

"I'll take your word for it. I don't think there's much left to discuss." She didn't want to get involved with him again, or listen to him feel sorry for himself.

"I'd just like to see you. I miss you." She missed him too, once in a while, but not often enough to want to see him again. And what he had done to Antonia, and the way he had treated her, Lara thought was unforgivable. She couldn't imagine loving him again, or how she ever had. But when she'd married him, she had no idea how disturbed he was, or how cruel he was to his daughter. Looking back, she saw hints of it here and there. But in retrospect, as a whole picture over many years, she saw it clearly, and it was an ugly picture.

"If you ever want to have a drink or a cup of coffee, let me know," he said sadly, and she hung up a minute later.

Her father's letter arrived in June, the week of Dash's first birthday, when Antonia was feeling particularly low. She kept thinking back to a year before, when she and Hamish went through Dash's birth together, how beautiful it had been, and what it meant to both of them. It had bonded them even closer.

She was startled to see an envelope in her father's handwriting in her mail. It was marked personal, so Hamish's assistants hadn't opened it. They were still working for her. There were so many legal aspects of Hamish's estate still to deal with. She opened the letter herself, and it was surprisingly warm, telling her how sorry he was about Hamish's accident, and apologizing to her for how unkind, even cruel, he had been to her at times, without meaning to be. He said he had been blinded for years by his anger at her mother, which had nothing to do with her, and he begged her forgiveness.

He offered his help if there was anything he could do for her now, and he congratulated her on the birth of her son. He had a lot to make up for and catch up on, a birth, a death, and more than twenty years of neglect and abuse. She tried to view it kindly, and put the letter aside to answer when she felt up to it, which wasn't now. There was no rush. She recognized that it had been nice of him to write to her. She wondered if Lara had told him to write. She suspected she might have. But even if she had, at least he'd done it. Given everything he'd said to her, a year before he would have refused. Hamish's sudden death had woken him up. But it was too late for Antonia too. She felt nothing for her father.

The final details of Hamish's last movie, and hers, lingered all through the summer, and some of it kept Antonia busy. She was trying to decide what to do about so many things. Hamish's London house was lovely, and they had talked about buying a country home once they had children, but hadn't done anything about it. While he was single, he had never wanted to be bothered with owning a big country property, and rented vacation homes whenever he felt like it. She had been happy in London with Hamish, but London wasn't her home and she wasn't English. She didn't want to give up Hamish's house, it was so much a part of him, and they'd been happy there. But she'd been thinking that maybe she should go back to the States, and buy a farm in Connecticut or Massachusetts, where she could live in seclusion and bring up her children. She didn't know what she was going to do yet, and he had left her enough money to do what she wanted. She owned the plane now too, but didn't think she'd need it. Hamish had used it all the time. She wished he had used it to go to the insurance meeting, and not a helicopter.

She felt dazed every time she thought of all the decisions she had to make, and there was no one to help her now. Not like Hamish. The fairy tale that her life had been for three years ended the day he died. She had no idea what would happen next.

Chapter 15

The delivery of Antonia's second child would be very different from her first. Most of all because she wouldn't have Hamish with her. The paparazzi still pursued her when she went out, even to the grocery store, hoping for tragic pictures of her, preferably crying. They followed her when she had Dash with her, or went anywhere. She hid in the house most of the time, and didn't even let the nanny she'd hired take Dash to the park.

She didn't feel up to caring for him herself. Some days she didn't even get out of bed, and he was an exuberant seventeen-month-old as the date for her delivery drew closer. She didn't feel like she could face photographers bursting in on her in the hospital or worse the delivery room, or hunting down the baby in the nursery.

She knew Hamish wouldn't have approved, but the circumstances were different now. She contacted the midwife who had delivered Dash, and asked if she would be willing to do a home birth. She said she did them often, under a doctor's supervision and consultation.

Antonia had had no complications at the last birth, and expected none this time. She was twenty-five years old and in good health, and the baby seemed smaller than the last one. Hamish had hoped they'd have a girl if they had a second child, and Antonia hoped so too.

The midwife agreed to meet her at her doctor's, although the due date was only two weeks away, to see if he'd agree to a home delivery. When they met in his office three days later, he had no objection to a midwife birth at home, and would be available himself in an emergency. There was always the possibility that something could go wrong, but on the whole, he saw no reason to oppose it, and gave the midwife the green light to do the delivery at home.

She came to the house the next day and explained to Antonia what they'd need. They would deliver her in her own bedroom, they needed plenty of plastic sheets and old towels, and she would bring an assistant midwife with her and a nurse. She was licensed to administer certain medications relating to the birth. Antonia was relieved not to have to leave her home. And Margaret and Brigid bought all the supplies. Antonia felt more peaceful and less anxious as soon as she made the decision, and the midwife came to examine her every few days to make sure that nothing had changed, and the baby was in the right position. So far it was head down, and already engaged. But her due date came and went and nothing happened. Dash had been a few days early, and this one was late, which was no surprise since she had been under incredible stress ever since her husband died. The midwife wasn't concerned, and the baby wasn't unduly large and hadn't moved from the optimum position.

A week after her due date, she still hadn't delivered. The midwife suggested long walks, but she was accosted by paparazzi the moment she left the house, so she was confined to her home, and the weather in November was stormy and terrible. All she could do was sit and wait, while the nanny played with Dash.

She was ten days overdue when her water broke with a gush and she found herself standing in a pool of water in her bathroom, and called the midwife. She came to check her, and it took another six hours for labor to start. Nothing was moving quickly this time, but it didn't seem to matter. Whenever the baby came, Hamish wouldn't be there to see it, she would be alone, and there would be no one to celebrate it with her except two midwives, a nurse, and Dash's nanny. It seemed like a joyless event to her, which would only make her sadder, so she didn't care how long it took or when it started.

Labor had started quickly the first time, and moved at a steady pace. This time it started slow, did nothing for several hours, and then hit her like a tidal wave, with pains so violent that she could hardly breathe when they were happening, or speak between them. She could hardly walk by the time the midwife arrived, twenty minutes after she called her.

"The pains are really awful this time," she told the midwife, as she helped her into bed and was hit by another one. And it was agony when she examined her.

"The baby is coming down the birth canal very quickly," she explained to Antonia, who was clutching the nurse's hand and trying not to scream. "Maybe a little too fast," the midwife said to her, and told her not to push, as she had last time, but this time it was impossible not to. She was screaming a minute later, and the midwife examined her again, and suspected what had happened. "The baby

wants to come too fast, Antonia. You can't push now. It's got a shoulder wedged, and I'm going to have to move it, so we don't wind up
with a broken shoulder. We don't want that." She sounded professional and cool, glanced at her assistant and the nurse, and rapidly
began the procedure, which was excruciating for Antonia, as they
tried to dislodge the baby's shoulder and shift its position. She succeeded after an agonizing quarter hour and by then Antonia was
screaming and gasping for air between contractions.

"Can you give me drugs?" Antonia begged in a hoarse voice.

"It would slow things down," the midwife said sympathetically.
"Let's just get the baby out quickly." She told Antonia she could push
then, which was nothing like the last time. Every push was an agony
beyond belief, every contraction felt like it was tearing her apart.
Several times, Antonia thought she was dying and about to lose
consciousness. It was the worst experience of her life other than
Hamish dying. At the end of two hours, she didn't care if she lived
or died, or if she ever saw the baby. All three women were urging
her to push with all her strength or she would have to go to the hospital for a C-section. She didn't care about that either, but the nurse
was pressing down right above the baby, and shouting at her, and
Antonia gave one last heroic push through the haze of excruciating
pain, heard a wail that wasn't her own, and quietly passed out.

She awoke a moment later with an oxygen mask on her face, feeling like her nether regions had been torn to shreds and beaten with
a club, and she saw them wrapping a baby in a pink blanket, but she
was too weak to hold her. The midwife told her that she had lost a
fair amount of blood, but nothing to be alarmed about, and the baby
was fine, it was a girl.

"That's what her father would have wanted," Antonia said and nearly passed out again. They put smelling salts under her nose, gave her more oxygen and a shot for the pain while they sewed her up, and an hour later she was drifting drowsily, listening to them talk in the distance, but not caring what they said. The delivery had been as horrible as everything in her life was these days. Everything was painful, sad, tragic, terrifying. This was just one more thing, and she felt none of the unbridled joy and peace she had felt when Dash was born, with Hamish at her side. He had been born in the midst of a glorious sunrise of vivid colors, as though he'd come straight from Heaven. Their daughter had been born during a storm in the dark of night, with the wind shrieking, as though Hell had overtaken them, and indeed it had, for many months now, ever since April, when Hamish had died.

Two hours later, they let her hold the baby, when Antonia's vital signs were more stable. The baby girl had a small angry face and cried loudly, as though she hadn't enjoyed what had happened either. They had displaced and dislodged her, and her little face was full of fury, and none of the gentle peace when Dash was born. When Antonia tried to put the breast to her mouth to comfort her, she screamed even louder. They finally took her away to calm her. But she cried for a long time.

"Some babies take longer to settle down," the nurse said soothingly, but Antonia suspected that maybe this one was not going to be the easy, happy baby that Dash had been when he arrived. And who could blame her, with no father?

"What are you going to call her?" they asked her. She only weighed seven pounds, two ounces, but she had been much harder and more painful to deliver than her brother, who was two pounds bigger. Antonia wondered if it would have been as excruciating if Hamish had been there.

"The first time I was pregnant, her father liked Olympia for a girl. I thought I'd call her that. Olympia Lara." They all agreed it was a beautiful name and said she was a pretty baby. They gave Antonia something for the pain and to help her sleep then, and the nurse and assistant midwife were going to spend the night to check them both. A baby nurse had been hired to take care of Olympia. She was arriving in the morning. Antonia had called her as soon as her water broke. Everything was organized and she could spend the next month recovering and getting her strength back, and then it would be Christmas, which was a nightmare Antonia didn't want to think about now, since Hamish wouldn't be there, or for the rest of her life.

The recovery from Olympia's birth was harder than it had been from Dash's. But she had Hamish to fuss over her then, and share the joy with her. Antonia was anemic, exhausted, and the baby cried all the time. Olympia was colicky, hard to feed, lived on gripe water, which the British used for colicky babies, but it did nothing for Olympia, and she had a hard time nursing, so Antonia ended up with engorged breasts and painful mastitis, a breast infection.

Everything about the entire process was difficult with Olympia. Antonia wasn't sure if it was due to her own depression, or the baby's personality. But she was one of those babies parents talk about years later, remembering how hard the early months were, or even the first year. Antonia eventually ran out of milk and stopped nursing after her third breast infection. Every step of the way was hard now.

She decided not to celebrate Christmas, which would have made her feel even worse, and her children were too young to know the difference, so she gave herself a break and didn't let anyone put up decorations. She and Hamish had decorated the house themselves the year before, and didn't let anyone else do it.

In the bleak January weather, she made a decision. Hamish had been gone for nine months and she felt worse than ever. She was going to close his London house, but not put it on the market yet, and go back to the States and look for a country property, like a farm in Connecticut or Massachusetts, where her children could grow up. She wanted to go home, but had no home to go to. Hamish's associates were buying his studio and equipment from her. And once she got back to the States, she was going to sell his plane. She didn't need one. She wanted to stay home and take care of her children as they grew up. She had started writing again, but her acting career was over. She had told Fred several times. He said it was a crime to waste a talent like hers, and Hamish would have been upset about it, but he couldn't convince her.

"I'm not an actress, Fred. I never was," she told him. "If I'm anything, I'm a writer, and maybe one day a director, but I'm never going to act again." She was in hiding, and wanted to become invisible again, much to the dismay of her fans.

She went to New York in February, without the children, and Lara introduced her to real estate brokers in Connecticut and the Boston area to look for a large property where her children could grow up.

It took three weeks, but she found the perfect spot in Connecticut. It was a hundred-acre farm with beautiful old trees on it, a barn, stables for horses, a small lake, and a big, beautifully built farmhouse where a family with six children had lived before they grew up and disbanded. There was a nearby private school with a good reputation, and a picturesque little town. George Washington had supposedly lived in the area at one time, and a few well-known politicians, and a famous writer lived nearby. The farm was in perfect condition. It was expensive, but with what Hamish had left her, she could afford it. She set the wheels in motion to buy it, thanked Lara for her help, had lunch with Jake between voice-overs he was recording, and flew back to London on Hamish's plane.

Margaret and Brigid helped her organize everything for the move. Jake had told her that she was crazy to move out of the city at her age, that she couldn't hide forever, but she insisted it would be good for her children.

She left London at the end of February, moved into a hotel in New York, and spent a month getting the house at the farm ready. The property was called Haven Farm, which suited her intentions. She was looking for a haven, a peaceful place to hide. She felt lost in the world now without Hamish to guide and protect her.

They moved at the beginning of April, almost exactly a year after Hamish's fatal accident. It had taken her a year to come home. She gave Margaret and Brigid a year's salary to give them time to find other jobs after years of working for Hamish. The London house was closed. And she put the plane on the market. She wasn't going anywhere.

When Lara came to visit, she said she could see why Antonia

loved it, although it was very secluded and remote for someone so young. She mentioned that she had seen Antonia's father twice for lunch, but there was nothing there for her anymore. It was over for her. She would never be able to see him the same way again. He had killed it for her. She was dating one of her real estate clients, a widower who had bought a beautiful penthouse. And she said she was perfectly happy living on her own, just as she had been before.

Jake came to visit her at the farm too, and he thought it was beautiful, but he hated to see Antonia bury herself alive in the country. But she seemed happy there, she had a room to write in, and a hundred acres for her children to grow up on. He knew her too well.

Hamish had brought her out of her shell for a few years, and given her extraordinary opportunities, an amazing career, and two beautiful children. But the die was cast now that he was gone. Antonia was invisible again. It made Jake sad for her as he drove back to the city. He wondered if she'd ever come out of seclusion again.

Chapter 16

Haven Farm was just what Antonia had needed to start a new life in the States with her children. She had bought some beautiful early American pieces to furnish it, and kept it simple. It was a home where one lived outside a great deal. Dash and Olympia were still babies, but they wouldn't be for long. She was going to buy horses for them when they were older, and sign them up at the private school in the area. She could envision her life there for a long time, until she was old herself. She had hired a housekeeper, a maid, and brought the nanny with her, and there was a team of people to care for the grounds under a property manager who came with the house.

Fred Warner was discouraged when he came to see it.

"You're burying yourself alive out here," he complained to her, just as Jake had said. "Hamish gave you a fabulous acting career. Are you really going to throw that away?"

"It was never what I wanted to do. It was his dream for me, not mine. I'm not going to just sit here and pick apples off the trees. I'm going to write, and if you help me put a picture together one day, I'd like to direct too. Hamish was the finest director I've ever seen. I learned a lot from him, not just about acting."

"Show me what you can do, and I'll put it together for you. I don't want you to sit and rot out here. You're too young to give up a career and just raise two kids. Hamish wouldn't have wanted that for you."

"I did the acting for him, because he wanted me to. I'm going to do the writing for me, and make him proud of me too. I just don't want to be in front of the camera, or out in the world, showing off in evening gowns and high heels on the red carpet." She had hated that, even with him at her side.

"You look damn good in them. Let's not go all Daisy Mae just because you bought a farm, please." Fred rolled his eyes and she laughed.

"I have an idea for a screenplay, Fred. Give me some time to get settled here, and see what I can do."

"I'll be at my desk, waiting for the phone to ring," he said, waving one of his Cuban cigars at her.

"I'll call you. I promise. And come out and visit us."

"There's too much fresh air out here. It makes me nervous. But yes, I'll come to visit. I want to see you and the kids." He was still heartbroken about Hamish. They both were. And she was only just beginning to feel like herself a year later. It had been the worst blow of her entire life.

* * *

She had hired some of the staff who had worked on the farm before. It was a very large, luxurious property, and needed experienced high-end maintenance. She had kept the two men in the stables, who were going to help her buy horses. She wanted the children to ride when they got older. There was a housekeeper to clean the house, with a maid who was a young local girl. She already had the nanny for Dash and Olympia she'd brought from England, and there were people to take care of the grounds, run by the efficient property manager. It was all she needed for now. And she felt safe here. It was a wholesome little community, although she rarely left the property. People were curious about her, once they knew she was there.

She had a view of the lake from her new office window, and she had just sat down at her desk on a sunny May morning to work on the screenplay she had told Fred about when she saw a battered pickup truck pull up, and a woman get out. Antonia had no idea who she was. She was wearing a short, tight black skirt and a low-cut blouse you could see through. She had thick, long dark hair that looked like it was dyed black, and she was mincing across the gravel in high heels that made it hard to negotiate as she got to the front door. Antonia wondered what she wanted, if she was selling something, and then forgot about it and started writing at her desk, and two minutes later the housekeeper knocked on her office door.

"There's a woman who wants to see you," she said simply, and Antonia tried not to look annoyed. She missed the efficiency of Margaret and Brigid in London, but she didn't need them. The housekeeper she'd hired locally was of a different caliber. She had worked for the previous owners for years.

"Do you know who she is?" Antonia asked her.

"No. She didn't say." Antonia had the feeling she was selling something and didn't want to deal with her, but the housekeeper didn't seem to be equal to the task, so she got up from her desk and ran rapidly down the stairs. She wanted to get back to work. She was excited to be writing again. It made her feel free. She could do whatever she wanted.

The woman was sitting in the kitchen where Alva, the house-keeper, had left her. She was looking around, interested in her sur-roundings. And she gave a start when Antonia walked in. She looked a little worse than she had from Antonia's office window. Her hair was badly dyed jet black and appeared painted on. She was wearing heavy makeup at ten o'clock in the morning, and her face was lined and weathered. You could see her bra through the blouse. She had a generous bosom. She was wearing bright red lipstick, and had a full sensual mouth. She seemed tired or used, as though she had seen too many good times and some hard ones, and the room was filled with the smell of cheap perfume. Antonia guessed her to be in her mid or late fifties.

"I'm Antonia Quist," she said in an authoritative voice. She used her married name except for her writing, where she still intended to use her maiden name. "May I help you?" She hoped the woman wasn't going to be hard to get rid of. She seemed like she had a mis-sion. And she had a cheap plastic purse under her arm, decorated with rhinestones, most of which were missing.

The woman was staring at her intently, which made Antonia un-easy. She hoped she wasn't crazy. She didn't seem dangerous, just kind of sleazy.

"You're Antonia Adams, right?" Antonia could hear her French accent immediately, but her English was fluent.

"Yes, I am. And you are?"

"Fabienne Wheeler," she said, narrowing her eyes at Antonia. "I used to be Fabienne Basquet . . . and Fabienne Adams. Does that mean anything to you?" she said in a wheedling tone. "I'm your mother," she said, as though Antonia was supposed to rush into her arms and embrace her. Antonia was shocked but didn't let it show. Her acting lessons served her well. She had waited eighteen years for this moment. But the woman looked nothing like the woman Antonia remembered and had hoped to find. She wasn't beautiful anymore. The years hadn't been kind.

"I recognize the name," Antonia said coolly. She didn't invite her to sit down again, or offer her a cup of coffee. "I haven't seen you in a long time." She didn't know what else to say eighteen years after she'd walked out on her, with no news since.

"Yeah, I've been busy. I moved to L.A., then I moved to Vegas. I'm an actress," she explained as though Antonia knew nothing about her. "I moved to New Orleans for a few years. I got married and moved to Buffalo. Then I got divorced, and moved to Connecticut." She'd been all over the place and the marriage explained why Antonia couldn't find her under Basquet or Adams.

"I tried to find you in L.A. when I was in college, but you weren't listed and I didn't know where else to look."

Fabienne nodded but didn't show any interest in what Antonia told her.

"I was an actress, and I want to get back into acting again. I know your husband was a big deal moviemaker. Sorry for your loss, by the way." It was the phrase Antonia had most come to hate, it was like a dismissal when people didn't really care, or know what to say. "And he put you in some movies, so you're an actress now too. I figured you have some good connections and maybe you could help me." She looked hopeful as Antonia stared at her in disbelief.

"That's why you came here? Eighteen years after you left me, never called, never even sent me a postcard, and now you come here and want me to get you work?" Antonia could feel anger begin to rise up in her like bile.

"Yeah, well, I guess you inherited my talent. And since I'm your mother, and you know the right people, maybe you want to help me." Antonia wanted to ask her if she was crazy. But she could see now that what her father said about her was true, she was so narcissistic and obsessed with herself that it didn't even dawn on her how inappropriate it was, and he was right, she did look like a cheap tramp too. She figured that Fabienne must have been much better-looking when her father met her. He wasn't given to dating trampy-looking women, but she'd obviously seen eighteen years of bad road in the meantime, and had probably fallen on hard times when she left him and things hadn't panned out for her in L.A. She didn't ask Antonia how her father was, or even how she was. She had a single-track purpose.

"I'm not in the business anymore, and my husband died a year ago. And I can't imagine why you'd come here and think I would want to help you. It took me a long time to get over your walking out on us, and my father never forgave you. You ruined his life." She didn't add "and mine." Hamish more than made up for it in three short years.

"Yeah, I guess that's right. I saw you in a movie, you were pretty good," she said, as Antonia tried not to lose her temper.

"I went to the movies every week from the time I was nine, hoping to see you. I never did," Antonia said coldly. She was still shocked that she was actually talking to her mother.

"I had a screen test in L.A.," Fabienne said proudly. "But nothing ever happened from it. So you're not acting anymore?"

Antonia shook her head. "I'm not an actress and I don't want to be."

"Too bad." Fabienne looked disappointed. "And you don't know anyone I could call? I borrowed a friend's truck, when I read you live here. I didn't know how to contact you before."

"You could have called my father."

"Yeah, he was pretty pissed at me."

"He still is. Thank you for your visit, Mrs. Wheeler." Antonia decided she'd had enough of her.

"Yeah, nice to see you. You should keep acting. You've got my talent." Antonia didn't comment as Fabienne teetered to the door on her stilettos. She was only fifty, but she looked older. Drugs or booze in the last eighteen years probably hadn't helped either.

Antonia watched her make her way through the gravel on tiptoe to her beaten up truck, and she could feel the air go out of her, as though someone had pulled a plug. That was the woman she had longed to see in the movies as a child, and had gone to the movies every week hoping to catch a glimpse of, and had wanted to see in L.A., just once to ask her why she had walked out on her. It was easy to see why now. It was because she was so obsessed with herself and out of touch with reality that all she wanted from Antonia was help getting into the movies. Twenty years later, she was still chasing the same dream, and only interested in herself.

She heard the truck speed away on the gravel. She could see that Fabienne must have been pretty, in a cheap, sexy way, when she was a young woman, but there was nothing left now, except too much makeup, a see-through blouse, and cheap perfume. She knew her father would have been mortified if he could have seen her. She almost wanted to call and tell him, but she didn't want to start anything with him. She had answered his condolence letter after Hamish died, but she hadn't heard from him since. He was probably embarrassed because Lara had left him.

She called Lara as soon as the disreputable-looking truck passed through the front gate. It made her think that they should start locking it and install an intercom system. She didn't want any more visits like that one. But in a way, it freed her. It was like finding your birth mother if you were adopted, after years of fantasizing about her, and discovering that she was someone you really didn't want to know, let alone be related to. Her father had been no peach, but her mother was horrifying, as much for what she wanted from Antonia as how she looked, and the low life she must have led. She hoped she never came back again, but doubted she would. The visit had given her nothing, and no encouragement for the future.

When she called Lara, she told her about the visit and she was stunned.

"Did she try to hug you or anything?"

"Thank God she didn't, I'd have smelled of cheap perfume for a week. Actually, she was pathetic. I don't know where she crawled out of, but it can't be a good place."

"I'll tell Brandon if you want me to. It will embarrass the hell out of him."

"No, don't bother. I'm not dying to see him either. I have enough on my plate."

She went back upstairs to her office then, to work on her screenplay. She had a lot of work to do, but she had nothing but time now. She forced the image of her mother from her mind, which took some doing. And the worst of all was her father thinking she was like her.

Chapter 17

It took Antonia a year to finish her screenplay and get it just exactly the way she wanted it. Her last movie had come out by then, but she never went to see it. Fred had invited her to the premiere, but she didn't want to go. It would just upset her. She would remember every scene with Hamish directing her. It would make her too sad to see it.

Hamish had been gone for two years by then. Dash was three and Olympia was a year and a half and had just started walking. She was still difficult and not the sunny baby Dash had been.

Antonia sent her screenplay to Fred, and warned him first. He said he couldn't wait to read it. She hadn't seen him in months, but he called regularly to see how she was.

Fred called her as soon as he read her screenplay and said he loved it. He said it was a masterpiece. He was going to see what he could do to get it produced. It took him six months to find a group that was interested, some of them old associates of Hamish. They called him back as soon as they read it, and he called Antonia immediately.

"They'll do it," he announced victoriously. "And they agreed to let you direct it."

"Fantastic!"

"It'll probably take a while for them to get the money together and start picking the actors they want. You'll be part of that, of course. We're not heading for the studio and cashing checks yet."

"I'm in no hurry. I can wait."

In the interim she drove Dash to school every day, played with Olympia, and spent all her time with them. Olympia had never been an easy baby, and wasn't an easy toddler. It was just her personality. Antonia prayed that she wouldn't turn out like Fabienne.

It took the producers another six months to get everything organized and in shape. They had a shooting schedule over the summer, and they'd be shooting it in New York, which was easy for her.

They had attached some very big actors to the project. She was excited to be working with them, and had additional suggestions herself.

When they started, she was on set directing the entire time. Everything she had learned from watching Hamish was useful, and she got some magnificent performances out of the cast.

When the film finally came out, it got great reviews, and Antonia was working on another one by then. She knew she had finally found her niche, she was where she was meant to be. She had always known that she was meant to write, and she was doing it now, in just the way she wanted.

She went with Fred to the premiere of her first movie that she'd directed, and then went home to Connecticut and got back to work.

He sold her next movie even faster than the first. She was on a roll after that, doing one movie after another. And when she wasn't directing a movie, she was at home in Connecticut, writing, and spending time with her kids.

By the time she turned thirty, she'd had three successful movies, and been nominated for a Golden Globe. She still missed Hamish terribly, but she was doing okay on her own. She never regretted giving up acting. It was a moment in her life, something she had done to make Hamish proud of her, but it had never felt like she was doing the right thing. Acting had never been her path, no matter how much Hamish wanted it to be. Writing and directing were what she did best and were her passions.

Antonia was shocked by how fast her kids grew up. By the time Dash was fourteen and Olympia thirteen, she'd been writing screenplays and directing for a dozen years. The time had flown. She had sold Hamish's house by then. She had no reason to go to London and never used it. It gave her a pang of sadness when she sold it, but keeping it didn't make sense. She hardly ever left her Connecticut farm, except when she was shooting a movie. Fred and Jake both accused her of becoming a recluse. But she was happy and fulfilled with her children. They loved the farm too, especially Dash, who loved the outdoors and rode every day after school.

Jake had been in and out of a marriage by then, and had two kids. He had moved back to San Francisco and was sorry he had. He had given up acting once he had children, and was working for an insurance company. Like her children, he had grown up. And so had she. She was thirty-eight now, and Hamish had been gone for thirteen years, which was even harder to believe.

Her father had just turned seventy-one. He had retired and moved to Palm Beach. Antonia saw him sparingly, about once a year so he could see his grandchildren, and that was enough for both of them. Jake had been right, she didn't need a father, she needed herself.

She had come into her own when writing and directing movies. Lara was still living and working in New York, and came to the farm to visit a few times a year.

Hamish would have been sixty-one that year. There was no man in her life, just tender memories of him, her work, and her kids.

Dash had stayed as sweet and easy as he was as a baby. Olympia had stayed true to form too. Something was always out of line for her. She always had a complaint, a problem, something to argue about, and at thirteen, she was constantly crossing swords with her mother. She looked like Antonia, but Antonia always worried that her grandmother's genes were in there somewhere. Olympia wanted to be an actress, said she didn't care about college, and she wanted Fred to be her agent too when she grew up. Antonia wouldn't let her audition for anything until she graduated from high school. But she had the sinking feeling that when the time came, she wouldn't be able to hold her back. Dash had no interest whatsoever in the movie world. He loved animals and wanted to be a vet, which was fine with his mother.

The children went to the exclusive private school nearby, and had grown up on the farm. It was a healthy life, and had been the right decision for all of them. Antonia never regretted it for an instant, although it was a reclusive life for her, which suited her.

When Olympia was fourteen and Dash sixteen, she took them on a photographic safari to Africa. It was life-changing for Dash. He fell in love with the animals in the wild. Olympia complained about every moment of the trip. The bathrooms, the tents, the heat, the guides, she thought the food was disgusting. She was terrified of the bugs and snakes, her hair went limp in the heat, and she ran out of her favorite shampoo and conditioner, a catastrophic event. She made everyone's, and particularly her mother's, life a living hell on the trip.

She went to drama camp when they got back, which suited her much better. And Dash told his mother after their trip that he knew what he wanted to do with his future. He wanted to be a vet on a game preserve in Africa, and specialize in endangered species in veterinary school. She could see that he meant it. He was a dreamer, but he was determined and persevering, and she told him that everyone should have a dream and follow it. He took her advice to heart, and wrote a paper about their trip and what his dream was when he got back to school.

Olympia came back from drama camp more difficult than ever, heading like a heat-seeking missile for the stage.

Faithful to his goals, two years later, Dash left to attend UC Davis in California, headed for veterinary school as a graduate student. It had one of the best veterinary schools in the country. And Olympia was the star of her high school drama club senior year. She was refusing to apply to college and wanted to go straight into acting at eighteen.

She begged her mother for a part in one of her movies, which Antonia refused.

"If you're serious about it, the first movie you're in needs to be someone else's. You won't learn anything from me, but you will from someone else." Olympia sensed that she was right, and stopped arguing about it. Antonia told her that there would be plenty of time to work together later on, if she was really intent on an acting career, as she appeared to be. Nothing would stop her if that was the case.

As hard as it was to believe, Antonia had been widowed for seventeen years by then. There had been no man in her life since Hamish, and she didn't really want one. She never thought about it. She was busy directing films, and spending time with her children, with no time for anything else. She was forty-two years old, and she had changed very little. She was still tiny and slim with long blond hair. She didn't feel any different, and she still missed Hamish, and was grateful for the years they had shared. She thought it would be hard to adjust to someone else by then, and didn't want to try. She had never met a man who measured up to him. And ever since his death, she had kept well out of the public eye. She had become invisible again, which suited her better. She had no one to keep her safe except herself, so she did what felt best to her. She couldn't imagine her life run by a man again, even one as loving as Hamish was. She had trusted him completely, but no man since.

She and Fred argued about it at times. He wished, for her sake, that she was willing to have more in her life than just her children and work, but she wasn't. She was comfortable as she was, too comfortable, in his opinion. She always told him that a man would distract her from her work, and upset her children.

"Your children are grown-ups, for chrissake," he had said to her recently, when she came to his office to sign a contract.

"No, they're not, but they're getting there."

"Dash is away at college, and Olympia will be out in the world next year, if she doesn't go to college. That's pretty damn grown up. And you'll be alone, with nothing in your life but work. Is that what you want?"

"It's how things worked out. I'm okay with it," she said peacefully. She was content with her life. She treasured the three years she'd had with Hamish and knew that nothing else would ever come close to that.

"You're still a beautiful woman, Antonia. Don't waste it."

"What are you suggesting? Billboards and signs on bathroom walls?" She laughed at him.

"You're still young, for God's sake. Enjoy it. Live it. Stop hiding. Hamish wouldn't have wanted you to bury yourself."

"I'm not buried or hiding, Fred. I'm just comfortable, and I'm busy." She was, but she was also alone, with her memories of the only man she'd ever loved.

"You're goddamn hiding and you know it, you're invisible," Fred said bluntly.

She smiled when he said it. "It's a choice."

"It's a bad choice. You're one of the most beautiful women on the planet. It's a crime to waste that." She kissed him on the cheek, then signed the contract she had come for, and left his office a few minutes later, to go back to the farm. It had been a refuge for her for so long.

In the end, Olympia got her wish. Fred got her first part in a movie for her as soon as she graduated from high school at seventeen. It was a small part, but a good start. And he signed her as a client. She was thrilled.

It was a grueling part, and a challenge for a young, inexperienced actress, but she managed it beautifully, and Antonia was proud of her when she went to watch her on the set. She knew the director, and they chatted for a few minutes when she dropped by.

She was a very tough director who guided Olympia perfectly and got the best possible performance out of her, and didn't put up with any nonsense. Olympia wouldn't have learned as much from her mother. Antonia knew the other director handled her a lot better than she could have, and she was glad that Olympia was having the experience of working for a stranger who set high standards and expected Olympia to meet them. And she hadn't let her down.

Olympia's second role was in one of her mother's movies, and they celebrated Olympia's eighteenth birthday on the set. The whole cast sang "Happy Birthday" to her and she absolutely glowed. She thrived on a movie set. It was home to her. There was nothing shy and retiring about Antonia's daughter. She loved the attention and being center stage. She loved everything about acting that her mother had hated. Antonia was infinitely more comfortable behind the camera, just as she had told Hamish so long ago. He had tried to send her in another direction, but it hadn't lasted long. It had taken her forty-three years to find her place, her voice, and the role she knew was right for her, pleasing herself, not someone else. She had come into her own.

She had a new assistant director working with her on the set of her latest movie, Boden Locke, and he handled Olympia better than Antonia did too. He had a gentle, firm way about him. She was happy to have him with her. He'd been helpful and resourceful so far, but she wasn't used to him yet. Her old AD had moved to Europe a month before. She'd been lucky to get Boden through a producer she knew.

"She's got an incredible talent," he whispered to Antonia after a particularly difficult scene of Olympia's, which she handled masterfully.

"She must have gotten it from her grandmother, not from me." She smiled at him, remembering Fabienne's visit. She had never returned.

"I've seen all your movies. We both know where she got it from," he said. He was forty and looked like a boy to her. He had a youthful style and energy, and couldn't believe his good luck to be working with her. She was one of the best directors he'd ever seen. And no matter how difficult she was, Olympia had talent too. And time and life might soften some of her sharp edges.

Olympia held up well during the filming, and watched the other actors intently during their scenes, which was also a good way to learn how people worked. Antonia was pleased with what she saw her do.

And Boden had proven himself to be an able assistant, who tried to anticipate her needs, and understood a lot about camera angles, and how she liked to work. She was grateful for his help, and was coming to trust his eye and his suggestions. He was profoundly respectful of her talent as a director.

They wrapped the film just before Thanksgiving, and as they left the set, something occurred to Antonia, and she turned to Boden with a smile. She thought he had moved to New York recently from Boston or Chicago, or some other city, and she wondered if he had anywhere to go for the holiday.

He looked mildly embarrassed when she asked him, and he felt like a loser but decided it didn't matter.

"Actually, no, I don't," he admitted. "My parents moved to Florida last year, and they don't want my brothers and me home for the holidays. They go on cruises instead now. My brothers live in Montana, in a place that's murder to get to. And I just moved to New York. So, the short answer to your question is no."

"Then why don't you come to my place? We always have a mixed bag of friends over for Thanksgiving lunch." She noticed he looked like a cowboy himself, tall and lanky with an easy style. She wondered if he came from Montana. He was grateful for the invitation, and accepted with pleasure. He liked being with her.

When Dash came home from UC Davis for the holiday, he told his mother almost as soon as he came through the door that he was going to South Africa for six months on a special project for school. Four students had been chosen, and he was leaving in January. She was happy for him, he was following his dream, which she had en-couraged him to do.

"Can I come and visit?" she asked him.

"Sure," he said with a shy smile so like her own. They were so much alike, so much more so than she and Olympia, who always reminded Antonia of her mother, although she scarcely knew her, and her memories of her weren't happy ones.

On Thanksgiving, when he showed up with a bottle of wine, Dash and Boden got into a serious discussion before lunch about the game preserve where Dash was going to be working as an intern for six months. Fred joined them for major holidays, since he had no family of his own, so he was there too. He liked being around her kids and her.

It was always a warm family gathering at their table, despite the occasional snide remark from Olympia, or criticism aimed at her mother, which she could never resist. Antonia still hoped she'd grow out of it one day and soften up. At eighteen, there was still hope that she might. Antonia had invited Lara too, but she was going to friends in Dallas this time with a new man in her life. She had never remar-ried and always said she didn't want to.

Boden thanked Antonia for inviting him before he left. It had been interesting seeing Antonia at home, where she seemed so com-fortable, aware of everyone, and tried to make them feel welcome. She was much more intense on the set, constantly checking the cam-era angles, and creating a bond with the cast to get the best perfor-mances out of them she could. She had learned that from watching Hamish direct.

Boden was looking forward to working with her on post-production. She had a reputation for being a taskmaster, but got extraordinary results. And post-production was important too.

"I'm glad you could join us," Antonia said easily as he was leaving.

"You have wonderful kids," he said, smiling at her. He was a good-looking man, and was older than he appeared. He had a boyish style about him, with a ready smile and warm brown eyes.

"That depends on the day," she said about her kids with a grin, and he laughed. "But generally, you're right. I'm pretty crazy about them myself."

He had enjoyed talking to Fred Warner too, and knew who he was. He was a famous dramatic agent. He had a good sense of humor and had everyone laughing at dinner. At first, Boden had wondered if he and Antonia were a couple, but he eventually figured out that they were good friends and there was no man there attached to Antonia, which surprised him. She was such an attractive woman and her husband had been dead for a long time.

It had been a nice Thanksgiving, everyone had had a good time, and Antonia, Dash, and Olympia sat relaxing for a few minutes in the living room after all the guests had left.

"I like your new AD, Mom, he knows a lot about animals. He lived in Africa for two years after college," Dash commented.

"Good to know," she said vaguely. "I think he lived in Italy too. He speaks Italian. I heard him talking to one of the soundmen on the set. I think he lived in Florence. I haven't talked to him much. He just started with this film when Harry McAvoy left. And things have been moving pretty fast on the set. He just moved here from somewhere."

"Toronto," Olympia filled in. "He was working on movies in Canada. There are a lot of studios there." Antonia smiled that he had spent time talking to her kids.

The three of them ate leftovers for dinner that night, as they always did on Thanksgiving night. It was a tradition. And they watched a movie afterward. It was one of Hamish's. Olympia picked it. She always wished she had known her dad. He sounded like such a cool person. Neither of the children had known him. Dash was too young when he died to remember him. But he lived on through his movies, his children, and the love of those who still remembered him, like Fred and Antonia. He was someone one could never forget, an enormous talent and a remarkable human being, who had died much too young.

Chapter 18

Dash left for South Africa in January, while Antonia was already deep in post-production on her last film. She and Boden and the rest of the crew worked late every night.

They finished editing the film in February and she was planning to visit Dash in a few weeks. Olympia already had a part in another film.

Antonia was on her way to the studio one morning when she got a call from the dean of students at Davis that Dash had been chased by a hippo. He had survived but broken his leg. She rushed to the studio she'd built in Stamford years before, and let the crew know she was leaving. They only had a few details left to attend to and could finish without her. She left precise instructions and drove home. She was startled when Boden came to the house a short time later while she was packing, and asked if he could come with her.

"To South Africa? Why? I'm just going to see my son." She told him about the broken leg.

"It's a long way to go, I thought maybe you'd like company and someone to protect you. I'd be happy to come along as a friend. I know Africa pretty well. I lived there for two years, in Mombasa for a year, and in Cape Town for the second year." In truth, she would have taken Olympia if she was willing to go, but she would have hated it, and she had to start shooting her next film in a few days. And Fred was too old now to drag to South Africa. Boden had a good point. It might be smart to take a man with her, but she didn't want to impose.

"I can manage on my own," she assured Boden, more confidently than she felt.

"I'm sure you can. You're a brave woman, Antonia." He already knew that about her. "But maybe for once you don't have to do everything hard alone." It was a powerful statement, and the kind of thing Hamish would have said to her. It jarred her memory to a distant time when she heard his words, and their eyes met.

"Are you sure?" she asked him and he nodded.

"I'm ready to go if you want me. I don't want to intrude but I'd like to help."

"All right." She wasn't sure why she'd agreed, but she had liked working with him for the past months, and it might be good to have a man along. She hadn't thought about that in years, but she was comfortable with him, and she was going halfway around the world to visit her son at a hospital in South Africa. It seemed smarter not to go alone.

They left the next morning for the long flight. He had a small rolling bag with him and she had a small suitcase to check in.

They spoke very little on the flight. It was early, and she was worried about Dash. And then she turned to Boden while they were having breakfast on the plane.

"It was nice of you to come. Going to Africa by myself probably wouldn't have been smart." She was used to doing everything alone, and had for years.

"Not anymore. I lived there almost twenty years ago, it was easier then."

"It sounds like you've lived all over the place," she chatted as they ate.

"My father worked for an oil company. We lived in some pretty cool places when I was a kid. India, Pakistan, Morocco, Kenya, Saudi Arabia. We spent a year in France before we went home. And I did a year in Florence when I was in college. And then my parents came back to New York, which seemed pretty dull." He smiled at her.

"You said your brothers live in Montana. Were you from there originally?"

"No. They own a cattle ranch there together. That sounded even worse to me than New York." He grinned. "I went to USC film school for grad school. Princeton before that. We all went there. My father did too. Family tradition. I wanted to direct movies all my life. I worked at some of the studios in L.A. after I came back from Africa. I've been in Canada for a couple of years. I just moved back to New York in time to get this job working on your movie. Blind luck." He smiled at her and she felt at ease with him.

"Good luck for me too. My AD just retired before you came along."

"I love the movie. You've done a great job with it."

"It's kind of a modern day Western. That's different for me. I like trying new things." It was about a woman in a man's world, who wins their respect by being as brave as they are.

"So do I. It's a bad habit, though. Wanting to do and learn something new all the time kept me moving around. At some point you have to slow down, and stay in one place. I've just recently figured that out. I turned forty and woke up alone."

"I've done that for the last seventeen years in Connecticut. I moved back from London when my husband died, and bought the farm where we live now." She looked serious as she said it. "It's been good for the kids."

"And for you?" She didn't say much about herself. He had the feeling that she was always hiding, keeping out of sight and watching everyone else. He wasn't wrong. She was an observer of life.

"The farm is a good place to write. It's peaceful."

"Do you go into the city much?" He was curious about her. She was famously private.

"Almost never," she said about the city. "I'm too lazy. And I don't like dealing with the press and paparazzi, so I stay on home turf." The press still pursued her when she showed up in public or at an event. Her reclusiveness kept them interested in her. And she was a star now as a director.

They both slept for a while after that, and then he watched a movie, and she read. They had another meal, and then they finally arrived. Her office had arranged a car and driver for them. They dropped their bags at the hotel, and left for the hospital immediately after they got directions, and found Dash's room.

He was stunned when his mother walked into his room, she

hadn't told him she was coming, and his face broke into a broad smile. He looked like a little kid, and she hugged him. Boden was hovering in the doorway, not wanting to intrude, and Dash told him to come in and seemed happy to see him too. He remembered him from their talk on Thanksgiving. Dash had a cast on one leg from thigh to toe. He had broken it in two places.

"I got chased by a hippo," he told Boden.

"It's one of the most dangerous animals in Africa," Boden told him, and Dash nodded. "And they're fast as hell."

"I'll know next time," Dash said sheepishly. "It almost ran me over. We had a guide who knocked me out of the way." He could easily have been killed, and Antonia was grateful he hadn't been. She couldn't have borne losing him too.

"How long do you have to stay here?" Boden asked him.

"Five days or a week, I think. The food is disgusting. I want to go home. I'm not sure yet if I'll go back to Davis for the rest of the semester or stay in Connecticut. But I can come back here next semester. I want to do that. I want to work with some of the big cats."

"I see sleepless nights in my future," Antonia said, "worrying about you when you're here." It was the nature of motherhood she knew well.

"It's all really well set up, Mom. No one ever gets hurt." She pointed at his leg and they all laughed. "Well, almost never. I wasn't being careful enough. I didn't know hippos could run like that."

They stayed with him for two hours, and he looked better when they left and went to their hotel to clean up and get something to eat. Antonia agreed to meet Boden in the bar in an hour. She looked fresh and crisp when she appeared in a white linen dress and sandals. As Boden watched her, he thought that she went from seeming like a little girl to being an elegant woman at the drop of a hat. He liked that about her, she could wear many hats. He had to force himself not to stare at her at times, she was so beautiful. He had loved her movies, the ones she acted in, and had seen all of them. She had distinctive looks and was a real star, no matter how much she denied it.

Over drinks, he asked her if she thought she would do any more acting. And she was definite about it.

"I just did it to please my husband. Once he was gone, I was done. I'll never go back to acting. Directing and writing are what I love."

"You were so good at acting. It's a shame to stop. But you're gifted at what you do now too."

"There has to be evolution, progress, like in anything," she said seriously. "If it all just sits there forever, it turns to stone. Or you turn to stone, which is worse. You have to use the talent you've been given." It was obvious to him that she hadn't turned to stone. She was warm and interesting and connected, and a wonderful mother, from what he could see. Coming on this trip with her was a rare gift, and gave him great insight into her. He was inside the palace walls, and she kept high walls around her. She was famous for that.

They spent an hour at the bar, just talking, and then they went to see Dash again, and had promised to bring him food. They brought him some kind of barbecued meat he'd asked for. He was delighted and devoured it. He said he was starving.

They kept him company while he ate, and then went back to the hotel. Antonia said she was going to her room. She was too tired to eat after the long day, and the trip. But she was less worried about Dash now that she'd seen him.

Boden walked her to her room and made sure she got in all right. She smiled sleepily at him as she closed the door, and minutes later she was in her bed and asleep. And he didn't take much longer when he got to his room. He was thinking about Antonia as he drifted off, and how remarkable she was.

The next day, Boden went to explore the city, and Antonia went to the hospital to sit with Dash for a few hours again, and have some time alone with him.

"That was nice of Boden to come with you," Dash said casually.

"Yes, it was. I didn't think of it, but he volunteered. This is probably a fairly dangerous city," she said, and Dash nodded.

"I think he was happy to do it, Mom." He grinned at her, and she made a sound that dismissed it. "I think he likes you," Dash insisted with a knowing smile at his mother, which she ignored.

"He has to like me. I'm his boss."

"That's not why he came with you." He was sure of that.

"If that's why he came with me, he came a long way to be disappointed. I didn't come here for romance. I came for your broken leg."

"Do you ever go out on dates, Mom?" He was curious. He didn't know. He'd never asked her and had never seen a man in her life, except Fred, her agent, or the guys at work on the set.

"No, I don't," she said.

"Why not?" He looked serious when he asked her. She hesitated for a long time before she answered.

"A lot of reasons. I loved your dad, and I don't think anyone could measure up to him. And I was busy with you and your sister for a lot of years. I work hard. I haven't gotten close to anyone. I have you and Olympia."

"I like Boden," he said, and she laughed.

"Is that a message, a suggestion, or your seal of approval?"

"All of the above. He's nice to talk to. He's a good guy. He's smart, and he's done a lot of cool things, and I think he likes you a lot."

"We don't know each other. He likes you too. He can come and see you anytime," and she meant it. She liked the way he related to her kids.

"I think he'd rather see you, Mom." He looked more serious than she intended to be on the subject.

"Stop shilling for me. I'm fine as I am," she said, laughing.

Boden was waiting for her at the hotel in the lobby, after she'd visited Dash. He told her about his adventures around the city, he hadn't been there in a while. And then he suggested they have dinner that night. He'd found a small French restaurant near the hotel he thought she'd like.

They went back to see Dash to bring him dinner before they went out to eat. She was wearing a blue dress the color of her eyes and red sandals. Boden was always surprised by how young she looked. She didn't look old enough to have a son Dash's age. And yet, whenever they spoke about life, or her work, she was very wise, beyond her years. Her life experiences, especially the hard ones, had served her well.

They had a nice time at dinner that night. They both liked the restaurant, and the food was as good as Boden had hoped it would be. He talked about his travels and the different places he'd lived.

"We lived so many places when I was a kid that I had a hard time settling down for a long time. But you can't do that forever. My brothers hated it and they love their small-town cowboy life. They couldn't wait to come home, get married, and have kids. I was afraid of that. I wanted to work in films and be a director. I couldn't see myself doing anything else. And maybe all the experiences I had traveling were good for something. I've worked with some amazing people, you among them." And so far, no one else had measured up to her, but he didn't say it. He didn't want her to think he was flattering her. She had enormous talent, and he had already learned a lot from her in a few months.

"Hamish taught me everything I know. He always thought acting was the right direction for me. I knew it wasn't." She had the looks for it, but it was obvious now she hadn't loved it. She didn't have the ego for it. In some ways she had no ego at all. "I wanted to be the window the light shone through, onto others. I didn't want the light shining on me. It was blinding."

"You have to be very strong to keep yourself out of the limelight. Very few people can do that, or want to," he commented.

"It works better for me." She smiled at him. "Hamish wanted me to be a star. It was an interesting experience, but it would have worn me out and bled me dry. Directing and writing feed me, they give me a strength that I can share with others. I think I would have stopped acting eventually anyway. I never thought of it as a job for a lifetime, like what I do now. And the way things worked out, I stopped acting when Hamish died. He's the only director I ever worked for. I couldn't have done it for anyone else. I suppose he was my Pygmalion, I was so young. I was in school when I met him, in college. He gave me all my fabulous opportunities and changed my life. And there was a lot of negative energy in my family about acting.

"My mother was an actress, probably a very bad one. She left my father to chase stardom in L.A. He kind of went nuts over it. My father threw me out when Hamish gave me my first real part in a movie. I was on my own after that, and Hamish took me under his wing, like a little lost bird." She smiled at Boden. He was intrigued by the story. It explained the way she had worshipped Hamish, but he was worthy of it. He was considered a genius in the industry, almost a god, even years after he died.

"What happened to your mother after she left?"

"Not much, I suspect. Or nothing good. I never heard from her again. She left when I was seven, then showed up on my doorstep at the farm in Connecticut when I was grown up, widowed, and had kids. She came to ask me to use my connections to get her a part in a movie. She never asked about my dad, or how I was after she left. Pretty incredible. In some cases, narcissism knows no bounds." She smiled at him, but there were tears in her eyes, thinking about it. "I don't want Olympia to end up like that."

"She won't. She has enormous talent," he said confidently. He was shaken by the story she had just told him. He had had parents who were always there for him growing up, and loved him, sometimes too much. And he could easily sense what a loss her mother had been for her as a small child.

"I'm not worried about her talent," Antonia said. "She'd roll over anyone and everyone to get what she wants. She's all about her. It goes with her age, and she's young. But I don't want her to be heartless or unfeeling and selfish the way my mother was, particularly if she's successful or becomes a big star. That can be pretty ugly. We see it in our business every day. I'm not sure you can change that, but maybe you can soften it a little. Stardom is very heady stuff. It ruins people, and lives." He knew she was right about that too. They'd all seen it.

"It didn't ruin you," he reminded her. But she was a very different woman than her mother must have been, or her daughter, as much as he liked Olympia, but he could see Antonia's point.

"Olympia and I don't have a lot in common. Hamish wasn't like that either. He was a very humble man, always looking for ways to improve things for others, and focusing the attention on them. I didn't want all that attention. I just hope that I didn't poison my daughter with my mother's DNA. There wasn't much worthwhile there. She destroyed my father. He never recovered from it. He's been an angry, bitter man ever since she left. I got a wonderful stepmother out of it in my teens. She's not with him anymore. And I see as little of him as possible. He's still toxic. It's not healthy to be around people like that." He could imagine what her childhood had been like, and was only getting a tiny glimpse of it. It explained many things about her, and how modest and self-effacing she was, and gun-shy about stardom. She was the anti-narcissist.

"I think Olympia will be okay," he said, "with some careful guidance from you," which she was providing.

"And a few hard knocks and tough directors to cut her down to size." She smiled at him, and he didn't disagree. He wasn't totally blind to Olympia's character as well as her talent. "Dash is a whole different story, an entirely different personality. He can't do enough for everyone around him. He's a gentle person, and the kindest kid I know. He's a lot like his father."

"And you," Boden added.

"It's why he loves animals so much. Olympia gave him a hard time when they were little kids. She was always tougher than he was, even though she's a year and a half younger. I had to keep an eye on her or she'd have steamrollered him completely. It's who she is. And she hated me when she hit her teens, and even before that. She's better now. But she was very precocious, and she's been fighting to get onstage almost since she was born.

"I wanted to be behind the camera, she wants to be the whole frame, with the spotlight full on." Boden laughed at her description of her daughter, but it was accurate. And she knew her son too. Boden liked both of them, with a special fondness for Dash, because it was easy to see what a sweet kid he was, and a little too brave, like his mother. He had proven that with the hippo. Boden could sense and understand better now that Antonia had been fighting hard battles since she was a child. It was just terrible luck that Hamish had died so soon, when she was so young. He must have seemed like a savior to her, and then he was gone in a few short years. Their happiness and his protection of her had been too brief.

"We barely had four years together," she said when they talked about him, "married for three of them. I had just told him I was pregnant with Olympia the day he died." Boden could sense the pain she had lived through losing him. He had experienced nothing like it himself in his lifetime. He considered himself lucky, and had lived a good life, with solid parents, even though they had lived all over the world, which he considered a rare opportunity and a gift. By the end of dinner, Antonia knew that he spoke five languages, including Hindi, which he admitted he rarely got to use. He spoke French, Italian, and Spanish too, which were more useful.

"You're going to have a hard time settling down to a normal life," Antonia predicted as they walked back to the hotel.

"I think I've been through all that. I've adjusted. It's a wonderful background to have, and very colorful, but in the end, it's nice to stay in one place, have roots and a family and a real home. My brothers aren't entirely wrong. I'm just not crazy about Montana. It's a little too rural for me. You get snowed in all winter. They both married local girls. They're nice women, but they've never even been to Chicago or New York. I'd have a tough time with that. But they're happy. One has five kids, and the other one three. They don't want to be anywhere else. They hated all our moving around. I loved it."

"What about you?" she asked him. "Do you think you'll stick around, or want to start traveling again?" It interested her, in light of the important position he had with her now that he had fallen into by chance, as her main assistant director. She was relying on him.

"I'm staying," he said, and seemed as though he meant it. "Except maybe for the occasional repeat visit to my favorite places, but not to live. I love Paris, and I wouldn't mind seeing Rome and Venice again. Other than that, New York is home now. I took a temporary apartment when I got back to the States from Canada." He smiled at her. "I've been looking for something in Connecticut, which makes more sense if you keep me on in the job. There's no point commuting, with you living in Connecticut, and your studio in Stamford. I'm searching for a small house in the area. I'd better find something soon. My lease on the furnished studio ended two weeks ago, and I'm going to be homeless when we go back."

"I've got a cottage on the property, if you need a place to stay while you look." She liked the idea that he wanted to find something permanent, and she wanted to encourage him. She needed an AD who was stable, reliable, and easily accessible. "My property manager lived in the cottage for years. He just bought his own place five miles down the road. The cottage is empty for now."

It sounded fantastic to Boden. "You wouldn't mind having me on the property, underfoot?" His face had lit up at the suggestion, and her farm was like a little piece of Heaven.

"Not at all. And Dash would love it. You may have to bar your door. He likes you." She smiled warmly.

"I like him too. I can give you a hand if he needs help while he's convalescing." Dash had decided to be home for a month before he went back to school. He'd have a smaller cast than the cumbersome one he had now, and they had advised restricted movement so the bones set well. He had pins in the leg that would have to be removed in a year.

At the end of the week, Dash was released from the hospital in South Africa. It had turned out to be a surprisingly pleasant trip. Antonia spent many hours with Dash every day while Boden went exploring, and then he and Antonia had dinner every night, and got to know each other. It reminded her of unraveling bolts of colorful cloth and spreading them out around them. They knew each other much better by the time they left South Africa, and he was excited about moving into the manager's cottage on her property. It was a stone's throw from the main house, but far enough away to give them mutual privacy. Dash was delighted. Post-production would be almost completed by the time they got back, so he'd have some free time to spend with Dash, waiting for Antonia to get started on the next project. She already had some in mind, but nothing was firm yet. She was still exploring new options, reading a lot of books, and working on some original screenplays.

Boden was extremely helpful getting Dash home on the plane. His cast was hard to maneuver with. They traveled through the airport with a wheelchair, but he had to manage on the plane with crutches. Dash was a tall, solid boy, and Boden was strong enough and big enough to help him. Antonia couldn't have done it on her own.

By the time they headed back to the States, the three of them were good friends. Antonia sat with Dash, with Boden across the aisle from them, so they could talk for some of the flight. And they landed in New York in a snowstorm. It was beautiful, but complicated for Dash and his wheelchair. Two of the boys from the stables had come to pick them up, and it was a long drive home.

When they reached Haven Farm, Boden helped get Dash upstairs and settle him in his room, and Antonia realized how helpful it would be to have him nearby. Once they got Dash settled, and had eaten something, Antonia offered to drive Boden to his new digs. He had left his car at the studio, and she got hers out of the garage to drive him to the cottage. The snow was deep on the paths, but they got there in a few minutes. She unlocked the cottage, turned the lights on, and had had the housekeeper turn the heat on before they arrived, so it would be warm for him. The bed was freshly made, there was a stack of towels in the bathroom. The furniture was simple but nicely done. The cottage had a masculine feeling to it, since her property manager was single and she'd done it for him, and Boden turned to her with a grin, and looked like a kid on Christmas.

"I can't believe you're letting me stay here." He smiled at her gratefully. "It's a lot nicer than my dismal place was in New York."

"Stay as long as you like, till you find what you're looking for," she said generously, smiling at him. It would be nice having him there. He added a touch of warmth and someone intelligent to talk to in her daily life, which she hadn't had in years and didn't even realize until now that she had missed. The arrangement suited them both.

"I'll call you before I come over," he promised, "and call me at any hour if you need help with Dash." It was crucial that he didn't fall and damage the leg again while the bones were setting. "I can run over in a minute." And she was much too small to help him or keep him from falling, or pick him up if he did.

"Thank you for being here," she said before she left him to go back to her house. She actually hated to leave him. It was comforting having him there.

"Thank you for having me," he echoed back to her. "Will you be okay driving back?" He was worried and she smiled. She wasn't used to having anyone worry about her. No one had in so long. It felt nice, in moderation. She was used to being the person who took

care of others, and no one thought about. But he did. It reminded
her of Hamish again, although Boden wasn't a father figure. He was
an equal, which was better for the age she was now. She had grown
up in the eighteen years since Hamish died. She'd been almost a
child then, with two children to raise.

"I think I can manage it." She smiled at him, referring to the short
drive to the house in the snow.

"Sorry, I didn't mean to imply you couldn't." But the road had
been slippery getting there, and he worried about her, even if he
wasn't supposed to. She was a perfectly capable woman, and his
boss. But he had a kind of well-brought-up gallantry she liked.

They both lingered at the front door, and he walked her to her
car, and they stood there with the snow falling before she got into
her car. The scene was incredibly beautiful and her large comfortable farmhouse lit up like Christmas loomed invitingly in the distance, with his cheerful little cottage as an extension of it.

"I loved being in South Africa with you. Thank you for letting me
go with you," he said, not knowing what else to say. He couldn't tell
her he had fallen in love with her, she would think he was insane.

"It was nice having you there," she said softly, and glanced up at
him. As their eyes met, words disappeared, and they didn't need
them. It didn't matter what they said, he pulled her gently toward
him and she didn't resist him, as they kissed standing in the falling
snow. Neither of them knew if it was a terrible mistake or what
they'd been waiting for, for years, and didn't know it. But did one
ever know? Hamish could have been a mistake, and had turned out
to be the biggest blessing of her life, even for such a short time. But
she wouldn't have missed it. And neither Boden nor Antonia could

tell where they were headed now. There was no stopping what they felt, and they both knew it. It seemed worth the risk.

"Good night," he said softly, as she looked up at him and they smiled.

"Thank you," was all she said, instead of "I love you," which was suddenly a given they both understood.

He kissed her again, and she got into the car with the snow heavy on her hair and her clothes, and on her eyelashes. She was so beautiful it made him long for her as he looked at her. He didn't want to frighten her. As brave as she was, he always had the feeling that if he moved too fast, she would run away. She liked to observe, but not be seen.

He stood watching her and waved, as she backed out of his driveway, heading toward her house. He stood there until the car disappeared around a bend.

Boden helped Antonia with Dash until he went back to school in March after spring vacation. Boden hadn't found a house yet, but she had kept him busy with projects at the studio. They spent countless hours talking, and she let him read some of the projects she was considering. She was working on a new screenplay, which was very powerful. It was the one he liked best, and in June she went to Fred with it, to have him put the production financing together, which didn't take him long, since it was hers.

Boden had stopped looking for houses by then, and they took long walks on the farm, and rode in the hills together. He seemed to fit into her life perfectly, like a puzzle piece that had been missing.

He gave her life depth and color, and on a summer afternoon, when Dash was in New Hampshire with friends, and Olympia was in L.A. rehearsing for a movie she had just been hired for, Antonia and Boden wound up in his cottage, and the inevitable happened. He was the first man she had made love with since Hamish, and the second in her life.

But she felt there was room for him in her life now. There wouldn't have been before that. But she was ready now, and so was he.

They were discreet for the rest of the summer, while Fred worked on the financing for her new film. Boden was taking on more and more responsibility in the studio, and she consulted him about everything now. Her children were coming home for Labor Day weekend, and she told him to stay in the main house and not move back to the cottage. He had started spending the nights with her sometime in July. It was just easier.

"Do you think they're ready for that?" Boden asked her about her kids, and she smiled.

"Are we?"

"I think so," he answered with his arms around her. "I'm not going anywhere, unless you want me to." She no longer seemed skittish with him, and he no longer had the feeling that she was about to disappear.

"I want you here with me," she said simply. "They'll get used to it. They love you too." She felt lucky when she looked at him every morning. He was a beautiful man, but that wasn't what tied her to him. She felt safe with him, just as she had with Hamish. Boden let her be herself. He had no ulterior motive, no hidden plan, no agenda for her. He wanted nothing from her.

"I used to want to be invisible," she confided to him one day, "so no one could hurt me, if they didn't see me."

"And now?" he asked her.

"I feel safe most of the time. With you anyway. I suppose there will always be times when I need to disappear. I don't like people focusing on me." He knew that about her, and let her come and go as she needed to, like when she was writing and needed time alone.

"You can be invisible any time you want. And I'll be here when you want to be visible again."

"I always want to be visible with you." She smiled at him and he kissed her. "I think you should forget about looking for a house. If my kids survive the weekend, you can move in. And I think they'll be fine about it."

She said something to both of them about it that weekend. Dash was thrilled and said he loved him, and Olympia laughed at her.

"Old news, Mom. Do you think we're both blind? You two have been crazy about each other since last Thanksgiving. I was waiting for you to say something months ago, but you never did."

"I hadn't figured it out yet," Antonia said, looking embarrassed.

"Well, I did. And so did Dash when he went to South Africa with you. Boden's crazy about you, Mom, and I think he's very cool." Antonia had thought that no one had noticed, but the kids were onto them, maybe even before they were themselves.

"I guess I'm not as invisible as I like to think," she said to Boden when he came home from the studio, and he laughed at her.

"You've got smart kids," he said as he kissed her.

Invisible

He stayed in her bedroom that night, with the kids in the house, and moved his things in the following week. It was as though he had always been there. He was the assistant director on her next movie, and the films she made afterward. She still disappeared when she needed to, into herself, but she was never invisible to him.

Chapter 19

The catering trucks began arriving at noon. They were giving the biggest party Antonia had ever given at the farm. It was a combined celebration of Dash's graduation from veterinary school and Antonia's fiftieth birthday. She and Boden had just made their twentieth film together, and had been together for six years.

Olympia's acting career was booming, and she was in constant demand, with Fred representing her. She was a big name now. And Dash was going to Africa to work on an important rescue project for leopards and cheetahs. If it worked out, he would be spending six months a year there for the next three years.

The guests had been invited for seven o'clock, and the children had added more names to the list. There were two hundred and twenty people on the grounds around the farmhouse by eight o'clock, and two enormous cakes burning with candles were presented after dinner. There was a lively country band Olympia had picked that had a current single in the top ten. She was dating the lead singer, a stunningly handsome English boy. Lara was there and brought the man she had been living with for five years. Brandon had stayed in Palm Beach. He was eighty-three and housebound now, which Antonia knew when she invited him. She didn't really want him there. She and the children hadn't seen him in several years.

Boden's brothers and their wives had come from Montana, but his parents were on a cruise again and sent their regrets. They were older than Antonia's father and traveled all the time. Jake was in San Francisco and sent his love.

Boden saw her blow out the candles on her cake. He thought she looked uncomfortable when she did. She kissed Dash when he blew his out and then she disappeared. He thought he knew where to find her, and he walked down to the small lake, and found her sitting there, on a big rock, in the moonlight. They walked there after dinner sometimes, on warm nights, when they were in residence between films.

He could see her silhouette in the dark, with the fireflies floating around her. There was an August moon heavy in the sky. He walked over quietly and sat down next to her on the rock. Evenings of revelry where she was the center of attention were not her strong suit, but she had agreed to it for Dash, and the children wanted to celebrate her birthday too.

Boden put an arm around her, and she looked up at him in the moonlight with a peaceful smile. He knew her well now, and they lived their life in harmony. He knew the evening was a lot for her.

"You disappeared," he said softly and didn't sound surprised. She nodded and kissed him, happy sitting beside him, pleased that she was invisible to the entire world, but not to him. He always knew how to find her, and where she was hiding, and she knew he always would, as he kissed her again. She didn't need to be invisible because she was safe with him, just as she had been with Hamish. She still carried Hamish in her heart, like the blessing he had been so long ago, and Boden was to her now.

They stayed at the lake for a while, and then walked back to the house hand in hand, when she was ready. She felt peaceful and loved, exactly where she wanted to be, and where she belonged. Destiny had brought her home and put the right people on her path, one by one, and the wrong ones who didn't love her or understand were gone.

Danielle Steel

Have you liked Danielle Steel on Facebook?

Be the first to know about Danielle's latest books,
access exclusive competitions and stay in touch
with news about Danielle.

www.facebook.com/DanielleSteelOfficial

HIGH STAKES

Jane Addison is smart, young and ambitious. She's delighted to have landed a job with a prestigious literary and talent agency, Fletcher and Benson. Hailey West, her boss, is dedicated to her authors, but her home life is chaotic and challenging as a single mother following her husband's tragic death. Francine Rivers, the stern and bitter head of department, is also raising children on her own after an acrimonious divorce and has had to overcome financial hardship by paying the very highest price.

Meanwhile, Allie Moore seems to have it all. She relishes success and loves working with the talented actors she represents – until a passionate relationship with one of her star clients threatens to derail her career. And Merriwether Jones, CFO for the agency, appears to have the perfect marriage until her husband's jealousy over her career threatens her happiness.

Jane quickly realizes that there are damaging secrets behind the doors of the agency. She has the least power, but she is also the least willing to accept things as they are. And when she tries to put things right, the consequences will leave no one unscathed.

In this riveting novel, five women at the top of their game navigate the challenges of career and ambition, family and personal lives in a world where it's necessary to fight for what is right.

Coming soon

PURE STEEL. PURE HEART.